“How *dare* you, Sandoval Parrish?”

Tess took a step forward, thrusting her chin out. “I wouldn’t be in this *situation* if it weren’t for your desire to curry favor with that unprincipled killer!” She was too angry to care they were alone and she was very much at his mercy.

Sandoval’s head snapped back as if she had slapped him, and he paled. For several endless moments they stared at one another. “You’re right, you wouldn’t. You have every right to think the worst of me. The best thing you can do is trust me.”

“But *why*, Sandoval? What do you hope to gain?” she demanded, self-control slipping, tears of outrage and fear suddenly threatening to spill over onto her cheeks.

“I can’t tell you that, Tess,” he said. “You may not believe this, but I’m not a bad man.”

Something about the softness of his tone and the kindness in his eyes was her undoing, and Tess gave way to her tears. Then suddenly he was holding her….

Books by Laurie Kingery

Love Inspired Historical

Hill Country Christmas
The Outlaw's Lady

LAURIE KINGERY

makes her home in central Ohio where she is a "Texan-in-exile." Formerly writing as Laurie Grant for Harlequin Historicals and other publishers, she is the author of sixteen previous books. She was the winner of the 1994 Readers' Choice Award in the short historical category, and was nominated for Best First Medieval and Career Achievement in Western Historical Romance by *Romantic Times BOOKreviews.* When not writing her historicals, she loves to travel, read, read her e-mails and write her blog on www.lauriekingery.com.

LAURIE KINGERY

The Outlaw's Lady

Published by Steeple Hill Books™

STEEPLE HILL BOOKS

Steeple Hill®

ISBN-13: 978-0-373-82818-0

THE OUTLAW'S LADY

This edition published by arrangement with Steeple Hill Books.

www.SteepleHill.com

Printed in U.S.A.

God is our refuge and strength,
a very present help in trouble.
—*Psalms* 46:1

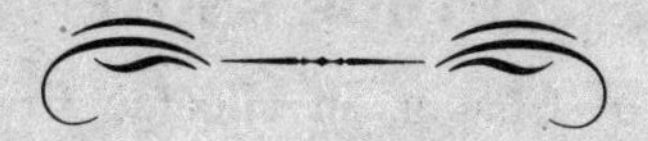

To Elaine English, my agent, with grateful thanks
for helping me to keep on believing in my writing,
and to Tom, as always

AUTHOR'S NOTE

The town of Chapin, in Hidalgo County, Texas, mentioned in this book is the present-day Edinburg. The name was changed in 1911.

Chapter One

Rio Grande Valley, Texas, 1880

Tess Hennessy stared down through the darkness at the image taking shape before her in the chemical bath. The photograph she had taken of the Spanish mission-style home in which she lived was to be a present for her parents on their anniversary tomorrow. She had captured it at a moment when the lighting was perfect, with the noon sun directly overhead so that the palm trees didn't cast their shadows over the house. She smiled, pleased at her work. They would love it, especially after she mounted it in the elegant oak frame Francisco, her helper, had prepared. She'd have to sneak out here to her developing shed after they returned from the party tonight, no matter how late it was, so that the picture would be ready for gifting tomorrow.

If only it were as easy to see her future develop before her as it was to develop a photograph. Her mother, she knew, expected her to marry. But what man would want to marry a girl who had an unladylike pastime that involved messy, finger-staining chemicals and long sessions in a darkroom?

Was there such a man? If only she could submerge one of her collodion plates into the chemical bath in the basin before her, and see his image take shape…

"Tess! Tess! Where are you? Now, where can that girl have gone, Patrick? I specifically *told* her we were leaving for the barbecue at one o'clock…."

Oh dear, she'd lost track of time again. It was so easy to do when she was immersed in photography, her passion. "Mama, I'm in the darkroom, developing a picture. Don't come in, please—"

But it was too late. Sunlight suddenly flooded the little shed by the barn as Amelia Hennessy burst in.

Tess groaned. Her mother's untimely arrival had just ruined the photograph.

"Tess! What are you doing in here?" her mother cried. "We have to leave for the barbecue, and you're not even dressed. Look at you!" Her mother spoke as if she expected Tess to look down and be surprised that she was wearing her serviceable navy skirt and waist.

Behind her mother she could see her father, looking sympathetic and uncomfortable, his eyes appealing with Tess to comply so peace could be restored.

She would have to give her parents an IOU for their anniversary present and take the photograph again. Her father would understand and apologize privately to Tess for not stopping his wife before she'd burst into her darkroom.

Amelia Hennessy tapped her foot, her face tight with impatience.

"I *am* ready to go," Tess replied in a level voice, wishing she could avoid the inevitable confrontation.

"Surely you weren't thinking of wearing *that* at the

Taylors' barbecue?" An imperious finger indicated Tess's utilitarian clothes, in contrast to her own elaborately lace-trimmed dress with a fancy, bow-topped bustle.

Tess took a deep breath, praying for calm. She *did* want to obey the commandment that instructed her to honor her parents, and with her father that was easy. No matter how often she explained to her mother what was important to her, however, Amelia Hennessy seemed incapable of understanding. Tess shot a look at her father, but though his eyes were full of sympathy, he said nothing.

"Mama, I'm not going as a party guest, but to *work.* I told you the Taylors hired me to take the photographs of them and their guests. The developing chemicals can be messy, and with all the bending and stooping while posing the subjects, what I wear is apt to get dusty and stained, so it's hardly practical of me to wear a light-colored, frilly dress."

Her mother sighed and put her slender fingers up to her head as if she felt a migraine coming on. "Tess, I do *not* understand you!" she said for surely the thousandth time. "You're a beautiful girl—or you would be, if you'd take some trouble to put yourself together. You could make a brilliant marriage, but you'll never do it if you insist on spending so much time on this little *hobby* of yours. You're always at your little shop in town. I don't know why your father ever let you take it over when James passed away. And when you're not photographing, you're drawing. Patrick, *say something* to your daughter to make her see sense!"

Patrick Hennessy put one hand on his wife's shoulder, the other on his daughter's, and smiled the charming smile that usually mellowed his wife's anxious reaction to his daughter's individuality.

"Yes, she *is* a beautiful girl. Thanks be to God, our last chick in the nest got your looks, Amelia—especially your blue eyes, and only my red hair," he said, with a quirk of amusement that lifted the corners of his mouth and eyes. "When—and *if*—" he added, with a hint of steel "—she's ready, our youngest has only to crook her finger to have any man she wants. But she's not a brainless belle with no thought but how many beaux she can collect. If she wants to be a photographer and carry on for James, I don't see the harm."

Amelia Hennessy's lips thinned and she sighed again. "You never do, when it comes to Tess, Patrick, but she's already twenty and she's going to end up an old maid, you mark my words."

"I always do, Amelia," he said, giving his wife an affectionate peck on the cheek. "But an old maid? Nonsense. Our Tess is the prettiest girl in Hidalgo County. A man would be a fool to think otherwise if he had eyes in his head. And now, we'd better leave or we really will be late."

Tess sighed, too, knowing the battle was only postponed, not won, and followed her mother out of the shed. As she left the dimness, the tropical heat of the Rio Grande Valley washed over her. For a moment she envied her mother's lightweight dress, low cut over the shoulders.

In front of them stood two carriages, the open victoria, with its matched bays and driven by Mateo, and a smaller vehicle that resembled a Civil War ambulance, covered on all sides and in back by heavy canvas and pulled by Ben, the same mule that had once pulled the wagon for Uncle James. Tess had requested that her photography wagon be ready at the same time as her parents' vehicle, and Mateo had done so.

"We're going to be the laughingstock of the party with

that wagon following us," Tess heard her mother grumble as her husband assisted her up into the carriage.

"Horsefeathers," her father scoffed. "They'll be lining up to have their pictures taken, and Tess will be very popular indeed."

"If it comforts you to think so," her mother sniffed. "But I just wish Lula Marie had had the decency to ask me first before hiring our daughter. I would have forbidden it."

"Sam talked to me," Patrick Hennessy told his wife. "I said it was all right." There was a warning note of finality in his voice. Tess heard no more objections. She climbed into the driver's seat and gathered up the reins.

Her heart warmed with love for her father. He'd always supported her dreams, God bless him. She loved her mother, too, and knew despite her mother's fretting about her future, that the feeling was fiercely reciprocated.

Tess understood that her mother had grown up in a simpler time. She'd been a belle in the truest sense before the charming Patrick Hennessy, an Irish immigrant, had swept her off her feet. Everyone said she was marrying beneath her, but apparently she had known what she was doing. Starting from scratch, Hennessy had built his empire in south Texas until he was one of the richest cattlemen in the state, even after the Civil War.

If only she could convince her mother that she, too, knew what she was doing. Tess had grown up on her uncle James's tales of working as a photographer for the famous Mathew Brady during the war. She had taken her first daguerreotype at her uncle's direction when she was only seven. By the time she was fifteen, she was working alongside him in his shop in nearby Chapin whenever she wasn't away at school, and by the time he died, he had taught her everything he knew.

Tess glanced backward into the wagon to assure herself that all her bottles of chemicals were safely and securely bestowed inside. "Giddup, Ben," she said, clucking to the mule. And the beast obediently took his place behind the victoria for the short drive to the Taylors' plantation.

"I tell you, Dupree, we're going to have to call the Rangers in again to deal with these Mexican cattle thieves like McNelly did in seventy-five," Samuel Taylor said, turning to the man sitting next to him. "He certainly showed Cortinas what was what."

"I'm sure you're right, Sam," Mr. Dupree agreed. "I'm sick and tired of losing cattle to these bandits, not to mention two of my best broodmares." He slapped his hand on his knee as if to emphasize his disgust.

Tess threw off the heavy, dark canvas cover under which she had been crouching and faced the two men she had posed standing in front of their wives and daughters.

"Please, Uncle Samuel, Mr. Dupree. You must remain still, or you will be a blur," she pleaded, striving for a tactful tone. She swatted at a horsefly that had taken advantage of her coming out from cover to land on her neck. "The exposure will take only a few seconds and then you may talk all you want."

"I certainly *hope* we'll be done so soon," Maribelle, one of the Dupree daughters, complained. Like her sister, she was sitting at her father's feet with her skirts spread out decorously in front of her. "I'm roasting here in this heat, and without my parasol, the sun will *bake* my complexion, I'm sure. I don't know why we could not have sat on the veranda where it's shady."

Tess had already explained the need to use natural light, so she didn't bother to do so again. "Just another minute,

Maribelle, and you can go back to the party. Just think, you and your family will always have this picture to commemorate the day."

Maribelle made a little moue of distaste, as if nothing Tess could create with her camera could possibly compensate her for her suffering, but then her eyes shifted to something behind Tess and her camera. Her eyes widened. Without turning her head, she spoke out of the side of her mouth to her sister. "Melissa, who *is* that?"

"Who is *who?*" snapped her sister, also irritable in the heat.

"Ladies," Tess begged. She had been about to duck back under the canvas again and take the picture.

"That man who just stepped off the veranda, the one who's now standing by the fiddlers' platform," Maribelle Dupree told her sister. "Don't look now, because he's looking this way, but my stars, he is quite the handsome fellow!"

"You know I can't see that far without my spectacles," Melissa whined, "and I could hardly wear them *here.*"

Involuntarily, Tess looked back over her shoulder, and saw just what had caught Maribelle Dupree's attention.

The man was tall, probably all of six feet, and whipcord lean. He wore no hat, and in the sunlight his hair gleamed raven-black and a bit overlong, brushing the collar of his white shirt in the back. His features were angular, his nose slightly aquiline. He held up his hand to shade his eyes, peering around as if looking for someone or something.

What a fascinating face, Tess thought. What she wouldn't give to photograph him, to try to capture those angular planes of his face, that magnetism and sense of determination that radiated from him.

"Oh, he's coming this way!" squealed Maribelle to her

sister. "Melissa, is my hair all right? Is it coming loose in the back?"

"Girls, please," Taylor implored, just as Tess was about to remonstrate with them again. "If you two chatterboxes could hush up while we get this picture done, I'll present him to you."

Even as the girls squeaked blissfully and went into their poses again, Mr. Dupree spoke up. "I'd rather you didn't, Sam. I don't like what I've heard of the man. They say Sandoval Parrish is two different people, depending on which side of the border he's on."

Taylor blinked in surprise, then said, "Very well, a father has that prerogative, after all. Now, if we could let Tess take her picture? I believe there are several others who also want theirs done. Tess dear, thank you for your patience."

"Of course, Uncle Samuel." Tess took one last, fleeting glance at the object of the Dupree girls' attention. The stranger had paused to accept a drink from a tray proffered by a servant, and was now lifting it to his mouth as he continued to look in their direction.

Had he seen her staring right along with the giddy Dupree girls? Tess ducked under the canvas with the same feeling a mouse must have as it darts into a hole to escape the scrutiny of a hungry hawk. Half a minute later, she had completed the exposure.

"I'm done now. You are free to move," she said, coming back out from under her cover. She watched the Dupree girls stroll away, their bustles swaying as they each took one last, longing look over their shoulders. Apparently they had lost their nerve and weren't bold enough to stay and hold Taylor to his promise of an introduction.

Tess wondered if the stranger was still standing where he had been, but she was much too busy now to look at him again. Carefully, she removed the glass photography plate from the camera and strode over to where her wagon stood parked in the shelter of three shady live oaks. Her darkroom while at a job consisted of a larger, dark canvas tent stretched over the square, shallow bed of the wagon, in which sat the developing bath. She had only ten minutes to develop the picture or the collodion in the plate would no longer be wet, and her efforts would have been in vain.

Tess wished Francisco, her assistant in the shop, could have come to the barbecue today to take care of the preparation of the collodion plates and the developing while she took the pictures so she could be done sooner. But he had told her he had to help his father today. She straightened her shoulders, reminding herself that Uncle James had often worked alone to photograph the aftermath of battles during the war. Whatever he had done in the hardship of the battlefield, she could certainly do at a barbecue.

"Tess, can you come out for a minute? There's someone here who'd like to meet you," Sam Taylor said, just after she had gone into the developing tent.

"I'm sorry, I'm afraid I can't right now, Uncle Samuel," Tess said, staying under the tent and using her metal dippers to lower the undeveloped picture into the dipping bath. "If I don't bathe this photograph right now, then hang it up to dry, the picture will be ruined. I'll have to be in here for a few minutes, I'm afraid. Why don't I find you when I'm done, before I start posing another photograph?"

Idly, she wondered who it was her godfather wanted her to meet. She feared her mother had infected him with her anxiety about the possibility of her daughter's spinsterhood. Tess hoped he was not trying his hand at matchmaking.

She heard a rich chuckle outside the tent. "Well, if the

picture needs a bath, it needs a bath," an unfamiliar voice drawled. The voice was deep and accented in such a way to suggest that while Spanish was the speaker's first language, he was equally fluent in English. For a moment, she was curious about the possessor of such a voice. Then, when she heard nothing more, she assumed the men had taken her at her word and moved off. She had work to do, Tess reminded herself, and in the shadows of the dark canvas tent, she concentrated on producing the best image she could.

Minutes later, the photograph laid out on cloth and pinned into place so it could dry next to the others she had taken, Tess backed out of the tent. Before she left the party, she would have to brush a coat of varnish over the images to fix and protect them from the dust and moisture, but that could wait until all the images were dry.

"Ah, there she is, our lady daguerreotypist," Sam announced as she emerged.

Tess blinked, her eyes momentarily blinded by the brilliant sunlight after the semi-darkness of the tent. As her eyes adjusted to the afternoon light, her jaw fell open.

"Oh—it's *you!*" she said, before she could think.

Chapter Two

He watched with great interest as Tess Hennessy's lovely oval face went pale, then flamed as she realized what she had said.

"I—I mean, I didn't think y'all were going to wait right here!" One hand self-consciously flew to smooth her hair, which was coming down after brushing the overhead canvas too many times. Her gaze fled to Samuel Taylor, standing next to him.

Taylor stepped forward. "Tess, I'd like to introduce you to an old friend of mine, Sandoval Parrish. That is to say, *he's* not old, but our friendship is. Sandoval, Miss Teresa Hennessy, youngest child of Patrick Hennessy, my good friend who owns the land next to ours. I'm her godfather."

Parrish saw Tess blink as she heard his name. Sandoval, she would be thinking, a Spanish name, yet his last name sounds Anglo.

"I am pleased to meet you, Miss Hennessy," he said, and remembering that Anglo women thought hand kissing too forward, offered his hand instead. "My given name is from my Mexican mother. My surname, as well as my height, is from my father, who was an Anglo."

She colored again as if embarrassed that he had guessed her thoughts. "I see, Mr. Parrish. But you haven't taken your mother's name, too, as I understand most Mexicans do?"

He smiled, pleased that she knew of the custom. "Yes, my full name is Sandoval Parrish y Morelos, but it's much too big a mouthful, at least on this side of the border."

"And on which side of the border do you live, Mr. Parrish?" she asked.

Parrish cleared his throat. "I have ranch property on both sides of the river, Miss Hennessy, inherited from each side of the family."

He watched her eyes narrow at his noncommittal answer. She probably thought he was one of the many *Tejanos,* Texans of Mexican heritage, whose larger allegiance lay with Mexico. When it came to the test, Anglo Texans didn't trust them.

Ah well, it was a pity she seemed to feel that way, but maybe it was better. He hadn't known he would find the lady photographer so interesting, but if she didn't share the feeling, he could carry out his plan without distraction.

His suspicion was confirmed when she took a step back and said, "It was very nice to meet you, Mr. Parrish, but perhaps I'd better get back to my job. There were several other guests who wanted their photographs taken before I leave today."

Now Taylor took a quick step forward. "Now, Tess, I didn't mean for this barbecue to be all work and no play for you! The party ain't half over, so there's plenty of time for you to get to know Sandoval a little better. Why not let him get you some lemonade and y'all go sit down in the shade and get acquainted?"

"I…I really should do what you hired me to do before I stop to enjoy myself, Uncle Samuel," Tess protested, "or I can't take the fee we agreed upon." She pulled a folded sheet of paper from the pocket of her skirt and brandished it at her uncle, almost as if it were a weapon. "There are still several names on my list…."

"Actually, I was interested in having a photograph taken myself, Miss Hennessy," Sandoval said suddenly, "if you think you would have time today. If not, I could perhaps make time to come to the shop Sam tells me you have in town," he offered. "It would be a present to my mother, whose birthday is coming soon."

She hesitated.

"Who's next on that list?" Sam demanded, grabbing the paper away from her with the boldness only an old family friend could get away with. "Ah, Sissy Dawson. Why, she's much too busy flirtin' with Fred Yancy's youngest pup to be bothered sittin' still right now," he said, jerking his head in the aforementioned Sissy's direction. Just as he had said, Sissy was giggling and fluttering her eyelashes at a young man who looked utterly captivated by her antics. "Why don't you take Sandoval's picture right now?"

Her eyes darted to Sandoval, then back to her godfather. There was no way she could politely refuse. "I…I suppose I could do that," she said at last. "Very well, Mr. Parrish, please make yourself comfortable on that chair and I'll just prepare another collodion plate…"

"Tess, Lula Marie's motionin' for me to come over and meet somebody," Taylor said, "so I'll just leave you two together. Make Sandoval look handsome, mind—his mama thinks he is, and nothing I could tell her will convince her otherwise," he added with a chuckle, giving them a last wave as he strode away.

Tess started after his departing figure with obvious dismay.

"Relax, Miss Hennessy, I do not bite," Sandoval assured her, amused.

She stared at him, her lapis lazuli-blue eyes widening. "I never thought that you did," she began, but he interrupted her before she could deny it further.

"I will cooperate fully, better than any of your other subjects today, so you will be rid of me in half the time."

He enjoyed the flash of amusement that curved her lips upward. He liked the way her lower lip was fuller than the other, and the way she was biting it just now with straight white teeth as if to hold back a laugh. He wanted to make her laugh some more.

"Well, you'd hardly have to do much to behave better than those Dupree girls, Mr. Parrish. They were fidgety before, but once they spotted *you,* they became impossible."

Was it a test to see if he enjoyed the admiring glances of women? He'd seen the silly chits eyeing him, but they held no appeal. It had been this woman he'd come to meet.

"Ah, well, there's no accounting for taste, is there, Miss Hennessy?" he said lightly.

She met his gaze as if she weren't quite sure how to take his remark. "Just make yourself comfortable, Mr. Parrish," she said, gesturing toward one of the two ornately carved chairs she had been using all afternoon for her subjects.

"We have been introduced, Miss Hennessy. You may call me Sandoval."

Tess Hennessy did nothing to indicate she had heard him, merely moved the second chair away from the one in which he sat, and ignored his murmur that he could have done that for her. "I'll just be a few moments preparing the plate," she said, disappearing once more under the canvas hood.

"So you are called Tess, not Teresa, Miss Hennessy?" he asked, trying to keep her talking while all he could see of her, from his vantage point in the chair, was her navy-blue skirt. "It suits you."

"By my *family.* Uncle Samuel is my godfather, so he has that privilege, too." As you do not on such short acquaintance, he knew she meant. Her voice was muffled by the heavy fabric, but he didn't miss the starch in it. Sandoval smiled inwardly at her attempt to put him in his place. Tess Hennessy had the tart tongue to go with the fiery hair that the knot at the nape of her neck barely restrained anymore. He settled into a pose, staring back at the camera with a half smile. He let her direct him in how to hold his head, where to put his hands. When she announced that she was finished, he stood and told her he would pick up the finished product in three days at her shop.

"But…perhaps you didn't understand. I can have it done by the end of the day for you, Mr. Parrish," she said, taking a step after him. "It will come complete with a matte and protective folder."

"Ah, but your grandfather tells me one can also purchase frames at your shop, custom-made for the picture by your assistant. I would like a frame suitable for the picture, a gilt frame, if that is possible?"

"Of course, we can make such a frame for it," she said. "You said you will pick it up on Tuesday?"

Sandoval nodded. Had he imagined the slight heightening of color in her cheeks when she realized she would see him again? "Would late morning be convenient?"

"I'll expect you then, Mr. Parrish." Her voice was brisk,

businesslike. A prelude to goodbye. She stared down at the notebook she'd taken out to note the appointment.

He wanted more than that from her, despite his realization that mutual interest might complicate things. "If you like," he went on, "I'd be honored to take you to lunch at the hotel across from your shop. I'm told they have good food." He said it to gauge her reaction to him. Both of them would be many miles from Chapin by then, if all went according to his plan.

Her chin jerked up again. "I...I don't know...I'll have to think about it," she said.

"Very well, Miss Hennessy. Until Tuesday, then." He felt her eyes upon him as he strode away.

"Aren't you done yet, Tess?" Amelia Hennessy shouted through the heavy canvas of the developing tent. The sudden sound caused Tess to straighten quickly and bang her head on the support post, exacerbating the pounding headache she already had. She didn't know why her mother thought she had to shout, as if the canvas were a six-foot-thick adobe wall.

"No, not quite, Mama, why?" Tess replied, purposefully vague, though she was brushing varnish on the last picture. If she left at the same time as her parents, her mother would insist on critiquing the party with her—who had worn what, who had been flirting with whom, the quality and quantity of the food, and so forth—which would require Tess to drive her vehicle abreast of the victoria. After spending most of a day with social chatter droning into her ears, Tess was looking forward to being alone with her thoughts. She already knew what—or rather whom—she was going to think about.

"It's late. Your father and I are ready to leave."

Under the canvas, Tess pushed an errant lock of hair off her damp forehead, feeling wilted and sticky. She resolved never again to accept any commissions that involved outdoor photography in the heat of a south Texas summer. It was no longer necessary to protect the photographs from the light, but remaining under the hood allowed her to protect the drying photographs from dust and insects.

"You go ahead, then," she said, praying her mother would do so without further questions. "I'll drive back when I'm finished. I won't be too much longer."

She heard Amelia loose a heavy sigh. "Very well, but be home before dark, won't you? Have Sam escort you."

Tess stifled the urge to remind her mother it was only a mile between the Taylors' place and Hennessy Hall. She was not about to ask Uncle Samuel to saddle a horse and escort her as if she were six years old and afraid of the dark. Would her mother ever treat her as a grown woman? Why, her sister Bess had been married at seventeen!

Tess was the youngest child, the only one left at home. Perhaps that explained her mother's overprotectiveness. She resolved to be more patient with her.

"You need your rest, Tess. Don't forget, church tomorrow, and your brother and his family are coming for Sunday dinner."

She always enjoyed going to the little church in Chapin they had always attended, and it would be good for her mother to see Robert and his family. They lived in Houston and weren't able to visit often. Having three lively grandchildren around would distract her mother, and surely Tess could gain some breathing room.

"Well, aren't you going to come out from beneath that thing and tell your parents goodbye?" Amelia asked, her tone reproachful.

It wasn't as if they were going to be parted for more than an hour, but Tess deemed her last picture dry enough, so she obliged her mother by throwing the flap open and giving her mother an affectionate kiss on the cheek.

When she drew back, she found her mother staring at one of the portraits she had just finished and pinned up to dry. Sandoval Parrish's image stared back at them, his eyes dark and probing, as if he wanted to penetrate the soul of whoever gazed at the picture. There was definitely something about the man that disturbed Tess's peace, though she could not have said how, precisely.

Amelia's peace had apparently been disturbed as well. "Sam Taylor introduced you to *that man?* He must have done it when I wasn't looking. Why, I'm going to give him a piece of my mind," her mother said indignantly, snatching the picture from where it was pinned on the drying board and whirling around.

"Mama, it's not completely dry. Be careful!" Tess pleaded, following her and hoping she would not have to tell Parrish her mother had ruined the picture and he would have to sit for it again. She couldn't help glancing around to see if Parrish was still around and had heard her mother, but she saw no sign of him.

Her mother, however, had spotted her husband and Taylor standing by the hitched and ready victoria, and was already sailing off in their direction, her bearing rigid with indignation, brandishing the photograph in front of her.

"Mama, please, he only sat for a picture!" Tess protested, not wanting Uncle Samuel to be the victim of one of her mother's dramatic scenes. She knew better than to mention that her godfather had practically thrown the two of them together. She was also unwilling to admit—even to herself—that there had been more in Parrish's eyes than the mere politeness and cooperation a subject would give a photographer.

"Sam Taylor, what were you *thinking?*" Amelia demanded.

"What's wrong, Amelia?" Taylor asked, his face honestly confused. He looked to Patrick Hennessy for enlightenment, but seeing his friend looking as surprised as he was at Amelia's outburst, turned back to her. "Did I do something to upset you, dear lady?"

"As if you didn't know," Amelia Hennessy snapped. "Introducing *that man* to our youngest *daughter.* Why, everyone in Hidalgo County knows he's little more than a bandito!" her mother cried. "I could not believe my eyes when I saw him strolling around the grounds today as if he were as good as anyone else. Why on earth would you invite such a man, let alone introduce him to an innocent girl?"

Her father peered at the photograph, and when he looked up, his eyes were troubled. "So that's who that was. Sam, I hear tell he's rumored to be a compadre of Delgado himself." The questioning note in his voice echoed his wife's concern.

It was no light charge. Delgado was a notorious Mexican outlaw who raided Texas ranches along the Rio Grande, then ran back across the border with his loot—horses, jewelry, guns, sometimes even a rancher's entire herd of cattle.

"Don't believe everything you hear, Patrick," Sam protested. "I've known Sandoval Parrish since he was just a sprout, back in my days as a Ranger. You surely don't think I'd introduce my goddaughter to a bad hombre, do you? I'd ride the river with that man anytime."

Tess blinked in surprise. In Texas, saying a man was

good enough to ride the river with was high praise. It meant he was as trustworthy as they came.

And saying it was enough, apparently, to leave her voluble mother speechless.

Seeing that, Sam pressed his advantage. "And like Tessie said, all she did was take his picture."

Tess smiled at the nickname, one she hadn't heard him use in years. But Amelia Hennessy was never speechless for long. Handing the picture back to her daughter, she said, "Tess is our youngest child, and I'll thank you to ask us before you introduce her to anyone, Samuel Taylor."

Samuel hung his head. "Yes, ma'am. I'm sorry, Amelia, I didn't mean t' ruffle your feathers."

Patrick sighed. "No harm done," he assured his friend. "As you say, she only took his picture."

"And a fine job she did, too," Sam said, glancing at it. "Not only Parrish's, but all the ones she took today. Everyone told me how pleased they were. I'm much obliged to your daughter, Amelia and Patrick. Tess, why don't you come up to the house and we'll settle up?"

The sun was sinking behind a distant line of mesquite when the mule pulled Tess's wagon off the palm-lined lane onto the main road. Despite her most diligent efforts to be on her way quickly, Uncle Samuel and Aunt Lula Marie had been in a buoyant, post-party mood and were loath to let her go until Tess finally insisted she must be on her way or her mother would make her father come back to fetch her.

Tess let Ben have his head, for the mule knew the way home. It had been a very profitable day, Tess mused. With the money she'd been paid today, and the enthusiastic response she'd gotten from the guests that would surely lead to further business, she was that much closer to her goal of traveling to New York City. Portfolio of her best work in hand, she would waltz into the studio of the famed Mathew Brady himself and offer her services. He would be so impressed he'd hire her on the spot.

It was an idea that horrified her mother, who prophesied a dire end to a young lady who ventured anywhere into the Dreadful North, let alone a huge, wicked city such as New York. She would starve to death without the Protection of a Man to see that she ate only in Decent God-fearing Establishments, be accosted by rascals bent on No Good, and her traveling funds would be ripped from their place of safekeeping in the hem of her skirts.

"You have to remember that your mother lived through the War Between the States, darlin'," her father always reminded her. "And while the Yankees never penetrated as far inland as Hidalgo County, it seemed for a while they might. Then we got word of her cousin Lucretia being murdered by bummers during Sherman's March to the Sea. You're her last precious chick in the nest, Tess darlin', and she's anxious to see you married and settled."

"But I'm never going to marry. I want to do something more with my life."

"Darlin', darlin', never say never," her father advised. "Some nice young man may well come along and change your mind. And it's not impossible you might meet him in New York," he'd added, surprising her. "I came ashore there, fresh off the boat from Ireland some thirty-five years ago, and it wasn't so bad a place. If you must go, I'll have Robert escort you there."

Not if, Papa—when. And when she went, she was going alone. She loved her elder brother, but he was just as overprotective as Mama and sure he knew the only right way to do anything. Besides, he had a family to look out for. It would have been fun to have another girl her age along, but once they had become young ladies, all of Tess's school friends had become obsessed with beaux and clothing, and affected to swoon at the idea of leaving all that for some musty old photography studio up north.

One minute Tess's wagon was rolling alone along the shadowy, mesquite- and cactus-lined road; the next, figures like ghosts had emerged from the scrub and formed themselves in lines in front of her wagon and behind it. All of them, dressed in the simple, light-colored clothing of Mexican peasants, were pointing rifles or pistols at her.

Chapter Three

"*Hola, señorita,*" a mustachioed fellow in the center of the road called out, smiling broadly. "*Buenas noches.*"

Tess began to shake—not out of fear—or at least, it wasn't mostly fear, but rage. Less than a mile from home, she was now about to forfeit the fifty dollars for which she had labored all day to a handful of banditos. She would have given anything she had for a Winchester carbine in her lap right now.

"I don't have anything you want," she said, hoping she could bluff it out. "Just a camera and a wagon full of chemicals for developing photographs."

The mustachioed man translated her words to the others. Laughter rang out as Tess fumed. She hadn't been put here to amuse them! One evil-eyed man, standing on Mustachio's left, sniggered.

"You don't have anything we want? Ah, *señorita,* I am not so sure about that," he countered with an insolent grin that flashed white teeth against his brown skin.

Tess tried to stare him down with her haughtiest look, but failed. Rage was fast transforming itself into pure, unalloyed fear as she realized they could do anything they wanted with her—*anything.*

With a pang, she made the decision to surrender the fifty dollars and hope they would be content with that. The idea hurt her, but not as much as it would have to give them the camera and supplies. She switched to Spanish. She'd learned it early in a household run by Mexican servants. "All right, I will give you my money, if you're so desperate, but you must leave me my camera and the wagon. It's how I make my living."

The man smiled at her fluent Spanish, but his reply was not conciliatory. "*Señorita,* do you take me for a fool?"

"I—I don't know what you mean," she said, setting her jaw so her teeth wouldn't betray her by chattering. "You're not…are you saying you want the mule, too?" Ben had been at Hennessy Hall since Uncle James had died, and she hated the thought of handing him over to these outlaws. *God, please send someone along this road. Anyone. These men would flee if I wasn't alone.*

You're not alone. I am with you.

The bandito just smiled at her. "*Señorita,* it is good news that you have money—it is added luck for us. But it is not your camera, Señorita Hennessy, that we came for."

"How do you know my name?" Startled by that, the rest of what he said didn't register at first.

"The lady photographer? *Señorita,* you are famous along the Rio Grande."

She was getting very tired of his grin. "But I told you, I make my living with that camera. You can't take it!"

"Oh, but we can, *señorita,*" he said, almost apologetically. "We are, after all, *ladrones*—thieves. It's how we make *our* living."

Now, because he was toying with her, she was angry

again. "Are you thinking to sell it? Don't bother—I very much doubt anyone between here and Mexico City would know how to use it!"

Señor Mustachio *tsk-tsked* at her. "*Señorita,* it is clear you have no high opinion of Mexicans." He shrugged. "What you say is true—we would not know how to use it. But *el jefe* has a fancy to have his picture made, as well as a picture history of his exploits, you see."

Nothing he was saying made sense, but she was willing to engage him in conversation as long as she could on the chance that someone might happen along to rescue her. *"El jefe?"* she echoed. "Who's that?"

"Our leader, *señorita.* Perhaps you have heard of him? His name is Delgado."

Delgado, the notorious outlaw her parents and others at the party had been talking about only this afternoon.

"But if none of you knows how to operate a camera," she said desperately, "or even if you did, how to develop the pictures…"

He beamed as if she had suddenly grasped the secret of their plan. "Then, obviously, you will have to come with us to take the pictures, Señorita Hennessy."

"C-come with you? Me? You're loco! I'm not going anywhere with you."

Mustachio laughed and said something in rapid-fire Spanish to his fellows. Despite the fury that sent the pulse throbbing in her ears, Tess thought she heard the word *pelirroja,* the same word she'd heard one of the Hennessy housemaids call her. *Redhead.*

As one man, they aimed their weapons at her again.

"You see, you have no choice, *señorita,*" he said. "But do not worry. If you come with us, you will not be harmed.

When Delgado has his pictures, you will be free to return to your home."

Tess had had enough of his carefree banter. "Well, that's just dandy!" she cried. "If you think for one cotton-picking moment I'm going to tamely disappear and frighten my mother to death, you'd better think again."

They were beginning to advance, guns still trained on her. Frantically she looked backward, then ahead, but there was no one on the road but herself and the bandits. With nothing else to do, she opened her mouth and screamed. *Please, God, let someone hear me!*

She had not guessed any of the bandits could move so fast, but in what seemed like the blink of an eye Tess had been yanked off the seat of her wagon by the evil-eyed man who had laughed at her. He stank of stale onions, garlic and sweat.

Tess went wild, screaming and kicking. She knew that one of her kicks must have connected with something tender when she heard the man grunt and loose his hold on her.

"Bruja!"

In that instant she broke free and, crazy with hope, began to run.

Tess had only covered a few yards when she was tackled by one of the bandits, knocking the wind out of her. Her cheek stung from sliding against a rough rock and her mouth was gritty with dust, but before she could gather enough air to scream again, Tess found herself gagged and bound at her wrists and ankles. In mere moments she was lifted into the bed of the wagon and laid out in the center, surrounded by her bottles of chemicals. She felt the wagon lurch forward and realized they were moving off the road and into the brush.

Where were they taking her? Would she ever see home again? If only she had listened to her mother and gone home when they had, or had Uncle Samuel ride along with her! Or were they so determined to capture the "lady photographer" that the presence of others would have been no deterrent, and might have resulted in her parents' murders? Now, bowling along over the rocky scrubland as night fell, covered by the heavy canvas, no one would see her being taken away from everyone and everything she knew. Her stomach churned with nausea and fear.

Tess began to sob, soundlessly because of the gag, but soon her inability to clear her nostrils made breathing too difficult to continue crying. Then she could only lie there, feel the lurching and jerking as the wheels rolled over the uneven ground, and watch the last hints of light disappear from the tiny chinks in the sideboards of the wagon bed. At last, exhausted by terror, she slept.

Tess woke because of a sudden absence of the rocking, swaying movement that had haunted her dreams. Were they stopping temporarily, or had they reached Delgado's hideout?

Before she could listen for clues to the answer, the canvas under which she lay was shoved back off the wagon bed, blinding her with a sudden blast of sunlight. With her wrists and ankles still tied, Tess could only clench her eyes tightly shut.

"Idiotas! Necios!"

The man went on yelling in Spanish so rapidly that Tess could only comprehend that someone was being berated. She assumed it must be Delgado. After all, he would not want his henchmen to manhandle the lady who was about to make him immortal. Now she kept her eyes closed because she was afraid to have her worst fears confirmed. The voice barked out another spate of words, clearly a command, and she felt the bonds at her wrists and ankles being severed.

Tess knew she could not shut out the reality of her situation forever. As soon as she could shade her eyes with one hand against the brilliant sunlight, she raised herself on one elbow and peered at the speaker.

And saw with astonishment that it was not Delgado or any other stranger, but Sandoval Parrish who stood looking at her over the side of the wagon.

"You!" Before she could put together a rational, prudent thought, she had struggled up onto her feet and launched herself at him, fingers curved into claws.

He caught her easily before she could do any damage, and holding her wrists gently, but with an underlying steely strength, kept them pinioned against the side of the wagon. His body was next to hers, rather than directly in front of her, so that even if she were foolish enough to bring up one of her knees, she couldn't hurt him.

"Calm yourself, Tess Hennessy," he said, in the same soothing, low voice one would use to soothe a fractious horse. "No harm is going to come to you."

"No harm?" Tess cried. "I've been kidnapped and transported to who knows where, and my family has no idea what has happened to me, and you call that *no harm?* Sandoval Parrish, you are every bit the scoundrel my mother said you were!" There were no words for the depth of her hurt and disillusionment with him. To discover he was the one who had orchestrated her kidnapping, when she had already been imagining him coming to her rescue. "How dare you do this to me? I demand that you escort me and my possessions safely home immediately!"

He gazed down at her, his dark eyes serious, but there was an amused little curve at the corners of his mouth that betrayed the fact that he was struggling mightily not to laugh at her.

"Tess, Tess, you are in *no* position to demand anything," he told her, and now there was no merriment playing about his lips at all. "As you have guessed, you are many, many miles away from your home, and only I stand between you and a camp full of very rough hombres indeed."

She looked beyond him and saw that what he was saying was too awfully true. There must have been a score, at least, of swarthy men in ragged clothing watching this interplay between Parrish and her, and each man looked more dangerous than the one next to him.

"How very comforting," she fairly spat at him. "And my name, as I told you before, is *Miss Hennessy.*"

"Miss Hennessy, then," he said in that musical, accented voice that seemed to caress her senses. "I would set your mind at ease about your parents. They have been left word that you are safe and will be returned unharmed."

"Unharmed if they raise a ransom, you mean? What sum are you demanding for me? Your men have already taken possession of the fifty dollars I earned from my godfather."

He raised an eyebrow, clearly surprised. "If money was taken from you, it will be returned," he promised, then called sharply over his shoulder, "Esteban?"

The man Tess had mentally named Mustachio stepped forward. "*Sí,* Sandoval?"

"Give the lady back her money. I told you nothing was to be taken from her, and you have disobeyed. Just as you did by transporting her in such a position of discomfort."

Esteban smiled sheepishly at her and held out a small,

cloth drawstring bag which clinked as Parrish took it from him.

"And there is no question of ransom, Te—Miss Hennessy," Parrish went on. "You will be staying among us for a time to take pictures of Diego Delgado and his men, and possibly some pictures of our adventures—though I understand the limitations of the camera make it impossible to portray us in the midst of action."

"No, I would have to pose you amid your stolen booty, afterwards," she hissed at him.

He shrugged, as if her intended insult did not touch him. "Once Delgado is satisfied that he has pictures enough to record his adventures for posterity, you will be escorted safely home."

All she could do was stare at him, her brain reeling at the implications of what he had said.

"I'll find a way to escape," she whispered at least, hating the shakiness of her voice. "If not with my camera, then without it. I won't stay here in a camp of outlaws, with only your promise to protect me."

He lowered his head so that his lips were mere inches from hers. "I would not advise that, Miss Hennessy. You are across the Rio Grande, in territory foreign to you, and you're clearly a *gringa.* Not only Delgado's men roam this land, but other *bandoleros* much less civilized than these, not to mention Apaches and Comancheros. As I have said, I will protect you from all harm. I make this promise before God, and I consider it a sacred promise. And one other thing you have said is wrong, Miss Hennessy."

"Oh, and what is that?" she asked.

"That God does not know where you are. He does know, Miss Hennessy—Tess. And if the promise of my protection does not comfort you, the promise that He always knows where you are, and will keep you safe, should give you all the assurance you need."

Chapter Four

He could tell by her sudden stillness that his words had made Tess think. She looked down, blinking. When she lifted her face again, her expression was calmer, though her blue eyes still flashed with defiance.

She's afraid, he realized. What woman wouldn't be, in these circumstances? But she doesn't want to show it. Most women would have swooned by now, or succumbed to a bout of hysterics. His admiration for her spirit grew.

"You're right, He does know where I am. And if you believe in God, how can you take part in something like this?" She made a sweeping gesture as if to include everything—her kidnapping, the camp and all of Delgado's men.

He allowed his face to show polite regret and shrugged. "A man must earn his bread in the best way he is able."

"Having ranches on both sides of the river wasn't enough for you?"

Inwardly he winced at her scornful tone, much preferring the spark of interest he had seen in her eyes at the barbecue. He wished he could take her into his confidence, tell her she had no reason to fear him, that he was on the side of justice, but it was too dangerous. There were too many eyes on them right now.

"Ah, where is the zest in that? There is no excitement," he said, knowing his words would make her more furious still, but that she would control herself because she knew she must.

"So being a *bandolero* is a sport for you?" Tess exclaimed, but didn't wait for an answer before asking another outraged question. "You never did intend to come and pick up your framed picture at my shop on Tuesday, did you?" she asked then. "That was just a ruse. And you probably don't even have a mother, do you? Much less one having a birthday soon."

"On the contrary, Miss Hennessy, my mother is very much alive, living on my ranch north of Chapin, and will be very pleased with the picture you have taken of me, frame or no frame. You do have it with you, don't you?"

She nodded sullenly, pointing into the wagon.

"And if you had not driven home by yourself, then yes, the appointment on Tuesday would have been necessary—although a kidnapping raid in broad daylight in a town, involving seizing you, packing up your wagon and hitching up your mule, would have been much more risky, not to mention difficult."

Again, she appeared to consider his words, and it was a long moment before she spoke again.

"Do you think that my parents will just tamely wait for me to return?" she asked. "You don't know my father. He'll have the Texas Rangers after you—maybe even the army!"

He couldn't help grinning at the irony of what she was saying, and knew she would take it as insolence.

Which she did. "You think I'm joking? Mister, you just took hold of a tiger's tail!" she cried.

"Miss Hennessy, don't you think if the *Rinches*—the Rangers—or the army were capable of catching us, they would have long ago?"

He thought she would have another retort for him, but just then he saw her look behind him, and heard footsteps approaching.

"Ah, our guest has arrived at last, eh?" Delgado remarked in Spanish.

"Sí, jefe," Sandoval said, turning to face the outlaw leader, and switched to English, which Delgado understood as well. "Miss Teresa Hennessy, may I present Diego Delgado, leader of our band, and the reason you are here."

He saw Tess's eyes widen as she beheld Delgado, who had dressed for the occasion in the spotless uniform of a Mexican *coronel,* which had been cleverly laundered of its bloodstains and mended by Delores, Esteban's old mother, to hide the bullet holes that had caused the uniform's sudden availability.

Delgado swept her a bow as courtly as any European count could have made.

"Señorita Hennessy, I am delighted you were able to join us, especially on such…shall we say 'short notice'?" His English was as flawless as Sandoval's, though more heavily accented.

"Mr. Delgado," she replied, "the pleasure is all yours. I am here very much against my will."

He stared at Tess for a moment as if he was not sure he had heard her correctly, and then he threw back his head and roared with laughter. "'The pleasure is all yours,' she says!" he exclaimed, slapping his side gleefully. "Sandoval, you said she was a feisty one and you were correct, amigo! *Ay, caramba,* I like her!"

Delgado's eyes gleamed as, coming toward her, he

looked her up and down, as if she were an untamed mare that needed breaking, and suddenly Sandoval had to fight the urge to clench his fists. "*Jefe,* I have promised her she need not be afraid, for she will be safe among us," he said quickly, hoping Delgado would get the hint.

It seemed he did, for Delgado took a step back. "*Señorita,* you will be as safe here as in the midst of a church," he said, sweeping her another bow. "I, Delgado, have sworn it." He turned and repeated his words in Spanish for the benefit of his men. "Any man who touches this lady will answer to me, and will pay with his life, you understand, amigos?"

There was a resounding chorus of agreement.

Delgado turned back to Tess. "You see, they agree. You will be as their *hermana,* their sister." He made a gesture with his hand to indicate that he considered this problem solved. "And so you are here to take my picture, Señorita Hennessy? Why don't we start now, eh? Do I not appear magnificent in uniform?"

Now that her worst fears had been relieved somewhat, Sandoval saw the lines of weariness etched on her face. "*Jefe,* Señorita Hennessy has traveled a long way overnight bound and gagged. She has not eaten anything, I'll wager, since yesterday afternoon. Perhaps the picture taking could wait a little while until she has broken her fast and rested a bit?"

Delgado looked surprised. "But, of course! How remiss of me not to realize how tired she must be, and how hungry. Delores!" he called over his shoulder to the older woman who had been hovering nearby. "Cook this young lady some breakfast. She is famished! And then assist her to settle in. Get her some comfortable clothes—Alma's will fit her, I am sure." His face darkened slightly as he said the last, and Sandoval knew he was thinking of his last mistress, who had become so jealous and demanding that Sandoval had finally taken her back to the village from which he had lured her. "Perhaps I can pose for the *señorita* this afternoon instead? Until then, *señorita,*" he said, bowing again.

Sandoval saw Tess nod uncertainly as Delgado walked away. "Come with me, Miss Hennessy," he said. "I hope you don't mind if your breakfast is a little spicy. Delores makes the best *huevos rancheros* I've ever tasted. Esteban will unhitch your mule and bring your supplies to that adobe over there. It's where you will be staying."

Now that the outlaw leader was no longer favoring her with his bold stare, and the other outlaws were busying themselves elsewhere, Tess felt freer to examine her surroundings as she followed Parrish to where the old woman was stirring something into a skillet over an open fire. Beyond them, flush against the high red-rock walls that soared perhaps forty feet above them, sat three adobe huts. One of them was large, and stood on the left end of the row; the other two, including the one Sandoval had indicated as hers, were smaller.

"That one's Delgado's," Parrish said, pointing to the large one farthest from hers. "That one is mine," he added, pointing to the one in the middle. "The rest of the men sleep by the fire."

"So you really are Delgado's right-hand man," she murmured. "No humble bedroll for Sandoval Parrish." As she had expected, he only shrugged at her barb.

She was reassured by the fact that Parrish's building was situated between Delgado's and hers, but despite his earlier words, how safe was she, really, with Parrish?

Lord, protect me. She had a comforting sense of God's presence, but knew that sometimes evil things befell God's children for reasons they might never understand on this earth.

A creek, with a wooden plank bridge spanning it in the middle, mirrored the curve of the rock walls and served to separate the adobes from the rest of the camp. There were two corrals, one empty, one full of horses. Ben was now being led into the latter. Many of the horses had carried the men who had kidnapped her last night, but a tall, rangy black mustang she hadn't seen before pranced up now to challenge the newcomer, laying back his ears and snorting threateningly. Ben flattened his own longer ears against his skull, brayed and whirled around, lashing out with his heels. His hooves missed the mustang. The black horse turned and trotted away, still snorting.

Tess smiled, then saw that Sandoval was watching her. "My mule doesn't cotton to bullying," she said.

"And neither does his mistress, I'm thinking. Good for you, Miss Hennessy." They had reached the campfire now, and Parrish smiled at the older woman who turned to face them. "Delores, this is Señorita Teresa Hennessy, the photographer and our guest," he said in Spanish, then added, "and she speaks Spanish." He turned back to Tess. "It's a good thing, since Delores speaks little English."

"Mucho gusto, señorita," the older woman said, smiling warmly at her, then invited her to have a seat on a pile of old blankets behind Tess. Delores then turned back to the eggs, peppers, onions and tomatoes she was cooking. The wind carried a whiff of the savory, spicy smell and all at once Tess realized how hungry she was. It had been probably more than fourteen hours since she had eaten.

She sank onto the horse blankets, her aching bones

protesting at the long, bumpy ride, and smiled gratefully as the woman handed her a tin cup full of steaming hot coffee poured from a pot resting on hot stones within the fire ring. She caught sight of her dusty navy skirt as she drank, and was thankful all over again that she had been wearing sensible, modest clothing. She could only imagine how nervous she would have felt among these outlaws if she had been wearing the frilly, frivolous dress her mother had wanted her to wear.

She wondered what the clothes being loaned to her by the aforementioned Alma would look like, and if Alma would begrudge her the loan. She prayed the garments would be decent—if Delgado and Parrish thought she was going to parade around in revealing clothing like a cantina girl, they had better think again!

Minutes later Delores had deposited tin plates heaped with eggs and tortillas in both her and Parrish's laps, and refilled their coffee. Tess ate the spicy food ravenously, and saw out of the corner of her eye that Parrish was doing likewise. It was a surprisingly companionable moment. For a few minutes, at least, Tess forgot she was so angry with him for involving her in this strange situation.

After they both had finished, Parrish excused himself, and Delores took their plates away, returned and gestured for Tess to follow her into the small adobe building designated as hers. The wagon had been left right outside the door.

The door itself was a colorfully woven blanket, which Delores pushed aside so Tess could enter, though the lintel was so low Tess had to duck her head. The room was bigger than it had looked from the outside. Thin, makeshift curtains that had obviously been a pair of dish towels covered a small window. The interior was divided into a larger and a smaller room by means of an ornate screen—where had he stolen that? The larger room contained nothing but a rocking chair—probably also booty—and a pallet on the floor.

Delores mumbled something, pointing at the screen, and went back outside.

Tess went and peeked behind the screen. Here she found a pallet with threadbare but clean sheets, a pillow and a light blanket, and a large brass-bound trunk. Lifting the lid, she found a small, purple cut-glass stoppered bottle lying atop several items of folded clothing. Unable to resist her curiosity, she wiggled the stopper until it came out and held it near her nose. The bottle was empty, but the perfume it had held had been musky and overpowering—not the type of scent a demure woman would use. Had this been Alma's? Where was she now? What had happened to her?

Restoppering the bottle and setting it aside, she pulled out the garments and examined them. There were two skirts, one a much-laundered, faded-brick red, the other of a dingy hue that must have originally been green. Beneath them she found two bleached-muslin blouses with gathered, bright embroidery-banded sleeves and drawstring necklines. There were also a pair of fine white lawn camisoles beneath them and a lace-trimmed nightgown.

The last items in the trunk were the most surprising—a tarnished, brass-framed hand mirror that had a diagonal crack bisecting the glass, a black lace mantilla and a pair of combs. For all her practical habits when it came to clothing, Tess wouldn't have been female if the mantilla hadn't made her sigh with pure feminine delight and reach out to wrap the garment around her head. Instantly, she felt transformed into a woman who was mysterious, unpredictable—fascinating!

Tess sighed and refolded the garment. It wasn't likely

she'd ever have occasion to wear it, unless perhaps Delgado compelled his band to attend church on Sundays. The thought made her giggle.

It was getting increasingly warm as the sun rose higher above the canyon. Tess supposed she had better try on the borrowed garments so she would have something cooler to wear than the perspiration-dampened clothing she had arrived in. Peeking outside, she saw no one heading toward her hut, so she stepped back behind the screen and stripped off the dusty navy skirt and waist and pulled one of the blouses over her head. The soft, worn fabric felt soothing as it settled around her shoulders. Tying the drawstring at the neck in a bow, Tess studied herself in the cracked mirror, and supposed the neckline was modest enough, though if the drawstring were loosened, it would sink lower around her shoulders. The lower neckline of the blouse revealed the small, gold cross necklace which she always wore, reminding Tess that just as Parrish had said, God was with her, even here in this outlaw camp.

Next she dropped the skirt over her head. It also fastened with a drawstring. Alma must have been a few inches shorter than she was, for the skirt revealed her ankles, but she supposed if she kept her boots and stockings on, it would be all right.

She lifted the curtain again and gazed around the camp, seeing a few men caring for the horses, but there was no sign of Sandoval or Delgado. She wondered what Sandoval was doing.

Her brain ached with fatigue, her eyes felt heavy. The pallet looked so inviting. She hadn't slept soundly as the wagon had rolled over the uneven ground, and she was still tired. It wouldn't hurt to lie down until someone fetched her….

Chapter Five

"Is Francisco here?" Patrick Hennessy tried to sound calm, but he couldn't keep the anxiety from his voice. He exchanged a look with Sam Taylor, who had come with him. Sam looked as if he hadn't slept a wink last night, either.

"*Sí, señor,* I will call him," Francisco's father said, but before he could do so, the boy appeared at the door of their small house. He must have heard the approaching horses.

"*Hola,* Señor Hennessy, Señor Taylor," he said, smiling upward and raising a hand in greeting.

"Good morning to you, Francisco," Patrick said, but did not return his smile. "Francisco, Tess is missing," he said. "She never came home from Mr. Taylor's barbecue last night. The housemaid found a note in her room, saying she was all right, but it wasn't in her handwriting. Her mother is frantic, as you can imagine."

Francisco blinked and his eyes widened in alarm.

"Have you seen her?" Patrick asked.

"No, *señor.* What could have happened to her?"

Patrick could see his surprise at the news was genuine.

The boy looked as worried as he felt. He had reason to be grateful to her. After all, Tess was his friend as well as his employer. She'd taught him an unusual skill, developing photographs and mounting them, passing on a gift her uncle had given to her.

"We don't know," Patrick Hennessy said, wiping a weary hand over his face. "We're just checking to see if she might have stopped here, or told you she was going anywhere. She...she didn't say anything about going to New York, did she?" His heart told him his daughter wouldn't sneak off like that, without even saying goodbye, but he had to ask.

The boy shook his head vehemently. "She wouldn't have gone to New York, *señor,* this I know. She told me she wasn't ready for that. She said she had to have something...." He clearly struggled for the English word. "A...a collection of pictures, do you know what I mean?"

"A portfolio?" Samuel Taylor asked.

Francisco seized upon the word. "*Sí, sí,* a portfolio. To show Señor Brady, the great master of photographers. She said she didn't have enough good pictures yet."

Patrick's gaze sought Sam's again as he considered the boy's words. He felt waves of apprehension dancing down his spine.

Patrick saw the boy move a step closer to his father, as if he feared the two men wouldn't believe him, and managed, through his worry, to also feel regret that he had caused the boy to be afraid. The Hennessys and the Taylors and most of their Anglo neighbors had always lived in harmony with the *Tejanos* among them, but prejudice and bigotry were not unknown among the Anglos.

"You...you haven't heard of anything unusual happening, have you, Francisco? Señor Luna?" Patrick persisted, including Francisco's father in his question.

"Anything happening, *señor?* What do you mean?"

"Anything like raiding," Taylor answered for Hennessy, his voice stern, uncompromising, like that of the Ranger captain he had been in his younger days.

"*Señores,* one of my neighbors tells me Delgado's men were seen last night, riding along the main road about sundown. This man, he did not challenge them, but hid so they would not see him."

The very thing Patrick had feared. "Oh, no," he breathed. "Not Delgado! How am I going to tell her mother Delgado took her?"

Sam still looked as worried as he, but he spoke quickly. "I never heard tell of any bandit troubling to leave the family a note, and in English, at that. I don't reckon Delgado knows how to write Spanish, let alone English. No, there's got t' be more to this disappearance than that, but I'll be cussed if I know what."

"We've got to go see the Rangers," Patrick said. "They have to go after her!"

"Miss Hennessy?" Sandoval called, standing outside the blanket-door, but there was no answer. "Tess, it's Sandoval." Still no answer, so at last he stepped inside the hut. As his eyes adjusted to the cool darkness of the main room, he saw she was not here.

Where could she have gone? Could she have been so foolish as to try to escape already? But where would she have gone? It was not as if she could climb the steep vertical wall of the canyon, or walk right past his compadres who were dicing in the shade, cleaning guns or caring for the horses.

And then, as he stood still in the semidarkness, he heard the quiet, even sound of her breathing, beyond the blanket that divided the room. Moving quietly, he crossed the room in three quick strides and pushed the curtain aside to peer into the sleeping area.

Tess was lying on her side on the pallet, fully clothed in her new, borrowed garments, and fast asleep. One arm lay under the pillow, the other cradled her cheek. Her knees were flexed beneath the faded skirt so that only the tips of her toes stuck out. Her features were relaxed in slumber, the fear and anger that had marched across them earlier entirely absent. She looked so innocent....

As innocent as Pilar had looked before Delgado had ridden into Montemorelos, luring her into leaving with him. *As I live and breathe, Tess Hennessy, this will not happen to you,* he swore silently. He would not fail her as he had failed Pilar.

A wave of longing passed over Sandoval as he continued to look at her. He wanted to drink in the sight of her sleeping until she woke up, even if it took hours, but he knew he couldn't. Even if Delgado wouldn't become impatient and come looking for him, he didn't want to frighten her if she woke and found him staring down at her.

Sandoval stepped carefully and soundlessly backward, letting the blanket fall back into place across the doorway. He called again, louder this time: "Miss Hennessy? Tess? It's time to wake up. It's Parrish, and I've come to take you to Delgado. He's ready to have his picture made."

He heard her utter a quick, involuntary cry of alarm and the pallet rustled. Sandoval imagined her pushing herself up into a sitting position and stretching, perhaps trying to remember where she was.

"I...I guess I fell asleep," he heard her murmur. "Wh-what time is it?"

Sandoval smiled to himself. There were no clocks in the

canyon hideout. The banditos rose with the sun and, when not going raiding, ate and slept when they wanted.

"Late afternoon, Miss Hennessy. You slept through lunch. But no matter. I am sure you needed the rest after your journey, and Delores will be making supper before long."

"Oh! I—I didn't mean to sleep so long! I'll be right out."

He forced himself to sound casual, even disinterested. "Take your time, Miss Hennessy. Delgado merely thought you might want to take advantage of the afternoon light," he said, stepping back outside. "With your permission, I'll have Esteban and Manuel pull your wagon of supplies over in front of Delgado's hut."

She joined him three minutes later, one side of her face still faintly imprinted with the mark of the wrinkled pillowcase, and tendrils of escaping hair curling around her face. "Your new garments become you," Sandoval told her. It was the truth. Her dark-blue skirt and long-sleeved blouse had masked the delicacy of her bones and her womanly form. Her neck was long and elegant, rising above the gleaming, golden cross necklace he spotted just above the drawstring. She was more beautiful in these simple garments than most women would be in satin and lace.

He swallowed with difficulty, trying to look away. "I hope they are comfortable?"

She nodded, gazing down at them. "I daresay they're more practical than what I wore here."

"One might almost think you a *señorita* in a Mexican village, were it not for this," he said, reaching out and touching the thick plait that ran halfway down her back. "It's an unusual color for a *mexicana.*" He saw her blush then, and let go of her hair. What had he been thinking, to take such a liberty?

Then she looked very directly at him and asked, "Who's Alma?"

The question surprised him so much that he replied in the same straightforward way. "Delgado's former mistress. Why?"

She blinked at the information, but went determinedly on. "These are her clothes. I was wondering if she minds my borrowing them. Is she here somewhere?" She peered beyond the little creek as if she expected the woman to be standing just beyond it, glaring at her.

"She is no longer with us, Miss Hennessy," he told her.

Tess gasped. "He killed her? Why?"

He could have kicked himself for phrasing the information that way as he saw the color drain from her face and her eyes widen. "No! I meant that she and Delgado are no longer together," he said quickly. "The last I heard she was living in a village somewhere in the state of Zacatecas."

"What…what was she like?" Tess asked. "Was she beautiful? Why did she leave?" Her blue eyes, alight with curiosity, made her face even more appealing.

"Very beautiful. But very temperamental. She didn't leave willingly. Delgado got tired of her jealousy and her scenes, and left her there with a promise to visit her often. He's never gone back."

Tess looked thoughtful, and perhaps would have asked more, but at that moment Delgado stepped out of his adobe, once more dressed in his fancy Mexican colonel's uniform, complete with ornamental rapier at his side.

"Ah, there you are!" he called, catching sight of them. "Come, come, Señorita Hennessy. I know you will not want to lose the light."

It was many hours till sundown, but once Delgado was ready to do something, there was no gainsaying him, and they walked toward his hut, just as Esteban and Manuel arrived to move the wagon.

"You have had a little siesta, yes?" he said to Tess, as the two men muscled the cart over beside them. "I hope you feel rested."

She nodded.

"And you find your quarters *cómodo*—comfortable? You have everything you need?" His eyes raked over her, and Sandoval saw him taking in her different appearance now that she had changed from her Anglo garments. If he had any thoughts about her wearing his discarded mistress's left-behind clothing, it didn't show in his opaque gaze.

"Yes, it's fine. I—I don't need anything." She darted a glance at Sandoval, and her blue eyes flashed another story. *Except my freedom.*

"*Bueno.* We will commence then," he said, as the two henchmen carried out an ornately carved ebony wood chair padded in red velvet. It was practically a throne.

Tess posed Delgado in the chair, much as she had posed Sandoval—had it only been yesterday?—and took his picture, then disappeared under the canvas to begin the development process. Sandoval saw Delgado fidget as he waited, sweating in the heavy uniform, for Tess to reappear.

"Is that something I could do for you, Miss Hennessy?" Sandoval called, stepping forward.

"I—I suppose it would make things quicker," she said. "I'll show you what to do after I take the next picture. If you came in now, the light would harm this one."

When Tess emerged, she said, "Why don't we pose you in a more active way this time? You could draw your sword, for example."

Delgado beamed. "I believe you have the soul of an artist, Señorita Hennessy." Grinning, he struck a pose, his right arm holding the sword dramatically aloft, his left hand on his hip.

As he had suggested, after Tess removed the collodion plate from this exposure, Sandoval ducked under the canvas with her. It was hard to force himself to pay attention as she showed him how to use the metal dippers to lower the plate into the developing bath, rather than to savor her nearness in the murky half light, but he didn't want to ruin her pictures.

When she was ready to take the next exposure, she suggested, "This time, Mr. Delgado, why don't you do like so…?" She lunged forward as if to parry with an imaginary rapier.

Delgado was clearly delighted at her idea and slid into the pose. "*Señorita,* you are *un genio,* a genius, truly! I already know I will be very pleased with your work, for the world will see Diego Delgado for the warrior he truly is."

Tess couldn't help but smile at his enthusiasm but laid a finger on her lips. "No talking now, Mr. Delgado, until we have made the exposure."

Sandoval could hardly hide his own amusement as he ducked under the tent to develop picture after picture. If Tess was at all intimidated by her situation, she was hiding it well, and she was demonstrating a natural flair for appealing to Delgado's vanity and sense of the dramatic. Sandoval knew Delgado saw himself not as a mere bandit leader, but something more heroic, more like Robin Hood leading his merry men, and Tess had instinctively sensed that, too.

They had taken perhaps half a dozen pictures, and

Sandoval had just emerged from the tent after developing the last one, when Delgado decided he wanted to have Tess take his picture while he sat on his stallion.

Sandoval saw Tess glance skyward. "I'm afraid we are losing the light, Señor Delgado," she said, pointing to the sun, which was beginning to make its descent behind the canyon wall. "Perhaps we could do that tomorrow?"

"Ah, but tomorrow Delgado and his men ride at dawn," Delgado said, thumping his chest with one fist. "We will go on a raid, and there will be much booty! But perhaps that would be the ideal time for you to take my picture, eh? Both before, when I am ready to ride out on a victorious raid, and after, surrounded by fabulous plunder, *sí?*"

Tess nodded. "I will be ready to take the picture when you depart, Mr. Delgado."

"Please, Señorita Hennessy, you must call me Diego," Delgado insisted. He came forward and took her hand, kissing it. "And you must dine with me tonight in my quarters. I usually dine with my men, but tonight we must celebrate your arrival. And you will bring me the developed pictures then, all right?"

Sandoval saw Tess dart a frightened look at him, but before he could speak up, Delgado said, "Ah, you need not worry for your virtue, *señorita,* for I will have Sandoval dine with us. And Delores will be serving the meal, so that will be chaperones enough, *sí?*"

"*Sí*—that is, yes, I suppose that would be all right… Señor Delgado—"

Delgado wagged a finger at her playfully. "Ah-ah-ah, I am *Diego* to you, at least when the other men are not present," he said.

"D-Diego, then," she stammered. "Yes, I will have dinner with you and Mr. Parrish."

"*Bueno,*" he said, and turned on his heel, then halted. "Oh, and wear your hair down, eh? It is such a lovely color—I would see the full effect of its fire." It was a command, not a suggestion. He turned again and disappeared inside.

Sandoval felt his jaw clench and when he looked down, both hands had tightened into fists. He saw that Tess was staring at the bandit leader's door and gnawing her lower lip.

He stepped closer so he could speak in a lowered voice. "Don't worry, Miss Hennessy, I'll be there the entire time," he said.

"Until he orders you to leave," she fretted.

He made a dismissive gesture. "Don't worry. He likes to play at being the suave courtier, just as he reveled at posing as the master swordsman a few minutes ago," he said reassuringly, but inwardly he was not so sure. He was six kinds of a fool to have gotten Tess involved in this. He ought to have foreseen that, having banished his woman weeks ago, Delgado would find Tess's beauty tempting. He was going to have to walk a tightrope to fulfill both his promise to Pilar and to Tess.

Chapter Six

"Dinner is ready, Miss Hennessy," Sandoval called through Tess's door. "Delgado sent me to fetch you. Are you ready?"

She pulled the blanket door-covering aside, and he saw to his surprise Tess had not complied with Delgado's command—instead of wearing her glorious, red hair down, it was drawn up in an elegant chignon held in place by decorative combs. Was it meant to be a subtle bit of defiance?

Good for you, he cheered inwardly, but then he saw how the hairstyle, coupled with the simple drawstring neckline of the *camisa,* left an enticing amount of her neck and shoulders bare for a man's gaze. And perhaps she hadn't noticed the subtle hints of Alma's perfume that clung to the fabric. Sandoval smothered a groan. He was going to have his work cut out for him to protect Tess Hennessy without appearing to do so.

"The photographs are ready," she said, pointing to where they lay, pinned to a drying board on the earthen floor. "Should I bring them?"

Sandoval shook his head. "No, let's wait until after the

meal," he suggested. When we might need a diversion to distract Delgado from your very lovely self, he thought.

"I can always go get them for you," he said.

"And leave me alone with him? Don't you dare."

He saw that beneath her bravado, she was nervous. "Very well," he agreed. "We can send Delores for them."

Delgado opened his door—a real door—before they even had a chance to knock. "Good evening, Miss Hennessy," he said smoothly, beckoning them inside. "And to you, too, Sandoval, of course. But you put your hair up, *señorita!*"

"I'm sorry, but my hair is just so thick and heavy, and it's so very hot. I hope you don't mind," she said.

"Mind? Of course not!" Delgado exclaimed, and Sandoval saw that he, too, was unable to take his eyes from her graceful neck and shoulders. "I want above all things that you should be comfortable here, Señorita Tess. And it happens that I have just the thing for you," he added, crossing the room to a mahogany desk and opening a drawer. When he turned around, he held out an object to her—an ivory-handled fan.

"A gift for you, Señorita Tess," Delgado murmured, watching in patent delight as she opened it and admired the hand-painted floral design revealed when she unfurled it. The breeze she created with the fan fluttered the fiery-red, curling tendrils about her forehead.

"Oh, but I could not accept such a lovely thing. I'll just use it while I am here tonight."

"Nonsense, I want you to have it," the outlaw leader insisted. "Now come, dinner awaits you. I hope it will be to your liking."

Delgado gestured toward one end of a long, rectangular table lit by long beeswax tapers flickering in a pair of silver candelabra. Three place settings of elaborately painted china, heavy silverware, and cut-glass goblets stood at the ready. A nearby sideboard was heaped with an array of savory-smelling dishes.

Delgado held a chair for Tess on his right and indicated that Sandoval was to take the seat on his left, so that Sandoval was sitting opposite her. Delores came forward and filled the cut-glass crystal goblets with claret from a crystal decanter.

"I… Would it be possible for me to have water instead, please, Mr. Delgado?" Tess asked, looking uneasily at the blood-red liquid. "I…I don't drink spirits, you see."

Delgado blinked. "You are…how do you say it? A tee-totaler? I see," he said when she nodded shyly. "Delores! *Agua para la señorita, por favor,*" he said, and the old woman came forward with another glass and a pitcher. "That is most commendable, *señorita.*" He turned to Sandoval. "I think we should toast our lovely guest, do you not? *¡Salud!*" he said, lifting his glass, and Sandoval did likewise. "To our guest, Tess Hennessy, a long and happy life!"

Sandoval watched as a faint flush of color rose up Tess's cheeks. "Thank you," she said, leaving her eyes downcast. Sandoval suspected she had never been toasted before in her life, and marveled at the blindness of Anglo men.

"Delores has surpassed herself tonight," Delgado announced, indicating the dishes on the sideboard. "We have chicken with *mole* sauce, which I warn you is rather spicy, *carne asada, ensalada guacamole,* as well as the usual black beans and rice."

"All of this is for the three of us?" Tess asked, her eyes wide.

"*Sí,* to celebrate your arrival. Of course, my table does

not look like this every night, you understand," Delgado told her, obviously reveling in being the bountiful host. "On nights when we have come home late from a raid, I am lucky to get a bowl of warm soup, eh, Delores?"

The stolid-faced old woman nodded.

"Please, allow me to place a sampling of the dishes on your plate," Delgado said to Tess, "and when you have decided what you like, you must have more, eh? But save room for dessert at the end," he warned.

"Only a little, please," Tess pleaded. "At home we do not have such a big meal at night."

"Ah, but at home you do not sleep through lunch, do you?" Delgado asked with a chuckle. "Don't worry. I like a woman with a hearty appetite."

Sandoval saw Tess dart a look at Delgado that plainly said, "I don't care what kind of woman you like," but Delgado was concentrating on serving her and didn't see it. Once he had placed the plate in front of her, she hesitated, and Sandoval thought she was waiting for Delgado and himself to make their selections, too. But when they had both done so, she still did not lift her fork. Surely she wasn't refusing to eat? But then he saw her duck her head and close her eyes for a moment, and realized she was silently saying grace.

How long had it been since *he* had thanked God for what he put in his mouth? Pilar had always been the one to bless the family dinners.

He saw that Delgado had also noticed what she was doing. Then Tess raised her head, and both men picked up their knives and forks and pretended they had not been watching her.

"Tell me about yourself, *señorita,*" Delgado invited, after a moment or two. "I know little about you except that you are a lady photographer. Tell me of your family."

Tess shrugged, unconscious that the gesture called attention to her lovely shoulders. "There's not much to tell," she said, and went on to tell Delgado what Sandoval already knew of her family.

"Have you ever been away from home like this?" Delgado asked.

As Sandoval listened, Diego Delgado effortlessly drew her out. She told them about being sent away to a fancy finishing school, which purported to be all that was needed for a young lady of good family to be ready to make a brilliant marriage.

Who knew that a notorious outlaw like Diego Delgado could be such a good host, Sandoval mused. He could see Tess relaxing in the midst of Delgado's concentration on her answers and was glad for that, at least.

"But how did you develop an interest in photography?" Delgado inquired. "It is an unusual pastime for a lady, no?"

Spearing a piece of the spicy chicken and dipping it in the chocolate-based sauce, Tess told them about her uncle James, who had been a Brady photographer and had taught her all she knew, and about her goal of going to New York to work for Brady.

Sandoval pretended absorption in his beef as he fought the surprising sense of jealousy that twisted his gut. *He* should be the one plying Tess Hennessy with clever questions, drawing her out, not this scoundrel! She had been standoffish with him when they had met at Taylor's, but surely with time and charm he could have won the right to court her.

And so he might have been the one, if he hadn't decided first to use her to achieve his own goal regarding Delgado.

"Ah, you are a woman of amazing ambition," Delgado

purred, after taking a long draft of his wine. "Do you not wish for a home? A husband? Babies to dandle on your knee?"

Sandoval saw two spots of color spring to Tess's cheeks and sparks flash from her eyes. "*Jefe,* I think your question may be a little too personal..." he began, but Tess found her voice before he could finish his sentence.

"I'd like to ask *you* a question or two, Diego," she said, biting out the words. "Such as, how did you develop an interest in thievery? Especially thievery on such a grand scale?"

Slowly, deliberately, Delgado laid down his knife and fork in turn. The color had fled from his face. "How did I become Delgado, scourge of the Rio Grande Valley, you mean? This land is rightfully Mexican, Tess Hennessy. So I don't really feel that I am doing anything wrong—I am merely taking back those possessions which should belong to my people."

"But people have been killed who sought to protect their property from you and your men, Señor Delgado," she protested.

Sandoval could see the nerve jumping in Delgado's temple and knew the outlaw was perilously close to losing his temper at her outspokenness.

"I kill no one who does not resist us," Delgado said.

"That is your excuse?"

Sandoval knew it was time to intervene. Delgado had been so affable a host before they got on this subject that Tess had forgotten who and what he was. Beneath the table, he very gently but firmly put his booted foot down on Tess's foot. "I think you have said enough, Miss Hennessy," he warned. "Do not forget you are a captive here, and dependent on Delgado's goodwill."

Yes, that's it, he thought, when she transferred her indignant gaze to him. Show me your anger, not Delgado. It's much safer.

He increased the pressure on her foot, hoping she'd take the hint and not insist on having the last word.

Her eyes were disks of ice as she stared at him, her mouth a thin, tight line, but she held her peace.

"I believe you will be pleased at the pictures Miss Hennessy took today, *jefe,*" Sandoval said, praying Delgado was ready to let go of the conflict, too. He turned to Delores, who'd been half dozing in a corner of the room, asking the old woman to bring the photographs from Tess's hut.

Delores was back in a few moments, and Delgado was so thrilled with the results of Tess's first session that he was once again beaming at her, all his wrath forgotten.

"You are a true *artista,* Señorita Tess," Delgado enthused, kissing his fingers at her as if the past, tense moments had never happened. "A genius of daguerreotype, isn't she, Sandoval?"

"Indeed she is," Sandoval said, watching Tess warily.

"And it was masterful on your part to think of bringing her to me," Delgado went on, slapping Sandoval on the back. "Thank you, my loyal amigo!" He turned back to Tess. "And you will be ready at dawn tomorrow to take the pictures of me on horseback, just before we ride out on our raid, *sí?*"

Tess nodded.

"That being the case, perhaps I should escort Miss Hennessy back to her quarters so that she can get her rest," Sandoval said, rising.

"Oh, but we have not had our dessert," Delgado protested. "Delores makes the best *flan* in Mexico, perhaps in the world!"

Tess rose also, protesting that she couldn't eat another bite, as polite as any guest could be.

"Then go and get your beauty sleep, *señorita,*" Delgado said, bowing. "Sandoval, after you have seen her safe inside, summon my other lieutenants and come back. We need to plan our strategy, eh?"

Tess was silent until Delgado closed the door and she was alone with Parrish on the short path to her hut.

"I'm sure I can manage the rest of the way by myself," she told him, her voice burning with suppressed fury. "Go summon the rest of his lieutenants as you were told." She mimicked Delgado's accent mockingly. "You have strategy to discuss, don't you?"

"Woman, hold your tongue," Sandoval snapped, taking hold of her elbow so tightly she almost squeaked at the sudden, unexpected roughness. He yanked her along and pushed her roughly inside the hut, and to her alarm, followed her inside. The interior was dimly lit by a flickering tallow candle burning in a niche in the adobe wall above a pallet like the one Tess had slept on.

"Now, just a minute," she began, beginning to realize too late she might have pushed him too far. "I didn't invite you in—"

Chapter Seven

His dark eyes smoldered down at her, frightening her with their intensity.

"I had to come in, since apparently you have no more sense than to mock me right outside Delgado's quarters," he said in a low voice. "I don't care how you feel about me," he told her, "but don't you think he'd be listening at the window for what you might say? You can't take hints, evidently, so I came inside to tell you what you need to hear."

"Oh, and what is that, pray tell?" she retorted, with all the bravado she could muster.

"Don't think you can be insolent with Delgado, Tess. He may act the courtier at times, but don't forget he's an unprincipled bandit. You're going to have to mind that red-headed temper of yours and at least pretend to respect him and his men if you hope to get out of this situation unscathed."

"How dare you, Sandoval Parrish?" she demanded, taking a step forward and thrusting her chin out. "I wouldn't be in this *situation,* as you so charmingly put it, if it weren't for your desire to curry favor with that same unprincipled killer!" She was too angry at him to care that they were alone in this hut, and she was very much at Sandoval Parrish's mercy.

His head snapped back as if she had slapped him, and he paled. For several endless moments they stared at one another, breathing hard. Then Parrish walked past her and she thought he was leaving, but he only went to the door and stood there for a few moments, peering out into the darkness. Tess realized he was making sure no one was nearby.

He walked back to her. "You're right, you wouldn't. You have every right to think the worst of me, Tess Hennessy. And I can see why you'd think I had you kidnapped to make myself look good to Delgado—but I'm telling you that's not exactly the case. There's more to it than that, and it's up to you whether you believe me or not. The best thing you can do is trust me, and mind what I tell you. I told you I wouldn't let any harm come to you."

"But *why,* Sandoval? What do you hope to gain?" she demanded, self-control slipping, the tears of outrage and fear suddenly threatening to spill over onto her cheeks.

His gaze became more intent then, and she realized she had unconsciously called him by his first name for the first time.

"I can't tell you that, Tess," he said. "Not yet, anyway. I…you may not believe this, but I'm not a bad man."

Something about the softness of his tone and the kindness in his eyes was her undoing, and she gave in to her tears. Then suddenly he was holding her, patting her back as she wept. There was nothing disrespectful about the way he held her, but even so, Tess knew she should move out of his embrace. But it felt comforting and right, and she remained where she was until her tears stopped.

He took a step back from her then, regret that he must do so showing clearly in those dark eyes of his.

"*Buenas noches,* Tess," he whispered. "Go to bed now. Delores will be along as soon as she has cleared Delgado's table, and will sleep out here," he said, indicating the rolled-up straw pallet. "No one will bother you."

Dazed, Tess watched him turn and lift the blanket door, and then he was gone.

Leaving the candle lit in the wall niche for Delores, she walked into her bedroom area and saw that the lace-trimmed muslin nightgown she'd found in the trunk was laid out on the pallet for her. She changed quickly into it in the darkness, unpinned her hair, then lay down on the pallet, sure sleep would come with difficulty if it came at all.

Now that Parrish had held her—and she had allowed him to do so—she was more confused about who he was than ever before. What kind of a dangerous game was he playing with Delgado? She'd thought she knew why he'd kidnapped her, but he had said she was wrong, that she didn't know the real reason. Could she—*should* she believe that he was on the right side?

Yes, her heart told her. He'd had her under his power moments ago, and could have done anything he wanted to her, then fobbed Delgado off with some excuse for why it had taken him so long to return. He had only held her—but what strength and comfort she had found in his embrace. She had felt at home there. It seemed to her he had been showing her a glimpse of his heart, showing her that despite the reasons he had for thrusting her into this dangerous situation, he cared for her. Or was that only what she wanted to believe?

If he wasn't trying to get into Delgado's good graces, then what *was* his purpose?

Uncle Samuel had said Parrish was a "man to ride the river with." Was *he* merely under the spell of Sandoval's charm—and Tess had seen that charm was considerable—or did the older man have good reason to respect Sandoval Parrish?

Before she'd been kidnapped, the worst predicament she had ever been in had been at Miss Agnes's Finishing School for Christian Young Ladies, when it seemed she would fail her class in deportment, a subject that had bored her to distraction. Back then, she had solved the problem by getting on her knees, praying and then opening her Bible at random.

She still remembered the verse on which her finger had fallen—Philippians 4:13—"I can do all things through Christ which strengtheneth me." And it had proven true—she had achieved the third highest mark in the class, though studying after she had prayed probably hadn't hurt.

Now she was in genuine peril, and she knew Parrish had been right about not provoking Delgado too far. He had promised to keep her safe, but what if something happened to Parrish in this nest of cutthroats? Delgado's moods could be capricious—she had seen that for herself tonight.

What she wouldn't give for her Bible right now, to be able to open it up and find a verse that would comfort her! But, of course, her Bible was safely at home on her night-stand, likely covered with at least a week's dust. Tess realized with a guilty start she'd rarely touched it lately except to carry it to church. *Why* hadn't she been more diligent about memorizing Scripture?

She hadn't prayed in ages, either. She'd been so consumed with her photography she'd hardly given a thought to God except during Sunday-morning services—

and sometimes not even then, for it was far too easy to slip into daydreams about working for Mathew Brady in faraway New York City.

Had the Lord allowed her to be kidnapped to punish her for neglecting Him?

Her soul instinctively rebelled at that idea. She'd given Him her heart at an early age, and had always known He was a God of love. But perhaps He was allowing this circumstance in her life to draw her back to Him.

Tess got to her knees. *I'm sorry, Lord,* she prayed. *Please forgive me for finding photography or anything more important than You. Please teach me what You want me to learn through this experience, and bring me safely back home as soon as possible. And please help Papa and Mama not to worry!*

A sense of peace washed over her—a trickle first, and then an ever-increasing stream as the words of a Psalm came to her from some distant part of her memory—"God is our refuge and strength, a very present help in trouble. Therefore will not we fear…"

Night sounds floated in through the window—the distant sound of someone strumming a guitar and singing, the hoot of an owl, the lowing of cattle. She smelled the smoke coming from one of the campfires beyond the stream.

She heard Delores come in then. The old woman shuffled around the outer room for a few minutes, then blew the candle out. The hut was swallowed in darkness. There was a rustling as the old woman settled herself on the straw pallet with a grunt. Within minutes, soft snores emanated from the outer room.

At last, lulled by the regular rhythm of the sound, Tess slept, too.

* * *

In his own adobe, sleep eluded Sandoval. He couldn't stop reliving the pleasure of holding Tess, of savoring her trust—at least, her trust at that moment that he would not take advantage of her nearness, and that he intended to protect her from the danger posed by Delgado and his men. He wanted her to feel secure during the time she was with the outlaws. When she'd been tense and apprehensive, it had felt like a dagger in his heart. What more could he do to assure her of her safety?

Should he confess the truth, that he was a Texas Ranger on a mission to bring Delgado down? Or might that knowledge be too dangerous if Delgado suddenly had some reason to suspect him, and put the question to her? She couldn't tell what she didn't know.

It seemed as if she had only shut her eyes moments ago when she was being shaken awake.

"*Señorita, señorita,* it is time to get up. Wake up, *por favor.*"

Tess opened her eyes with reluctance and saw that Delores was bent over her. Once she saw that Tess was awake, she straightened and left.

Soft light filtered in through the makeshift curtain. Beyond it, Tess could hear the camp waking up. Horses whinnied. Men called to one another. Chickens clucked nearby, and a rooster crowed from somewhere above her, perhaps perched on the straw thatch roof. The smells of coffee and cooking bacon wafted to her on the breeze, causing an answering rumble in her stomach.

Tess dressed quickly, braided her hair and splashed some water on her face from the pitcher Delores had apparently left on her trunk.

Still sleepy, she hoped she would be able to get a cup of coffee before she began photographing, but a shout went up from the direction of Delgado's quarters as soon as she stuck her head outside. Tess saw that Esteban was holding the rangy black stallion that had given her mule such a rude welcome yesterday. The beast was saddled, bridled and obviously ready to go. Her wagon with its photographic supplies still stood next to the adobe.

"*Buenos días, señorita,*" Esteban said, his eyes clearly approving of her Mexican garb.

Beyond the stream, Tess saw that the members of the bandit band were saddling and bridling their horses, some already mounting them. Where was Parrish?

As she returned his greeting, Delgado stepped outside. Gone was the suave courtier of last evening. Here was a man ready for a raid, dressed in rough trousers, a dark shirt and boots, with two bullet-studded bandoliers crisscrossed over his chest and a gun belt with two pistols slung over his hips.

Behind him, Parrish exited Delgado's quarters, and Tess saw with a shiver that he was dressed similarly. His gaze raked over her, nothing in it betraying that he was anything more to her than another of her captors. There was something lean and wolfish about his angular features, the way his eyes narrowed against the morning sunlight, and the tight line of his mouth. Had Tess only dreamed of his tender embrace the night before?

"Ah, I see you are ready," Delgado said to Tess, all business. "That is good. Let us get on with it, for we must be off soon, eh, Sandoval?"

"*Sí, mi jefe.* Señorita Hennessy, I will lift the camera down from your wagon before going to get my horse ready."

Delgado mounted his horse. The big black pawed the ground as his rider took up the reins, clearly eager for a gallop beyond the canyon walls. As soon as Delgado settled himself in the saddle, the black curvetted in the dust, arching his proud neck. It was going to be difficult to get the beast to hold still long enough to take Delgado's picture, Tess thought.

"*Cálmense, mi amigo,*" Delgado said, holding him with some difficulty, but he seemed to share the horse's eagerness and impatience to be off.

Now, if she could just capture that emotion on one of her photographic plates, it would be quite a picture!

Tess worked as quickly as she could, knowing Delgado would not be endlessly patient, and had made half a dozen exposures when the outlaw leader raised his hand and pronounced, "Enough!"

Just then Parrish returned, leading his mount, a striking black-and-white pinto. Tess watched as Parrish mounted.

"Miss Hennessy," he said, once in the saddle, "Delores will see to your needs while we are gone. You have but to ask her." His eyes were impersonal—was it because Delgado was present? Or had he thought about her weeping last night, and decided she was but a silly crybaby?

"But do not seek to escape," Delgado said, wagging a finger at her. "It is impossible."

"I wouldn't think of it," she said coolly, and met Delgado's black stare without blinking, until at last he and Parrish wheeled their horses and splashed through the shallow stream to join the rest of the band, already mounted and waiting.

"*¡Vayan, muchachos! ¡Rápido!*" Delgado cried, and then the band was galloping out of the canyon's mouth. She thought she saw Parrish look back at her before the horses' hooves churned up a cloud of dust that soon hid them from sight.

Tess wondered where they were going to raid today, then realized with a stab of anxiety that not only were they going to cause danger to others, but what they were about to do would expose them to danger, too.

She didn't care so much about the other banditos, except in the way she would care about the fate of any human being. But, *dear Jesus, please don't let anything happen to Sandoval Parrish! Don't let him be wounded or captured.* He might not truly be an outlaw—as yet she didn't know what he truly was, but if he were taken by the Texans, they might not allow him time before stringing him up to explain what he had been doing raiding with Delgado.

And then she had to smile at the irony of it all. Here she was, having photographed an outlaw in his lair today, and she had just thought of the Texans, *her own people,* as "them." And she had prayed specifically for the safety of one of those riding out on the raid, even though Parrish might be nothing but an outlaw himself.

Chapter Eight

With the outlaw band gone and the new exposures drying underneath the canvas hood, Tess was finally free to break her fast, and crossed the little bridge to the campfire. Delores, wrapped in a black rebozo against the early morning chill, was already there, stirring something in a skillet. At Tess's approach, she poured steaming coffee into a tin cup and handed it to her.

Tess sank onto a log nearby and drank gratefully. Moments later she was devouring not only eggs but the remains of a loaf of bread that tasted freshly baked. How early had this woman arisen, to have baked bread already? The sun was only now rising over the canyon wall.

"This is really good, *señora,*" Tess praised, realizing she had never enjoyed breakfast so much at home. She gestured at the last hunk of bread in her hand. "How on earth do you manage to bake bread in a place like this?"

Delores beamed. "In that *horno,*" Delores said, pointing to a rounded-edged, shoulder-high earthen mass that Tess hadn't noticed before. "The Indians taught our Spanish ancestors to use them."

It was a good thing she'd learned to speak fluent Spanish from the servants at Hennessy Hall, Tess thought. Her mother knew only enough to give directions to Rosa, the cook, and Flora, the housemaid, and would have been helpless to carry on a conversation like this. Maybe Tess could learn something from Delores that would help her to find her way out of this predicament.

Delores rose, and gathering up the stack of dirty plates the men had left scattered about on the other side of the campfire, ambled in the direction of the stream.

"Let me help you carry those," Tess said, taking the stack from her. Delores nodded, picking up a nearby bucket and a cake of soap instead. Together they walked to the water and, kneeling, washed the plates, cups and forks with a couple of rags Delores produced from a pocket in her threadbare skirt.

"Have you been among the bandits long, *señora?*" Tess inquired.

The woman seemed surprised at her curiosity. "Yes, for about two years."

"Why did you come?" Tess was careful to keep her tone nonjudgmental, but surely there had to be something more for a woman up in years to be doing than cooking for outlaws.

Delores shrugged. "I am a widow. My son Esteban, who is my youngest child, chose to ride with Delgado. I had nothing else to do. If I came along, I could make sure he got enough decent food to eat, at least when they are in the canyon."

So the mustachioed young man who had led the kidnapping and initially taken Tess's money was Delores's son. And he was a youngest child, too. Delores was certainly pragmatic about her son joining the outlaws, even coming along herself to look after him, more than Tess's mother would have been!

The day was rapidly growing warm. Tess had removed her boots and stockings and was enjoying the cool play of the water over her feet. Delores had shed her rebozo long ago. Now, with the dish washing done, she yawned widely, then rose to her feet and told Tess she was going to take a siesta in the shade and that Tess should, too.

Here was Tess's chance to explore. She didn't know if they had posted a guard or were counting on her, a foreigner far from home, being too intimidated to try to escape, but she didn't believe Delgado's assertion that escape was impossible. She hadn't seen the opening of the canyon when she had arrived yesterday, but all she had to do was walk in the same direction where they had ridden off.

After putting her stockings and boots back on, Tess waited until the old woman had lain unmoving in the shade for several minutes before getting up and looking around. The camp was eerily quiet except for the buzz of insects and the occasional stamping of her mule. The fact that she couldn't see anyone as she peered around the camp didn't mean one of the men wasn't watching them from some vantage point right this very minute! But if she didn't spot a guard, she was determined to try to escape. She could always ride Ben out of the canyon bareback, if need be.

Tess walked quietly up the stream past the sleeping woman until a bend in the canyon wall hid her from sight.

She walked about a hundred yards down the rocky, curving mouth of the gorge and encountered no one. She could see ahead of her where the canyon opened. Could it really be this easy to get away? A rising sense of hope surged within her.

"Buenas tardes, señorita," a voice said.

Tess gave a stifled squeak of alarm, nearly jumping out of her skin. A figure of a man, clad in the usual unbleached cotton garments of a Mexican peon, separated itself from a rocky boulder on which he had been leaning, holding a rifle with casual negligence and grinning at her.

It was the rude, aggressive man from the night of her kidnapping—Tess had heard him called Jaime Dominguez.

"Going somewhere, *señorita?* Or perhaps you came to chat with me, eh?" His knowing eyes indicated he knew exactly what she was up to.

Tess bit back a thoroughly impolite reply. It wouldn't be wise to trade barbs with this one while he was the only man left at the hideout.

"No, I was just taking a walk," she said. "I—I'll just be going back to Delores now...." Tess reversed her position, walking for a few paces, then breaking into a run back into the canyon. The man's scornful laughter echoed off the canyon walls.

Tess didn't stop running until after she reached the sanctuary of her hut. Evidently she wasn't meant to escape—at least not yet—so she must look for the good in the situation. And as she sat in the shade of a clump of mesquite that afternoon, sketching with a bit of charcoal on a piece of paper Delores had found for her, it came to her what the "good" might be.

She had been looking for some way to distinguish her work so Mathew Brady wouldn't be able to resist hiring her when she arrived in New York City. There had never seemed to be any way to achieve that, living in the sleepy Rio Grande Valley where nothing ever happened. Brady would not be impressed by her portfolio of stiff portraits of local residents. Now, it seemed, being kidnapped had dropped an amazing opportunity into her lap.

By saving the negatives of her photographs of Delgado and his bandits, Tess could put together a photographic essay of life among the *bandoleros.* The fact that the photographer was a woman would only add to the collection's appeal, and she would have proved she was a woman who could seize the initiative. He would beg her to work for him!

There was no sign of the outlaws until sundown. Tess tried not to fret as the endless hours crawled by, but Delores went about her tasks unperturbed. Finally Tess decided to pass the time by taking photographs of the older woman and her typical activities—grinding corn for tortillas, shelling beans, mending a rent in one of her voluminous skirts. Delores seemed bemused to find herself the subject of Tess's lens, but when she showed the old woman the photographs, Delores's mouth gaped in amazement. She had probably never expected to see a photograph of herself, let alone several.

The first sign of Delgado and his men returning was a steady thunder, distant at first, gradually building until Tess looked upward to see if rain clouds had stolen over the evening sky. Then she heard the bawling of cattle and, over that, the occasional yips of the men as they drove along the stolen herd.

A rising cloud of dust heralded their imminent arrival into the canyon. Delores yanked Tess's sleeve, gesturing for Tess to follow her, and hastened across the bridge and into the hut. They watched from the window as the bellowing cattle, a mixture of rangy longhorns and fat Herefords, pounded into the camp. Scenting water, most of the cattle headed straight for the stream, stopping there and lowering their heads to drink, though some ran straight through the water and past the hut, looking for the way out. As soon as a few of the beasts finished drinking and lurched away from the stream, others took their place, and the banditos funneled the satisfied cattle into the empty one of the two corrals.

Peering through the gathering gloom, Tess looked for Parrish, but without success. She saw that Delores also appeared to be watching for someone—her son? She saw Delgado ride past on his black stallion. The horse's earlier fire was gone now, his flanks lathered, his head hung low. Jumping off his mount and handing his reins to one of his men, Delgado headed for his quarters without acknowledging her.

And then she saw the pinto—his bold white patches standing out in the shadows. His pace was slow because Parrish cradled someone else ahead of him on the saddle, someone whose light cotton shirt was splotched with dark patches of dried blood.

Beside her, Delores shrieked, *"¡Esteban! ¡Mi hijo!"* The old woman was running out of the hut, faster than Tess had imagined she could possibly move, wailing and skirting the milling cattle, heading toward Parrish and the wounded man he carried.

Tess followed, and was in time to help Sandoval lower the unconscious young man into Delores's waiting arms. The old woman sank down onto the dirt with him, moaning and murmuring while she frantically searched him for wounds.

Parrish dismounted, then spoke to Delores, his tone calm and reassuring, but Delores was far too upset to be comforted while Esteban lay insensible and pale in her lap.

Parrish turned to Tess, his face coated with dust, his eyes unspeakably weary. "His only wound is in the shoulder, but he's lost a lot of blood, and we're going to have to dig the bullet out if he's not to die of blood poisoning."

"But...but he needs a doctor," Tess protested. "Why didn't you find him a doctor?"

His dark eyes raked her, their depths lit with impatience. "You think we should have stopped the herd on the Texas side of the river and taken Esteban to some Anglo sawbones? The rancher we stole that herd from and the Rangers pursuing us would have appreciated it, I'm sure."

"Of course I don't mean that! I meant once you were safely across the Rio Grande," she retorted.

"Just how many competent *médicos* do you think there are between here and Mexico City?" he asked, his tone bordering on contemptuous. "Even supposing the *Rinches* hadn't pursued us across the river, which they did! They shot Pedro Sanchez right off his horse just before we reached the other bank. He was dead before he hit the water, I think. We had to ride hard until they finally gave up a few miles ago and turned back—didn't want to battle us in the dark in unfamiliar country, I guess."

Tess wasn't sure which of the outlaws Sanchez had been, but she saw the grim set of Parrish's mouth and bit back what she had been about to say. "I...I'll help however I can," she said.

"I've got a bottle of tequila in my quarters, hidden under my bedroll. Would you please fetch it? I'll be by the campfire—I'm going to need the light, as well as a place to clean my knife blade before I go digging for that bullet." Tess realized he meant to pour the liquor over the wound, not drink it. But what made Parrish think he could remove a bullet? He wasn't a doctor.

Because someone had to do it. There was no one else capable.

Over her shoulder, she heard Parrish call out to one of the banditos thronging around them to help him carry Esteban over beside the fire. Delores ran alongside, still moaning and muttering frantic prayers, until at last they could lay him down near the campfire.

Parrish's quarters were spartan and orderly—just a bedroll and a small trunk like the one in her hut.

When Tess returned, she found Esteban lying with his head pillowed in his mother's lap while Parrish cut away the bloodstained shirt with a bowie knife. She held out the bottle. Without thanking her, Parrish took it, uncorked it and poured tequila over the exposed, sinister-looking hole in the front of Esteban's right shoulder.

Esteban uttered a sharp, incoherent cry, rising up and swinging at Parrish with his other arm, then sank back into insensibility. The other men milled around the edge of the firelight, passing a couple of bottles around, watching.

"I hope he'll stay unconscious," Sandoval muttered. "Sit down here and be ready to help Delores hold him. He'll fight me—he won't know what he's doing, or that I'm trying to help him, only that he hurts like h—like blazes," he amended with a wry twist of his mouth. Tess obediently knelt down beside the wounded man. While Delores murmured in Spanish into her son's ear, Parrish held the blade of his knife in the midst of the flames for a moment, then bent to his task.

Esteban went rigid, screamed, then bucked and struggled against the restraining hands. It took all of Tess's strength to help Delores hold him down. One of the other banditos threw himself over Esteban's legs, preventing him from kicking at Parrish, until at last the bullet he'd been digging for fell out into the dust with a soft *plop*. Esteban sank back, completely unaware that Parrish was once again pouring fiery alcohol over the bloody wound. Tess looked away, feeling sick as the world spun around her.

She was vaguely aware of Delgado having returned, standing among his men, watching Sandoval and her with hooded eyes.

Delores, still crooning to her son, reached into one of her capacious pockets and produced clean, folded rags to use as bandages. Tess realized she had placed them there to be ready for the men's return, little realizing her own son would be the one who needed them.

"I need to have him taken to your quarters," Parrish told her.

"I can sleep outside," Tess agreed.

Parrish shook his head. "It wouldn't be safe." He nodded toward the door. "I meant Delores can watch over him in the outer area, while you sleep on your pallet." He spoke to the surrounding men, and several of them bent to the task of carrying Esteban into her hut. Delgado followed.

His eyes on the procession, Parrish let out his breath, almost as if he had been holding it the entire time. She saw his shoulders sag with weariness. She wanted to go to him, put a hand on his arm and tell him how brave he had been to take on such a hazardous task.

Then he turned back to Tess, and to her surprise, his eyes were warm with approval. "You did well," he told her.

Chapter Nine

Her eyes—those impossibly deep blue eyes—widened as if she couldn't believe what she had just heard. "I—*I* did well? But I didn't do anything. *You* dug the bullet out, not me."

He could tell by the way Tess paled she was remembering the way the crimson rivulet had flowed past his knife, and the heavy, coppery smell of the blood. Possibly she had never been exposed to such a sight before. Delicately reared young ladies were usually sheltered from such things.

"But you didn't cry or faint at the sight of all that blood," he told her. "You didn't make a nuisance of yourself—you made yourself useful. Thank you."

She raised her eyes to his, blinking as if trying to hold back tears. "Y-you're welcome."

Had she never been praised for bravery before?

Now Sandoval could see weariness taking over her features like a veil swirling between them.

"You'd best get some sleep," he told her. "Come on, I'll walk with you."

"Will he…will he recover?" she asked.

"Esteban? I think so, with a little luck, if no infection sets in. Delores has nursed wounded men before."

"Is there anything else I can do?" she asked, pausing just outside her hut. "Maybe I could offer to take over for Delores when she gets too weary."

He stared down at her in the darkness. Someone had built another campfire just beside the hut so Delores wouldn't have to go far from her son. The light of the campfire cast flickering shadows on Tess's earnest, upturned face.

"She'll let you know if she needs something," Sandoval told her. He wanted so much to kiss her, to caress her, to promise her everything would turn out all right.

"I'll pray for him."

Sandoval felt a tightening in his throat at her offer. She was a captive, but she was offering to pray for the recovery of one of the very men who had taken her prisoner on the road to her home. What kind of a woman was this? He wanted to say, Pray for me, too, while you're at it. But he didn't want to answer the questions such a request might raise. "Get some sleep, Tess," he said again, and walked away from her toward his own hut.

A moan from beyond the curtain wakened Tess just as dawn began to break. Was Esteban worse? Wrapping the sheet around her like a shawl, Tess pushed the blanket aside and went to where Delores knelt by her son's side.

Esteban's eyes were still tightly shut, his brown forehead pearled with sweat. Strands of black hair were pasted damply to his temples. His bare chest rose and fell rapidly under the light bleached-muslin sheet.

Delores murmured something to him, pouring a spoonful of dark liquid from a brown glass bottle and holding it to his lips. His mouth slackened, accepting the liquid, but he made a face as it trickled into his mouth.

"Is he feverish?" Tess asked, kneeling down on the other side of the man lying on the striped blanket.

"*Sí.* It is expected," Delores told her matter-of-factly. "The body protests both the invasion of the bullet and the knife that dug it out."

Tess reached out a hand to touch his forehead. Esteban's skin felt moistly hot, and her eyes went to Delores with alarm.

The older woman, her face concerned but not fearful, pointed to the brown glass bottle on the dirt floor beside her. "This will help."

Esteban passed once again into deep sleep, and Delores settled back against the adobe wall with a sigh. Had she been awake all night?

"I could stay with him while you sleep."

Delores smiled but shook her head, then pointed at the growing light stealing under the blanket door. "It is time for me to cook the men's breakfast."

Of course. Her son might be wounded, but Delores still had a camp full of hungry men who would expect to be fed.

"I'll sit with Esteban while you cook," Tess said. She wished she could offer to do the cooking, but though she'd learned a few basics at the finishing school, cooking was strictly the job of Señora Rosa at home. Her mother had made vague remarks about Tess needing to learn the skill "someday," but someday had never arrived. Perhaps that was something else she could learn a bit while she was here.

Delores smiled, her eyes tired, and rose stiffly to her feet. "*Gracias,*" she said, and went outside.

Time passed, and with nothing to do but watch the sleeping man, Tess had too much time to worry over her situation. How would she get free? What if something happened to Parrish, and she was left alone with the outlaws? Was there a posse searching for her, even now? What if they were killed trying to save her?

But once she had prayed for deliverance, what could she do but fret some more?

Finally she reprimanded herself. She might not be a competent cook, but she could pray for Esteban as she'd promised, at least. She knelt.

"Lord, please help Esteban to heal. Keep his fever down and please keep infection from the wound. He seems like a good man, even though he's an outlaw, and Delores loves him, Lord—"

Suddenly the blanket over the door was pulled open and a tall shadow blocked the doorway and the sunlight.

It was too tall to be Delores but, thinking it was Parrish, Tess's features had begun to relax when the figure spoke. "Ah, the angel of mercy, interceding with Heaven for a sinner. What an inspiring picture, to be sure. *Señorita,* it is a pity you cannot take your own picture."

Delgado. There was something about his voice that reminded her of a snake—the original snake in the Garden of Eden, beguiling with its lovely words, but the voice came from the same part of its body as the fangs.

"You give me too much credit, Mr. Delgado," she said crisply. "I merely agreed to stay with Esteban so Delores could perform her other duties." She wished Parrish would come, or Esteban would wake up, so she would not have to be alone with this man. His eyes were too intense as they roamed over her, missing nothing.

"Not at all," Delgado said, coming forward to where she

sat. "I realized while you watch over my injured compadre, you are not breaking your own fast. So I came to bring you some food." He lifted the blanket again, leaned over and reached outside on the ground, and brought in a tin plate heaped with tortillas, eggs and bacon and a mugful of steaming coffee, which he set down by her.

"Thank you."

Tess's hopes that Delgado would go after performing this service were dashed immediately when he lowered himself to the ground and sat across from her with Esteban between them.

"And how does the patient this morning, eh?"

Tess reached out a hand to test Esteban's forehead, and found it already cooler. "Better," she said. "He had a fever when I awoke, but Delores gave him something, and it seems to have broken."

"Ah, Delores is a wise woman, no? But it is also good of you to tend him."

Just then Esteban began to stir, saving her the necessity of a modest demur. As both of them watched, the wounded man opened one eye, blinking up at Tess, and then opened both eyes, his gaze shifting to Delgado. He smiled weakly.

"*¡Hola, Esteban, mi amigo!* How goes it, my brave man? Esteban's bullet was meant for me, did you know that, Señorita Tess?"

Tess shook her head.

"Esteban is a tough man. It takes more than an Anglo bullet to kill him, eh?"

Esteban grinned and weakly thumped his chest.

Tess nodded. "I hear one of your other men was not so lucky."

Delgado's mouth tightened. "Yes, we lost Pedro, gunned down by a cowardly Anglo dog."

Who was probably just trying to protect his property—Tess bit back the retort, aware Delgado was baiting her. Parrish had advised her not to argue with Delgado, and in any case she would not do so in front of a sick man.

"We could not even bring back his body without risking the loss of other men," Delgado told her, eyes hot with anger, as if she were somehow responsible merely by being a Texan. He pointed to Esteban. "You will take a picture of this victim of the *Norteamericanos*."

He waited, but when she did not respond to his taunts, Delgado got to his feet and headed for the door. "We will rest today and recover from our exertions. I will tell Delores her son has awakened, so she can bring him something to eat. Then you must come see the spoils from our raid, and make a picture of it all, eh? I have kept the men from taking their shares until you do this."

Later, when Tess emerged from the adobe, she found Parrish, Delgado and several others drinking coffee and standing around a blanket piled high with objects. Parrish watched her approach, his eyes guarded.

As she drew nearer, items distinguished themselves—jewelry, including a brooch, a pair of onyx earbobs and a string of pearls, a man's pocket watch, a pair of fancy tooled-leather boots, an ornate silver-studded saddle, an ormolu clock, a large gilt-framed landscape painting.

"Quite a successful raid, I see," she commented, wondering if all these items had come from one home or if they had struck several ranches. Esteban had been wounded, and another of the banditos had died for these things. Had anyone been wounded or killed, trying to protect their property? The idea sickened her.

"Yes. I have decided we will have a celebration tomorrow," Delgado told her. "We will enjoy some of that good beef over there," he added, pointing to the corral where the stolen cattle stood, some of them grazing, others standing idly, swatting flies with their tails. "We will ride into Santa Elena and invite everyone to come and feast with us—very enjoyable, no?"

She stared at him. There was a *town* nearby? A town where people knew of the hideout, but did nothing to bring the outlaws to justice? Were they afraid of Delgado and his men? Or perhaps they were indifferent to the idea of Anglos being raided. Most Mexicans regarded all of Texas as land that had been stolen from *them,* after all. Maybe they benefited from the goods Delgado stole, too. But if she could find *someone* among those who came to celebrate who would be sympathetic to her desire to escape…

"And I have something especially for you, something you will like," Delgado said, reaching into the pocket of his trousers and bringing out a gleaming gold necklace with an ornate cross pendant studded with sapphires—a necklace Tess had last seen around the plump neck of Mrs. Dupree at Uncle Samuel's barbecue. The fact that Delgado had it meant that the raiders had struck near Hennessy Hall.

"You didn't kill the lady this belongs to, did you?" she demanded, glaring at Delgado.

He chuckled and grinned at her. "No, do not fear. She was very willing to give it up when I explained the alternative to her. Here, let me fasten it on your lovely neck," he said, holding up the necklace and gesturing for her to turn around. "I thought of you immediately when I saw it—it matches your eyes."

Tess took a step back. "No, thank you. I already have one." She pulled out the plain, small gold cross that hung from a thin chain around her neck, the same one she had been given when she went away to finishing school.

"Oh, but this one is much more beautiful," Delgado said, dangling the sapphire cross in front of her as if he thought it might tempt her.

"This one is all I need."

Delgado shrugged, amused. "Then perhaps what Sandoval obtained for you will be more to your taste."

Tess's gaze flew to Parrish, and he reached inside his vest and brought out a small, black leather-bound book she recognized—*her own Bible.*

"How did you get that?" she cried, grabbing it. "Did you raid Hennessy Hall? Did you hurt my father or my mother?"

He held up a reassuring hand. "Your parents never knew I was on the property. Only one of the housemaids, who was very willing to get it for you without telling anyone I was there."

Tears stinging her eyes, Tess clutched the familiar book to her, suddenly very homesick. And touched that Parrish had thought to obtain the one thing that would bring her a measure of real comfort. Why had he done such a thing?

"You took a chance," she told him. "My father would have had you horsewhipped at the very least if he'd caught you."

Sandoval's eyes danced with mischief. "And the neighbors would have held a lynching," he agreed. "But he didn't catch me. And I also had the housemaid leave a note on your bed that you were alive and well and would return soon."

"Did he know it was from you?"

Parrish shook his head. "I signed it 'A Friend.'"

All at once she was conscious of Delgado watching them.

"As soon as the *señorita* takes a picture or two, let's ride to town and issue our invitation," Delgado said to Parrish. "I know Lupe, especially, will be happy to see you."

Lupe? Who was that? Some Mexican sweetheart of Parrish's?

His expression gave her no clue, but she shouldn't have found it surprising that a man as handsome as Sandoval Parrish had a girl nearby. He probably had one in each town on both sides of the river. She had no reason, she reminded herself sternly, to care.

But against all reason and common sense, she *did* care. She had thought he cared—there had been something in the air between them, she thought. But she must have been wrong about how he felt about her. The idea of Sandoval's sweetheart joining him in camp made her sick with jealousy.

Chapter Ten

The canyon hummed with the afternoon drone of insects. Everyone else in camp seemed to be enjoying siesta, though Tess had no doubt someone was on guard duty at the mouth of the canyon. Ignoring the trickle of perspiration down her neck, she labored to develop the pictures of the booty—and of Esteban, who had been assisted out in front of the adobe for the photograph. Afterward, she made up some new collodion plates, using the chemicals from her wagon.

Her photographic duties done for the moment, Tess retreated to her hut. Esteban had been assisted to join the other men, who had gathered in the shade. She could see Delores napping again under the shade of the biggest cottonwood by the stream.

Her Bible lay waiting for her on her pillow in the shadowy coolness inside the adobe. *God, please encourage me.* The Psalms were usually good for that, weren't they? Flipping through the gilt-edged pages, she paused at Psalm 62—"He only is my rock and my salvation; he is my defense; I shall not be greatly moved."

Thank You, Lord, for reminding me of that. Tess had intended to spend the rest of the afternoon reading, but lulled by the heat and shadowy stillness inside her hut, her eyelids drooped....

It was nearly dusk when she awoke to sounds drifting in through her window—men laughing and talking, the whinnies of horses, the clang of metal against metal. Had Parrish and Delgado returned?

She paused in the doorway, her eyes taking in the sight of several of the outlaws standing waist deep in a hole, throwing red dirt from their shovels. Evidently this was to be the barbecue pit tomorrow. Bawling as if they suspected their fate, half a dozen steers were even now being funneled into a smaller holding pen nearby.

Delgado came out of his quarters just then, flanked by a slender whip of a woman taller than he. She wore a silver-studded black riding outfit with a divided skirt and a short jacket that showed off an enviably narrow waist. Possessed of the same dark, sinister beauty as Delgado, the same sinuous grace, the same glittering obsidian eyes, she had to be his sister.

"Ah, Tess, there you are. Come meet Lupe." He turned and said something to the woman.

Lupe. It was a common enough Mexican name. Could it be the same Lupe who Delgado had said would be happy to see Parrish? But of course it was, Tess realized, when Parrish, ducking his head so as not to hit the lintel, followed her from the outlaw leader's adobe. So Sandoval had yet another way to earn favor with Delgado, by romancing his sister.

"Lupe María Consuela Delgado y Peña, I am honored to present Señorita Tess Hennessy, who has so kindly consented to immortalize our exploits in photographs," Delgado said, as ceremonially as if he were presenting Tess to a queen.

And Lupe considered herself a queen, Tess realized, watching as the outlaw's sister inclined her head regally, then inspected Tess from head to toe, eyes narrowed as if she were searching for minute stains on her clothing. Tess almost expected her to extend a hand to be kissed in obeisance.

"Buenos días," Tess said at last, when the other woman said nothing. Perhaps she spoke no English.

"So, you are the little…what is the word?—*photographer* my brother has hired?" Lupe purred, her voice unexpectedly deep and amused.

Little? Tess found herself bristling at the condescension in the woman's tone. She was shorter than Lupe-whatever-Delgado, but so what? "I am the photographer, yes, but I wouldn't say I was *hired,* precisely. Kidnapped, I would call it." She shot a look over Lupe's shoulder at Parrish.

Lupe allowed herself a husky, entrancing laugh, half turning to Parrish. "Ah, she is a fiery one, no? It goes with her hair. You did not get burned when you tied her up, did you, Sandoval, *querido?*" She laid a caressing hand on his cheek, gazing up at him through dark, thick lashes for a moment, then over her shoulder at Tess.

It was an unmistakable gesture of possession. Involuntarily stiffening, Tess studied Parrish's reaction.

His eyes gave away nothing. He did not seem to move so much as a muscle away from the caress, but he didn't lean into it, either. Was he merely too polite to display his feelings for the woman in front of Tess?

"Actually, I wasn't even there," he told Lupe. "I merely let them know where and when they could find her alone, and rode on ahead."

Unwilling to watch Lupe touching Sandoval any longer, Tess swung her gaze to Delgado, and found him studying her speculatively.

"H-how pleasant that your sister could come for a visit," she managed to say.

"Yes, she loves to come and visit her brother the famous *bandolero* from time to time, when living in Santa Elena grows tedious. She will come along with us on our next raid, when we will be gone for several nights."

"She…she goes raiding with you?" Tess repeated, incredulous.

"You find that remarkable for a woman, when you yourself are a photographer? Lupe rides like she was born on a galloping horse and is utterly ruthless, not to mention deadly accurate with a pistol. A most formidable opponent, as many Anglos have discovered to their sorrow. You might not know that her name means *wolf*."

"How very apt," Tess murmured, well able to imagine Lupe as a female version of her outlaw brother. So the outlaws would be away for a while—might she have the opportunity to escape while they were gone?

"And since Lupe will be with us, she can serve as a chaperone so you can come, too."

Tess's mouth dropped open. "*Me?* Come along on a raid? No, I don't think so! I'll stay back here in the canyon." Or at least I'll let you believe I'm content to do that, she thought.

"Come now, *señorita,* you can hardly expect me to leave you here with only a wounded man and an old woman to guard you," Delgado told her.

"But I could hardly hope to keep up with you, driving my cart full of heavy equipment," Tess pointed out. "Aren't you afraid I'll slow you down, cause you to risk capture or worse?"

Delgado shook his head. "On this expedition you will not bring your big camera and mule cart, only drawing paper. Delores showed me some of the sketches you did yesterday while we were gone. Your gift for drawing is nearly the equal of your talent behind the camera lens. No, for the raids, we will mount you on a swift horse—perhaps that sorrel in the corral over there."

"But…aren't you afraid I will escape?" Tess asked. Out of the corner of her eye, she saw that Lupe had stopped batting her eyelashes at Parrish and was taking in every word.

Delgado chuckled. "No, *señorita.* I have told you my sister is a crack shot, and utterly ruthless. She would not hesitate to shoot your horse out from under you, if you were to try such a thing."

"Why waste a good horse, *hermano?*" Lupe inquired, her eyes narrowed at Tess. "If it comes to that, perhaps I will just shoot the *gringa* herself. From what you have told me, she has already taken enough pictures."

Tess felt a chill entirely at odds with the July heat gripping her heart like a squeezing fist. Looking into the flat, soulless, dark eyes of Lupe Delgado, she did not doubt the woman would do exactly what she threatened without a qualm.

Delgado's hand snaked out and seized his sister's wrist, and he uttered a spate of low, hissing Spanish at her. Tess could only wonder what he said, but she saw Lupe's eyes flash angrily up at her brother before they turned with hot resentment on Tess.

Lupe snarled something at Delgado. Then she yanked her arm out of her brother's grasp and flounced back inside the adobe.

"Do not worry, *señorita,*" Delgado murmured. "My

sister now understands that you are under my protection, and any harm to you would touch upon my honor."

Tess could only stare in Lupe's wake. Despite Delgado's assurances, if looks could kill, Tess would be dead.

"Go smooth her feathers, Sandoval," Delgado urged. "You seem to have a way with my sister."

Parrish shot a look at Tess she couldn't interpret, then ducked his head to reenter the adobe. Tess didn't see him alone again for the rest of the day—only later, at a distance, walking with Lupe down by the stream.

The townspeople of Santa Elena began arriving in late afternoon the next day, on foot, on donkey or horseback, and by oxcart. Everyone from the oldest graybeard to the youngest child able to toddle was dressed in their festive best. They treated Delgado with the respect due a *patrón* opening up the grounds of his spacious estate rather than a local bandit inviting the peons to a party in a dusty canyon.

Many greeted brothers or sons or cousins among the outlaws. Several men arrived with guitars strapped to their backs, and soon the air was filled with lively strumming as well as the savory aroma of roasting beef. The women had brought platters of sliced mangos, oranges and bananas, bowls of salsas and sauces, as well as mounds of freshly baked red-and-green striped cookies, and laid them out on a makeshift table of planks and sawhorses. Fat-cheeked, black-eyed children ran everywhere, shrieking merrily or staring at Tess as she indicated to a trio of banditos where to place her photography wagon.

At first she and the wood box she set up on its tripod were the subjects of much staring, pointing and whispered commentary, but all at once, Parrish materialized at her side.

"This is Señorita Hennessy," he announced, after clapping his hands to obtain silence. "She is a friend of Señor Delgado. She's here to take pictures with her camera."

Suddenly everyone was crowding around Tess, all smiling and talking at once. The children, even less inhibited, began jumping up and down and pulling at her sleeves. Only a few of the older women backed away, muttering and making odd gestures in Tess's direction.

"Some of those older women think your camera is the evil eye, out to capture and imprison their souls," Parrish explained. "But the rest of them all want their pictures taken."

"But I don't have enough chemicals and paper for all of them," Tess said, eyeing the growing throng with dismay. She didn't want to disappoint anyone, especially the laughing, excited children. "I wouldn't be able to take any more of Delgado, and he still seems to want more."

"Maybe you could arrange them in a group—the tallest men standing in the back, the women kneeling in front of them, the children sitting in front of the women?" Parrish suggested. "Then you could make just one photograph of all of them. It would probably hold the place of honor in the local cantina for the next hundred years."

Tess chuckled, imagining it. "That might work," she agreed. "You'll have to explain the necessity of remaining very, very still once I give the word. I'm not sure those children can do it. They all seem to be part grasshopper."

Sandoval grinned, then called out instructions. In a couple of minutes, most of the townspeople of Santa Elena had arranged themselves in orderly rows. Even the children froze in their places, staring into Tess's lens with all the solemnity of statesmen. A couple of minutes later, Tess emerged from under her canvas and told Parrish the photograph had been a success.

"How did you manage to get the children to hold so still? They were better behaved than the Dupree girls at Uncle Samuel's party!" Tess praised him.

He smiled down at her. "There is a very badly chiseled stone statue of Santa Anna that stands in front of the cantina in the village. I told them to pretend to be that statue."

"I'll have to remember that ploy," she told him. When he smiled at her like that she could almost forget what was happening—forget that he was the very man who had arranged her kidnapping, forget that he had brought his inamorata to camp, forget that thanks to Parrish, she was utterly at the mercy of an outlaw leader whose moods were as changeable as the wind.

"I am ready for you to take *my* picture now, *gringa*," Lupe announced from behind her.

Tess nearly jumped out of her skin. How did the woman move so silently, especially dressed as she was? Lupe was clad in an elaborately frilled gown of low-cut black satin which clung lovingly to her impossibly narrow waist. The hem was shorter in the front to show off lacy, white-ruffled petticoats. She carried a pair of castanets.

"And unlike these peons, I have been photographed before," she hissed. "So make it the best picture you have ever done, *gringa*."

Or what? Tess wanted to ask, guessing Lupe had seen Parrish smiling at her and hadn't liked it one bit. "I have always tried to make each exposure better than the one before," she said, her voice calm. "How would you like to pose?"

Lupe narrowed her eyes suspiciously at the mild reply,

then stood a few feet away and struck a dramatic attitude, her arms gracefully raised with the castanets held in her fingers, her face in profile, gazing upward.

"Sandoval, remember when we danced the flamenco together? We were like twin flames, eh?" Lupe said, slanting her eye at him. "Come and pose with me as if we're dancing again," Lupe invited, running her tongue over her lush, full lower lip. Tess saw the woman dart a glance at her as if to see if she had caught the implications of her silky words.

Parrish shook his head, indicating his dusty trousers and shirt. "I'm not dressed for it, Lupe. I'd detract from your picture."

"Nonsense," Lupe said, pouting. "Come, *querido,* I want you to be in the picture."

But Parrish stood firm in his refusal. "No, you go ahead. I've already posed for Miss Hennessey."

Lupe stuck her lower lip out farther. "Very well, *querido,* but stay right there where I may see you for inspiration."

Tess had to duck hurriedly under the canvas so Lupe would not see her rolling her eyes. How could Parrish stand there with a straight face? But perhaps he enjoyed such antics from this woman.

Lupe pronounced herself displeased with Tess's first, second and third photographs, threatening to seize them and rip them up. "I don't know how you did it, *gringa,*" she snarled. "But do not make me look fat or stupid again or you will regret it."

Only Parrish's wink behind Lupe's back kept Tess's temper in check. Perspiration had begun to run down her back in rivulets and her hair clung to her damp neck.

Finally, on the fourth attempt, when Lupe saw that everyone else was sitting down to eat, she declared herself satisfied.

Chapter Eleven

Patrick Hennessy's shoulders slumped in discouragement as he rode up to the house. He and Samuel Taylor had ridden all the way to the closest Ranger headquarters, which was at Brownsville, only to be told by the captain there that Governor Roberts, who was trying to get along with the government in Mexico City, wouldn't authorize him to send a search party across the Rio Grande.

"But that's my *daughter* he's taken, man," Hennessy had protested. "Are you a father? If you are, surely you'll understand how distraught her mother and I are! How am I to go back there and tell her you won't even look?"

"That's not the way we used to do it in McNelly's day," Taylor had growled by his side.

"It'd be different if we knew exactly where to find her," the captain had said. "Then we could notify the Mexican officials we were coming, and secure their cooperation."

"I doubt very much they know the meaning of the word," Taylor snapped. "They've been turning a blind eye to Delgado's raids on Texas soil as long as he's been making them."

"Yes," the captain was forced to agree. "But if I know Delgado, he won't be able to resist raiding again, and soon. And if we can catch him in the act on Texas soil, we're within our rights to pursue him across the river."

"*If* you catch him! The man strikes like lightning and is gone that fast, too!" Hennessy retorted, despair nearly robbing him of reason. "And he might not have Tess with him! She's a beautiful girl—he might have sold her to someone, can't you see that?" Imagining his precious daughter in the hands of evil men, Patrick sank down on a nearby chair, his head in his hands.

"We have...*ahem!* Shall we say, *sources of intelligence* in Mexico? Perhaps someone will spot her. The way you described her—red hair and blue eyes—she won't blend in, Mr. Hennessy. Don't give up."

But now, as Patrick Hennessy dismounted in front of his home, giving the reins of his lathered horse to Mateo, he saw Amelia running down the steps, and his heart sank.

"Is there any word of her? Are they going after Tess?"

Putting his arms around his wife, Patrick told her what the Ranger captain had said, and let her weep in his arms. Then when he thought she had cried herself out, she lifted her head and told him what had happened while he and Taylor were gone. Delgado's men had struck the Duprees, who lived about five miles away. One of the bandits had been killed, another wounded, but after taking all they'd wanted, they'd ridden off as fast as they had come. And after they had gone, the maid had brought Amelia the note about Tess.

Sandoval wondered, as the day of the fiesta went on, what Tess must be thinking. At times, she appeared to be taking pleasure in the moment, and there was much about the day to find pleasurable—the simple joy of the children and the smiles of the adult villagers at this unexpected party, the delicious food, the lively music. Maybe she appreciated the opportunity to forget that she was a prisoner. But Lupe stuck to his side like a burr to a blanket and he had no opportunity to speak to Tess. Once, he saw her looking at Lupe and him with a strange expression on her face. Did Tess think he found the constant attention of Delgado's sister appealing?

He'd met Lupe only once before, when he'd first become allied with Delgado and his band, and even at that first meeting she'd made it very obvious she found Sandoval attractive. He hadn't felt the same about her, but he'd been able to pretend he didn't notice the seductive signals she'd sent him with her glances and seemingly accidental touches.

Now Delgado had invited her to stay with them for a prolonged visit, and because of it, Sandoval would have to walk a tightrope, appearing to find Lupe's lures irresistible without actually giving in to them. In time Lupe might be able to accept Sandoval's lack of interest—especially if others in the band were panting after her—but if she ever suspected Sandoval's growing feelings for Tess Hennessy, she would react with all the fury of a woman scorned, and it would be Tess who would suffer.

Dusk now deepened into dark in the canyon, and the ground was littered with empty whiskey, beer and tequila bottles. Sandoval spied Tess sitting at the edge of the firelight, looking weary and a little uneasy as the music got louder and the songs more raucous. At last, Delgado, who had been standing next to Sandoval and Lupe, leaned over and murmured, "Lupe, why not dance for us now?"

Preening, Lupe feigned reluctance to leave Sandoval's

side. Sandoval knew what she wanted, and he gave it to her. "Please, Lupe, I'm sure everyone would enjoy seeing you dance."

"Even *you, querido?*" she murmured, looking sidelong at Sandoval.

"Oh, especially me, Lupe."

"Very well, then..."

"Sanchez!" Delgado shouted to the guitar player. "Play some flamenco for my sister to dance to, eh?"

Obligingly, the guitar player switched to a more lively tune and the audience began to clap in time.

As if she were mounting a stage, Lupe pranced into the center of the circle with a swishing of skirts. She struck a pose, head up, throat exposed, and began to move, twirling around and clicking her castanets in time to their clapping. She whirled this way and that, dipping low to entice the men, then flipping up her petticoats and dancing away as if taunting them. The emphatic stamping of the dancer's feet, so much a part of traditional flamenco, was somewhat muffled on the hard dirt beneath her, but the enthusiastic, rhythmic clapping of her audience more than made up for it.

Knowing what was required of him, Sandoval stared at Lupe and waited, hoping Lupe would get so caught up in her dancing she'd forget about any individual man watching. In time she did just that, closing her eyes and swaying as if her life began and ended with the rhythm of her stamping and the villagers' clapping.

Moving gradually, he stepped behind Delgado and moved to where Delores was sitting with her son. Leaning down, he used the music to cover his voice, and said, "*Señora,* please tell Tess this would be a good time for her to retire to her hut. These men are only going to grow drunker, and we would not want her to have to discourage any unwelcome attentions, would we?" He winked at her. "Once she's in there, I'd appreciate it if you stayed with her and moved your pallet in front of the door."

Delores winked back. "I will be happy to do that for you, Sandoval."

The old woman read him too well. It was fortunate he could trust her. If only Delores could discourage Lupe from bothering him, also. After her dance, Lupe would seek him out, expecting him to feel amorous. He was going to have to feign a drunken slumber at the campfire.

It was a long time before the music and the hooting and laughter of the celebrants died down enough for Tess to fall asleep. She thought she had only just nodded off when Delores gently shook her awake. She saw from the light behind the towel-curtain that it was morning.

Delores held out a folded garment to Tess, mumbling something about Lupe. Apparently the skirt belonged to Delgado's sister, but Tess was to don it. Once dressed, she saw the breakfast of tortilla-wrapped strips of beef Delores had left on her trunk.

Now, as she stepped from the hut, bringing her sketching pad as ordered, the rising sun illuminated the forms of rebozo- and horse-blanket-wrapped villagers sleeping everywhere on the ground.

Delgado, standing next to Esteban, who held his black stallion, grinned approvingly at her skirt. "*Buenos días.* I hope you slept well and are ready for a long ride, Señorita Tess. Sandoval is saddling your horse. We will soon be on our way."

His high-handed, authoritative tone sparked Tess's temper.

"Señor Delgado, you had me brought here to take your picture. I've done that. Several times. Why can't I just go home now?" She knew it was futile to ask, but she didn't want him to be in any doubt about her unwillingness.

"Because I want you with me, *señorita,*" he said, and the gleam in his eyes when he said it sent a chill of foreboding spearing through her.

"But...what about them?" she said, indicating the sleeping villagers.

Delgado shrugged. "Many will wake up with sore heads, but Delores will feed them and send them on their way to Santa Elena. They will talk of this fiesta for weeks. No more arguing, *señorita.*"

Parrish returned, leading his pinto and a sorrel mare. Lupe followed, holding the reins of a prancing white gelding. Lupe scowled as she saw Tess standing by her brother.

"I hope you can ride, *gringa.* This will not be a gentle outing in a park."

"I have ridden since I was old enough to walk," Tess told her, striving to keep her tone neutral. "My father taught me. Thank you for loaning me this riding skirt," she added politely.

Lupe's full lips twisted into a sneer. "It was one I had grown tired of," she proclaimed. "So don't think I will hesitate to shoot you out of the saddle if we're pursued and I think you lag behind on purpose."

"Lupe! Remember your manners!" Delgado snapped.

Over Lupe's shoulder, Sandoval caught Tess's eye, his look warning but full of sympathy. It heartened her and gave her the will to hold her tongue and nod meekly, as if Lupe had succeeded in intimidating the *gringa.* She saw Parrish's shoulders relax.

The mare, which Parrish called Dulce, nuzzled Tess in a friendly fashion. Tess soon found that Parrish had chosen her mount well. Dulce's trot as she rode out of the canyon was easy to sit, and when they accelerated, Dulce's canter was as smooth as a rocking horse's. If only this were a pleasure ride! One glance at the bandits riding on all sides of her, however—a crisscrossed bandolier full of cartridges decorating each chest, pistols in holsters and rifles strapped to their saddles—made that pretense impossible.

They headed northeast, crossing the Rio Grande at a shallow point where the muddy water reached only as high as the stirrups. Tess was relieved—she knew if the horses had had to swim, her wet thighs would chafe, slapping against the soaked leather of the saddle.

Once across, Tess looked around her. She was once again on Texas soil. If only she knew exactly where she was—how close to any town! The scrubland on the northern side of the river, however, looked much the same as it did in Mexico. They rode on, occasionally passing isolated shacks, some with a bony horse or two standing in a small, weathered corral, but they kept going. Evidently the pickings weren't rich enough to tempt Delgado.

The sun was directly overhead when they spied a ranch in the distance with a pasture full of fat cattle and horses. The ranch house, built of fieldstone, was large and sprawling. On either side sat an outbuilding; one of them like a smaller version of the house, the other, more crudely built, looked like a bunkhouse. Behind them stood a large barn.

"Ah, there is a worthy target, eh?" Delgado said to Parrish.

Parrish shrugged. "I don't know…maybe we ought to ride farther north, hit a small town—concentrate on money and jewelry, things we can carry. Once we're driving horses and cattle, though, we have to hurry back across the river to one of your hideouts before they can put together a posse or summon the Rangers. Why not hit this place on the way back?"

Parrish wanted to penetrate farther into the interior of the Rio Grande Valley? Why? Tess wondered. If they did that, there was a risk of the bandits being cut off and taken. She sought his gaze, seeking a clue. Did he want to give her the chance to escape? But Lupe was studying him with narrowed eyes, and Parrish didn't look Tess's way.

"No, we strike here. Now," Delgado pronounced, his jaw set. "Look how easy they make it—they haven't even posted a lookout."

Parrish shrugged again. "A bird in the hand…"

Lupe reined her mare next to Tess. "You stay with me, do you hear, *gringa?* We will hang back until the gringos are subdued." Her scornful eyes made it very clear she begrudged the fact that she had to guard Tess instead of being in the thick of things with her brother.

Tess nodded, apprehension crawling up her spine like an icy spider. *Please, Lord, don't let the outlaws kill anyone. Protect Sandoval, please.*

Delgado looked over his shoulder at his men. "Ready, *muchachos?*"

"*¡Sí!*" they chorused, pulling pistols out of holsters and rifles from their bindings behind their saddles. Lupe gave Tess a dark, threatening glare.

Just then a cowboy ambled out of the barn carrying a pitchfork, and stopped stock-still, staring. Dropping the pitchfork, he let out a shout and ran for the bunkhouse.

"Curse him, he'll alert the others," growled Delgado. "But no matter!" He uttered a hoarse cry and threw his arm forward. As one man, the outlaws charged, the air ringing with the ear-splitting report of their rifles.

Shutters slammed back from windows on either side of the bunkhouse door, and puffs of smoke erupted from rifles firing at them. Through the haze of gunfire, Tess saw a window thrown open in the house, too, and red flashes as a rifle began to spit bullets from there, too, even as a bandit on the left flank fell limply from his saddle. She lost track of Parrish.

Undeterred, the bandits kept going. As they closed on the house and bunkhouse, a cowboy was unwise enough to poke his head above the windowsill, and one of the outlaws took aim and fired. Tess heard a scream and the cowboy disappeared. A pair of bandits split off from those riding toward the house, and hanging low over the far side of their mounts like Comanches, using their horses as shields, they shot directly into the bunkhouse windows. All return fire ceased.

Within the main house, Tess could hear women shrieking and a man trying to shout over them, though she couldn't make out the words. She felt tears streaming down her cheeks.

"Come out with your hands up and no one else will be shot!" Delgado shouted at the house, while the outlaws who had shot at the bunkhouse dismounted and yanked the bunkhouse door open. Seconds later two cowboys emerged, pale-faced and trembling, their hands raised high. One of them wore only pants held up by suspenders over his bare chest.

Parrish reappeared out of the floating smoke. Lupe grabbed a rein of Tess's mount and rode forward, her eyes gleaming in avid triumph.

A trio of trembling women emerged from the ranch house, one of them gray-haired, another younger, the third probably the cook, judging by the apron she wore around her rotund waist. All of them held their hands high; the younger woman wept.

"Don't hurt us," the older woman begged, clutching a shawl around herself. "Please. You can take what we have."

"Yes, I can, *señora,*" Delgado agreed, smiling broadly, "Who was firing at us from that window in the house?"

The older woman straightened. "I was," she said, staring stonily at Delgado.

"Sandoval, go in and see if she tells the truth," Delgado ordered.

Tess watched as Parrish dismounted and complied, his pistol at the ready. A minute or so later he reemerged, using his pistol to push a shambling, balding man with his hands raised high. In his other hand Sandoval held a rifle. She saw Parrish saying something into the man's ear.

"I thought there was no one else, *señora?* He was the one firing, wasn't he?" Delgado taunted.

Parrish threw the rifle down on the ground. "It's empty," he said. "That's what he was firing with."

Both women fell down on their knees, shaking, tear-drenched eyes darting between the outlaw leader and Parrish's captive. "Please, don't kill him! He's all we have."

Delgado stilled, staring at the man, and raised his pistol.

The man in front of Parrish trembled, too, his eyes bulging in terror. Seconds ticked by, but they seemed like an eternity to Tess.

Suddenly the man's eyes rolled back in his head and he collapsed in the dirt. The women shrieked.

Parrish bent over him, then straightened and spoke to the women. "He's fainted."

Delgado's laugh dripped with scorn. "What a brave man! He'd rather pass out like a girl than fight to his last breath to save his women. Mendoza, Jimenez, tie up those cowboys, the women and that pitiful excuse of a man. Guard them while we do a little exploring inside," he said, pointing at the house.

Tess watched, agonized that she couldn't help the two women, while the two banditos did as Delgado had instructed them, and a handful of the other bandits disappeared inside the house. Parrish, however, remounted his horse.

"Watch her, *querido,*" Lupe told him, jerking her head toward Tess. "I believe one of the ranch women is hiding something I might want."

Parrish did as she said, his face a mask, while Lupe slipped off her mare, lithe as a cat, and stalked up to the younger woman, who had struggled to her feet.

"Very pretty," she murmured, using the long muzzle of her pistol to caress the woman's neck, then to pick up a gold chain at her throat. As she lifted the muzzle, the chain pulled out an oval ruby pendant set in gold filigree from within the woman's bodice. "Ah, I thought so," Lupe said. "Take it off."

The young woman set her jaw and did so, staring fixedly at a point in the distance. Then she deliberately dropped the necklace into the dust at her feet.

"Pick it up, *gringa,* or I'll make you very, very sorry."

The younger woman hesitated, then complied, her eyes stony.

Now the old woman seemed to see Tess for the first time. "You're not one of them, are you? How can you just sit there and watch?"

Chapter Twelve

Sandoval saw Tess pale and flinch as if the woman had slapped her.

"I…I'm not here by choice," she said, her voice barely above a whisper.

The woman looked unconvinced. "What's your name?"

"Tess Hennessy…of Hennessy Hall, near Chapin. Could you please send word to my parents that you've seen me? That I'm all right?"

"Liar! She's my brother's mistress," Lupe snapped. "I'll have those earrings, too." She pointed at the garnet pair dangling from the old woman's lobes, and held out her hand until the woman removed them and gave them to her, transferring her glare to the insolently smirking Lupe, who was not troubled by it in the least.

The bandits emerged a few minutes later, laden with booty—a brass candelabra, a pair of Colts with inlaid ivory handles, a gold pocket watch, a silver platter.

"Be thankful I left you the boxful of silverware," Delgado told the angry women. "A service for twelve, no? A pity it is so heavy, but we must ride fast. Be thankful.

Muchachos, it's time we were on our way. Drive the cattle and horses out of their pastures and let's get going."

"But you can't leave us tied up like this!" the younger woman protested.

"I say we herd these fools inside and fire the house," Lupe suggested to her brother, deliberately using English, Sandoval knew, so she could enjoy the horrified reaction on the captives' faces. "In revenge for Pablo, over there." She pointed to where one of the men was tying Pablo's body onto his horse.

"As much as I like revenge, Lupe, that would not be nice for our guest, would it?" Delgado asked, nodding toward Tess. "Don't be so bloodthirsty."

Lupe pouted.

"I left your knots a little loose," Sandoval told the woman, his voice curt and impersonal. "If you work at it awhile, you ought to be able to free yourself, and then the others."

"Of course, by that time we'll be safely back in Mexico," Delgado added. "*¡Adios!*"

They wasted no time reaching the river again, driving the stolen cattle and horses ahead of them as fast as they could go. At this crossing, the Rio Grande was so deep the animals had to swim. Once across, they didn't linger. It wasn't safe to dally on the other side—they had to put some distance between themselves and any pursuers. Rangers and posses of vengeful civilians had crossed the river before.

By late afternoon they reached one of the small, hidden valleys Delgado had used before on his forays away from his main camp in the canyon. Everyone was exhausted from the hard ride. No one spoke while several of them dug a grave for their fallen compadre, and no one wept. Dying was a known hazard in the life of a bandito. Sandoval saw Tess sketching the burial scene from the fireside, where she was tending a pot of cooking beans, and wondered what she was thinking.

After supper, night watches over the stolen livestock were assigned, and the men who did not have the first watch rolled up in their serapes and were soon snoring by the fire. At last only four remained sitting near the campfire and watching the sparks fly upward from its flickering blue-and-orange depths—Sandoval, Delgado, Lupe and Tess.

Tess looked strained, Sandoval thought. She stared with unfocused eyes into the fire, as if haunted by what had happened today. He willed her to announce she was going to her quarters. Then he could walk with her without being too obvious and speak to her alone, at least for a few moments. He clenched and unclenched a fist. Blast it, there was never a chance to tell her what he was thinking, to begin to tell her what was in his heart. Always, Delgado was around, or Lupe, or one of the men—and most of them, he thought, jealous of Sandoval's position as Delgado's right-hand man, would gladly do what they could to discredit him. Telling the outlaw leader that his lieutenant was paying too much attention to the pretty lady photographer that Delgado fancied would certainly accomplish that.

Tess remained where she was, perhaps hypnotized by the flames, perhaps too deep in her thoughts.

Delgado seemed determined to stay out here with Tess, too, so Sandoval continued to wait. He didn't want to leave Delgado with Tess—nor did he want to give Lupe an opportunity to seek *him* out alone.

"Where do we go tomorrow, *hermano?*" Lupe asked at

last, breaking the silence. "Into Ciudad Rio Bravo to sell the booty?"

Delgado took a puff of his cigarillo, shaking his head. "No, it's a poor town. I doubt even the *alcalde* has the price of that watch or the silver platter, much less the cattle. What would you think of riding up to Rancho Cordoba and spending a day there? I'm sure Andrés Cordoba would be delighted to buy the cattle and horses we took today."

"Diego! You are the best of brothers," Lupe exclaimed, throwing her arms around him and kissing him on the cheek. "I'm sure he will invite us to dine with him! Perhaps we could prevail on him to invite Sandoval, too?" She fluttered her lashes at Sandoval.

Across the fire, Sandoval saw Tess watching the brother and sister. He could practically see her mind working, and knew she was hoping that if the Delgados were going visiting, she would get her chance to escape.

Delgado chuckled. "Are you trying to make Cordoba jealous, *hermana?* He's never made any secret of his affection for you—maybe you ought to encourage him. You could become a lady of leisure, you know."

"Perhaps I will…." She shot another look at Sandoval, as if daring him to object; then, when he didn't rise to the bait, she said, "I don't know…perhaps I would be bored, not being free to go raiding with my brother the bandit, and his handsome lieutenant…."

"And we could not very well invite Sandoval without Señorita Tess, eh? I would be a very bad host if I left Tess behind while you and Sandoval and I dined with Cordoba."

Across the fire, Sandoval saw Tess's mouth tighten in frustration.

"I think you're more concerned I'll escape if you leave

me here," she said. "But aren't you afraid I'll tell this rancher that I'm your captive, and he'll demand you free me?"

Delgado threw back his head and laughed. "Hardly! Cordoba's father was killed by the *Norteamericanos* at Veracruz. He wouldn't lift a finger to help a Texan, even such a lovely one as you." He reached out a finger and casually chucked her under the chin.

Sandoval had to look away so Delgado and Lupe wouldn't notice his clenched jaw. Tess looked as if she wanted to slap the outlaw leader.

"I imagine he would find it fascinating to meet you, though, *señorita,*" Delgado continued. "It's too bad you don't have your photographic equipment with you, but perhaps you could offer to draw him, eh? Very well, tomorrow we visit Rancho Cordoba, so you ladies had better get your rest. The more beautiful you both are, the more Cordoba will be dazzled and pay me what I want for the livestock."

As if in mutual consent, the Delgados and Tess rose and started for their respective quarters. Sandoval trailed behind, watching sister and brother enter Delgado's quarters and Tess hers. He knew Delores was already inside.

Sandoval was well satisfied with the plan for tomorrow. If they spent the day at Rancho Cordoba, that was one day Tess would not be exposed to the dangers of raiding. And if Cordoba kept Delgado busy dickering over the price of the livestock, and distracted Lupe with flirtation, surely he could find some time to speak to Tess alone....

"You drive a hard bargain, Delgado," said Andrés Cordoba, a tall, urbane man whose proud, erect carriage hinted at his descent from Spanish grandees. They stood in front of the corral where the stolen cattle and horses had been driven for his inspection. "But I find it hard to haggle anymore in this hot sun if it means keeping your beautiful sister—" he winked at Lupe "—and the charming Señorita Hennessy from refreshing themselves in their guest chamber. A good siesta, and then later we will dine. I think you will find my cook has outdone herself in your honor," he said, bowing low and raising Lupe's hand to his lips.

Lupe giggled and fluttered her thick lashes at Cordoba; then, when the rancher turned his attention back to Delgado, shaking his hand to seal the deal, Sandoval saw Lupe aim a challenging look at him. But he shook his head subtly, as if hinting he couldn't show his feelings, and kept his features impassive.

"Very well then, we will see you later, *mi amigo.* It's a pleasure doing business with you," Delgado said. "Sandoval, you will station yourself in front of the chamber Lupe and Tess share, eh?"

Cordoba pursed his lips. "But I assure you, no one would dare bother a guest in my house. I'm sure that's not necessary."

Sandoval saw how he could use the rancher's interest in Lupe.

"But remember I have told you I am still trying to persuade Señorita Tess to remain with us," Delgado said, winking at Cordoba, as if entrusting the silver-haired rancher with his roguish secret.

"Yes, yes, of course," said Cordoba, glancing up and down at Tess, then winking back. "Very well then, until later…"

While Delgado, Lupe and Tess began walking toward the imposing house, Sandoval deliberately caught Cordoba's eye, jerking his head as if to indicate that he wanted the rancher to lag behind.

Fortunately, Andrés Cordoba guessed his meaning. "There was something you wished to talk to me about, Sandoval?"

Sandoval nodded. "I must tell you something, but first I want to assure you that while I am in her confidence, Señorita Lupe and I are merely friends. I am like a brother to her—except that she can confide in me more freely than she can to her real brother."

Cordoba waited, one eyebrow raised.

"The *señorita* is a woman of great passion," Sandoval said. "And I believe the object of that passion is *you,* Señor Cordoba. She begged her brother to bring her back here to visit you. The cattle were only an excuse."

Cordoba blinked. "Can that be true? She said so?"

Sandoval gave an elaborate shrug. "Not in so many words… But I believe if you were to press your suit while she is here, you would find the results very…rewarding." Sandoval glanced meaningfully in the direction of Lupe's gracefully swaying figure.

Cordoba's eyes widened. "You do not jest with me? You are serious?"

By this time the others had reached the wrought-iron gate to the courtyard and didn't seem to notice that the rancher hadn't kept pace with them. Sandoval stopped stock-still, forcing Cordoba to stop, too.

"Couldn't you tell by her flushed features, the light in her eyes, when she saw you?" Sandoval said.

Cordoba clapped his hand on Sandoval's shoulder, grinning. "Ah, Sandoval, that is good news! Being around Lupe makes me feel like a young man again. I thought I would never fall in love a second time, after my late wife died so tragically. She was never able to give me children, the poor woman…."

Sandoval grinned back. "I think that would not be a problem with the *señorita* in question, *señor.* Just look at her."

Cordoba did so, licking his lips. "So what would you suggest I do, Sandoval? Ask Delgado for the beauteous Lupe's hand in marriage after dinner tonight?"

Sandoval allowed his features to become grave. "I think the lady would like you to woo her first. You know how women are. They don't want to be handed over like a sack of cornmeal! Perhaps you should find a way to be alone with her this afternoon…."

"And how would I do that, Sandoval? She will be very effectively guarded by you, and chaperoned by the presence of that pretty redheaded Texan, *sí?* Speaking of her, I must admit that if it were not for my love of Lupe, I would beg Delgado to leave that little morsel with me!"

Sandoval forced himself to chuckle. "No, you have chosen the right one. You wouldn't suspect it to look at her, but that red-haired Texan has the very devil of a temper. I would suggest you come to their chamber in a little while and tell her that you crave a few precious minutes to speak to her." He waggled his eyebrows.

"But what of Señorita Hennessy?"

"She's guessed Lupe's feelings and is sympathetic. She won't tell Delgado you were there."

"Amigo, I am in your debt," the other man said, beaming.

"And I will be happy to dance at your wedding," Sandoval replied, praying his ruse would work. He *had* to find a time to speak to Tess, to let her know what he was planning. "Oh, and one more suggestion…"

"Yes?"

"I wouldn't mention to the lady that I told you all this. Ladies like to think their suitors' actions are spontaneous, you know what I mean?"

"Of course..." Cordoba pumped his hand.

The clean, smooth sheets and the luxuriously appointed room reminded Tess of her room back at Hennessy Hall, sending a wave of homesickness over her as she sat sketching at the table, while Lupe lay on the big bed. If she ever reached home again, Tess was sure it would be very hard to leave it, even if Mathew Brady himself issued her an invitation to come to New York!

"Stop rattling the paper, *gringa!*" hissed Lupe, turning from where she had been lying with her back turned to Tess. "The flickering candlelight is bad enough. How am I supposed to fall asleep?"

"I...I'm sorry, Lupe," Tess said. "Perhaps I should blow out the candle and lie down, though I don't feel very sleepy—"

"So I can feel you tossing and turning? Stay where you are!"

"All ri—"

Suddenly both women stilled as they heard a soft knock at the door.

"Who is that? Sandoval? What do you want?"

"No, it's I, Andrés," came the soft, cultured voice. "I must talk to you, Lupe!"

Lupe sat up, staring first at the door, as if she didn't believe who had come, then at Tess.

"I—I'm not alone, Andrés! That...that *gringa* is with me, you remember?" She glared at Tess as if she expected her to disappear if she looked hard enough.

"I know, my sweet," he called softly through the door, "but Sandoval has volunteered to take her elsewhere so that we may be alone for a while…."

"But, *señor*…" Lupe gave a girlish giggle. "I'm not sure it's entirely proper for me to be alone with you here… perhaps Tess should remain as my duenna?"

Tess heard Cordoba groan against the door.

"I swear you have nothing to fear from me, Lupita, *mi corazón,*" he declared. "My intentions are entirely honorable. We can go down to my chapel if you like. But I cannot speak freely in front of another…"

Lupe smiled, smug as a cat that had just captured a particularly choice mouse.

"No, I trust you, Andrés. I'll be ready in a minute, then…" Lupe called, then grabbed at the blouse and skirt she'd thrown over a chair. "*¡Gringa!* Help me get dressed and comb my hair!"

It was fortunate Tess had remained fully clothed, for Lupe threw the door open as soon as Tess finished combing Lupe's thick, ebony hair. Cordoba stepped inside. Tess caught a glimpse of Parrish standing just behind him, his expression hotly sulky as he watched the rancher bend to embrace Lupe.

He's jealous, Tess realized with a stab of pain. Lupe had monopolized Sandoval's time the first day she had come to camp, but since then, Tess had seen no more evidence that Sandoval returned Lupe's interest, and she'd begun to think Sandoval had only been polite to Lupe. But here was unmistakable evidence she had been wrong.

He does want Lupe Delgado for himself, she thought. How could he be so foolish as to care about Delgado's sister, with her bold eyes and loose ways? She doesn't care about Cordoba for himself—she just wants to make Parrish want her more!

For a moment she thought past the blinding pain and felt sorry for the older rancher. If he sincerely loved Lupe Delgado, he was going to hurt one day, too.

"We'll go for a walk," Parrish announced, pulling Tess outside. He called over her head to the other two, who were still clasped in an oblivious embrace, "If we return to find the door ajar, *señor,* we'll know you've left."

Cordoba kicked the door closed without answering.

Parrish took Tess by the elbow and marched her down the outdoor corridor that overlooked the inner courtyard.

Tess waited until they had descended the shadowy steps to the flagstone courtyard. "Take your hands off me!" She yanked her arm from his grasp. "Where are we going?" she demanded, when he kept striding on, not looking at her.

"To Cordoba's chapel," he said in a low voice. "That's the one place I'm sure no one will bother us. Even if they leave the room, Lupe won't want to go there."

The rancher's small, private chapel lay diagonally across from the chamber they had just left, but rather than cutting across the square inner courtyard, Parrish kept to the shadows beneath the overhanging balconies of the upper rooms.

He turned to see if anyone was watching, then pulled open the door and gestured her inside. He had thought it would be safer for her not to know everything, but he could no longer bear for her not to know the truth.

Chapter Thirteen

The chapel was small and dimly lit only by the sun penetrating one brilliant stained glass window in a corner and a candle burning on the altar beneath it. Tess stared up at Parrish's earnest, shadowed face.

"There's no need to be angry," he said.

That was the last thing she had expected to hear. "*Me? Angry?* I would have said it was *you* who was angry—at Cordoba, for desiring Lupe, too."

To her annoyance, he laughed. "'Too?' *I* don't want her."

She blinked up at him. "Y-you *don't?* B-but I thought you did, that you found her…" Her voice trailed off. She didn't want to say *entrancing, irresistible* aloud, for fear he'd change his mind.

"If that's the way I made it look, I was successful," he told her. "I wanted her to think I felt that way about her because it's what she expects from a man. It'd be hazardous for me to show her otherwise, particularly since she's Delgado's sister. And more dangerous still for you, if she guessed it's *you* I care about."

Her jaw fell open. "Y-you *do?*"

Sandoval nodded solemnly, his dark eyes black as night in the shadowy chapel. "It's not what I intended when I set this whole plan in motion," he admitted, "and I've been fighting it from the first moment I met you at Sam Taylor's barbecue, but I'm not winning that struggle. Something was telling me not to go through with this kidnapping scheme, but fool that I was, I went ahead. Now, of course, I wish I hadn't, but it doesn't do any good. We're in the thick of things and I have to keep you safe till I can get you out of it."

"I...I see," she breathed.

He turned and paced toward the altar, then back to her. "Lupe isn't content with mere adoration, of course, so I needed to do something to distract her from me. Delgado mentioned that the last time Lupe went raiding with him, he could see Cordoba fancied her, so I only had to hint to Cordoba that this time she might accept him. If he can woo her into staying here and marrying him, we'll only have her brother to worry about."

Tess nodded, considering. It was a lot to take in. He cared for her. What did that mean, exactly? And why had he made this plan to get her into Delgado's hands in the first place?

"I...don't blame you for being angry at me," he said. "I was wrong to do what I did, bringing you into his camp, involving you."

"I'm not angry. I...I was," she confessed, "at first."

"So...you don't hate me?" he asked, behind her.

"Hate you?" she repeated, turning back around. "No, I don't hate you, I—" She stopped short. Had she really been about to say she loved him? She did, but it made no sense. There was no future in loving Sandoval Parrish, a man whose loyalty lay with Mexico—a man whom she could never imagine wanting to settle down and be law-abiding, on either side of the Rio Grande, let alone raise babies with her!

"No, I don't hate you," she said again. "But I still don't know why you've made this choice to ride with Delgado, yet you like hobnobbing with Texas planters and ranchers as one of them, too. Aren't you afraid someone will recognize you when you go raiding?"

"I wear a bandanna over my face where I might be known. And no, I didn't choose what I'm doing. It's a matter of retribution."

Retribution. It was a chilling word, a word that echoed in the quiet stillness of the chapel. A word that seemed to have been ripped from the recesses of his heart. Parrish's features were suddenly wintry and hard.

"Retribution? Against Anglos? Are you one of those Mexicans still angry that Texas is no longer part of Mexico?"

He shook his head. "Not against Anglos. Against Delgado."

"But why?"

"That's what I brought you here to tell you. I've wanted to tell you for a few days now, but there's never been a safe place to talk to you, a place where we couldn't be overheard."

Parrish held up his hand as if to indicate that he would speak again in a moment, then walked stealthily to the door and threw it open. She saw him look up and down the shadowed, cloisterlike walkway. The abrupt gust of indrawn air made the candle flame dance wildly on the altar. Then he shut the door again and returned to her, taking a deep breath.

"No one is around," he said. "Tonight at dinner, I believe Cordoba will ask Delgado for Lupe's hand, if he's been successful in his courting," he said, nodding in the direction of the room across the courtyard and up the stairs. "That means Lupe will stay with him."

It would be wonderful to be free of the woman's hostile, sarcastic, ever-watchful presence, Tess thought—and to not have to watch her staring at Parrish with those avid eyes.

"We'll remain with Delgado," he went on, "till we return to the canyon camp. Then we'll escape."

"Wouldn't it be easier to make a run for it while we're across the river on a raid?"

"Yes, but there's something back at camp I need to get."

Tess let her eyes ask the question. Tess couldn't imagine what he could be referring to. Surely if either of them had something in camp to return for, it was she. But she could not imagine how they could flee with Ben and the heavy, slow wagon full of photographic equipment. As fond as she was of the old mule, he wasn't capable of speed. She hated the idea of leaving him and her precious camera behind, but she'd do what she had to, of course, to make it to safety and hope she could somehow get them back.

"You have negatives of the pictures you took of Delgado, correct?"

Tess nodded.

"I want a couple of those. One full-face, one profile. Maybe one of the developed pictures, too."

She waited, twisting a fold of her skirt in her hand.

"I want to be able to reproduce his image all over the Rio Grande Valley—farther, if need be—on Wanted posters, so Delgado can be captured. The problem has been that when the government has sent army detachments to capture him, he goes to ground, blends in with the peons. And when Delgado's not wearing that fancy stolen uniform, he's ordinary looking, isn't he?"

She nodded, realizing it was true. Take away his swagger and arrogant confidence, and Delgado *was* ordinary—totally unlike Sandoval Parrish.

"But why are *you* the one doing this?"

He sighed, and drew her to the only place to sit in the chapel, a wooden bench in the back.

"I'm not an outlaw, Tess. I'm a Texas Ranger."

She stared at him. So much made sense now—especially Uncle Samuel's trust of him, when so many of the planters in the Rio Grande Valley were suspicious of Parrish. Sam Taylor was a retired Ranger. And now she knew why Parrish had had her kidnapped. As she had known, it was to take pictures of Delgado, but not because he wanted to pander to Delgado's ego.

"But don't Rangers usually work with other Rangers?"

"Usually, yes, but a whole company of Anglo-looking Texas Rangers can't infiltrate a pack of banditos."

No, they couldn't. But Sandoval Parrish, with his Hispanic heritage, dark eyes and hair, who'd grown up speaking Spanish as well as English, could.

The peril of his task unnerved her. Hardly aware of what she was doing, she grasped his wrist with urgent fingers. "You're playing a dangerous game, Sandoval. If they find out, they'll kill you."

"Yes," he admitted, looking down at her hand, then covering it with his own. "Probably slowly and painfully."

"Then why take the risk? Why does it have to be *you,* Sandoval? Why do you need retribution?"

Tess could see from the way his eyes changed that what he said next would transform everything.

Parrish took a deep breath and stared at the altar. "Because of what he did to Pilar."

"Pilar?" she echoed. "Was she…was she your wife?"

"My sister." He closed his eyes as if fearing she would read the pain in them.

"Tell me," Tess urged quietly.

"Pilar was older than me by five years, the sweetest, most beautiful girl in Montemorelos, maybe all of Mexico. Delgado had already begun the life of an outlaw, and was riding all over northern Mexico recruiting young men to join him. He'd swagger into a village and promise them booty and women and fame, and many believed what he promised."

"But not you."

"Not me," he agreed. "I wanted to be a ranchero like my father, and carry on what he'd begun when he met my mother and settled down near Montemorelos. Delgado kept coming around, trying to persuade me, and then he saw my sister coming out of the church in town. He lost all interest in me, of course. He decided he had to have her."

She waited.

"Papa tried to run him off. Pilar was the apple of his eye, and he wasn't about to let a man like Delgado close to his angel. One day when I was away from the ranch, Delgado rode in and asked our father for Pilar's hand in marriage. My father refused, naturally. Delgado didn't settle for that—he seduced my sister instead. One morning we found her bed empty—she had left with him in the night. We never saw her again, and Papa died of a broken heart."

"You…you don't know what happened to her? Whether she died, or…"

He shook his head. "She must be dead," he said bleakly.

"It's been five years. Why wouldn't she have come back if she was alive? No, he must have killed her. And now you know why I'm with Delgado. I'm going to destroy him. For Pilar. But I'm going to do it legally. I've had any number of chances to shoot him in cold blood—but that would make me the same as him."

"But...he doesn't recognize you? Or your name?"

Sandoval shook his head. "I was a skinny, half-grown boy whose voice still cracked. I'd hardly begun to grow a beard," he said, rubbing his cheeks and chin with a thumb and forefinger. "My parents always called me by my baptismal name, Juan, and in order to qualify for a land grant, my father had taken my mother's surname, Morelos—though everyone in the village knew his last name was Parrish. Delgado never knew it, though."

"Oh, Sandoval," was all Tess could say.

"I only hope she didn't suffer too much," he said, and though he looked in Tess's direction, his gaze was unfocused—a thousand miles, or ten years, away.

"But you have to find out what happened to her," she told him.

"I told you, she's dead. She must be," he insisted, turning his head away from Tess.

"You don't *know* that," she argued. "And you can't let him go to his grave carrying that secret. You'd always wonder."

"Tess, what am I supposed to do? Tell him I'm that skinny boy from Montemorelos, the one with the beautiful, innocent sister he despoiled, and I'd like to know where he left her? Mexico is probably full of women with the same story." Parrish turned back to her, his eyes full of a frustrated anger. "Even if I had him tied up and put a pistol to his head, he'd just laugh at me like the demon he is. No, I'll have to be content with seeing him pay for his crimes."

"Maybe *I* can find out," she said.

Chapter Fourteen

"You? How in—how do you propose to find out something like that?" he demanded, hands outspread. "Even if you could get him talking, he probably doesn't even *remember* what he did with her when he was tired of her."

"He might not," Tess admitted. "But then again, he might. All I can do is try. After we leave here it'll be a while before we return to the canyon camp, right?" Tess said. "That should furnish plenty of evenings to get him talking—you know he loves to brag of his exploits, especially when he's drinking. I'll pretend to be fascinated with his stories, and after a while I'll ask him about the early days."

Sandoval pictured what Tess was saying, of her leaning toward him, murmuring words like, "Really? Go on…tell me more…" while Delgado sank deeper and deeper into his bottle of tequila. And he realized how even a drunken Delgado would react to her rapt interest. It might well go far beyond talking.

"No!" he cried suddenly, making Tess jump with his vehemence. "You'd be playing with fire, Tess! You don't know what he's capable of."

"I think I do," she argued. "I've seen some of it, and you've just told me a good deal more. We *must* find out if Pilar's alive, Sandoval, if it's possible."

She thought he meant Delgado's anger, Sandoval realized. He had to be plainer. "Don't you see, Tess, I don't want what happened to Pilar to happen to *you,*" he said, desperate to convince her.

"It won't. *You'll* be there," she told him, her eyes shining with confidence in him. A confidence he didn't deserve. "And we'll pray about it and ask the Lord to help us—"

He ignored her last words. "And what if Delgado shoots me, or stabs me when I step in to save you from his...*attentions,* shall we say? Then what? I don't care about me," he declared hotly, jumping up to stand in front of her. "I've long thought I deserved to die after failing to protect my own sister from that monster. But what would *you* do then? No, let Pilar rest in peace, Tess. Leave it alone. It's my responsibility to get you to safety and achieve justice for her."

"No."

"*No?*" He couldn't believe his ears.

She stared up at him, her eyes enormous in her pale face, but her gaze was steadfast and determined. "No," she repeated. "You've been with Delgado how long? And he hasn't happened to mention your sister, has he?"

"About a year," he admitted grudgingly. "Before that, I was learning the ropes as a Ranger, and showing them they could trust me, a man of mixed heritage, to be fully Texan in my loyalty. But I wasn't expecting Delgado to just blurt out Pilar's fate—I was hoping to set up an ambush so he and his men could be captured. But I haven't been able to, since he never picks his targets far enough in advance, or at least, announces his choices. Then I decided if we could publish his picture all over the Southwest, he could be captured when he tries to go to ground in Texas, as he's had to before. That's why you're with us, to help me do that."

"I've taken the photographs, so that's done," she said. "And now I'm going to help you find out about your sister."

Sandoval crossed his arms. "Forget it, Tess. I forbid it," he told her.

It was the wrong thing to say. He saw frustration kindle her temper, and in a heartbeat she had jumped up, too, her chin jutting out as she glared up at him. "Who are *you* to forbid me anything? What right do you have to talk to me that way?"

"No right." He threw the admission at her, his own anger sparked now. "But I love you, and I won't let you put yourself under the cat's paw like that."

His declaration in the midst of their mutual anger had shaken her to the core—he saw that. Tess grew paler still, and she blinked—once, twice, three times.

"You love me," she repeated.

"Yes. I can't imagine why. You're stubborn and full of Irish temper as fiery as your hair," he said, reaching out and lifting the thick red braid that lay over her shoulder, then dropping it as if it burned him. "And set on having your own way, even if it destroys you, woman," he shot back. "I'm not worthy of you, I know. But I love you, Tess Hennessy, and I would die for you. That's why you must listen to me."

If he thought his words would render her submissive to his will, he was doomed to disappointment.

"I love you, too, Sandoval Parrish," she said, her eyes still blazing. "And if your Latin blood convinces you to think you have only to raise your voice to get your way, then maybe you'd better think twice about loving me, because I'm not a silly little mouse who will tremble if you yell."

No, she was no mouse. She was Tess, *his* Tess, and she was magnificent, even when she defied him and her rash ideas made him fear for her.

For a moment they just stared at each other, their faces inches apart, and then he was kissing her, pouring his soul into her, holding her so tightly that he could feel her heart race with his.

"Sandoval—"

"Tess—"

He was about to beg her to listen to him, not to try to trick Delgado for information, if only because she loved him. Just then, however, they heard approaching booted footsteps, accompanied by the characteristic clinking sound that spurs make against stone.

They had only a second or two to spring apart—she to throw herself down on her knees before the altar as if she had been praying, he to stride quickly and noiselessly toward the back of the chapel, and then Delgado came in, carrying something over his arm. Sandoval hoped the shadowy dimness of the chapel would hide Tess's flushed cheeks.

"Ah, I thought I might find our devout little lady photographer here," he said. "Are you praying for my soul, *señorita?*"

"Oh, did you feel in need of that?" she asked.

Sandoval saw Delgado search her face for mockery, but it seemed he found none. "Certainly. Prayer for oneself is always appreciated."

The hypocrite, she thought. He sounded pious as a Franciscan monk.

"Perhaps I was only praying for *my* safety until I'm able to return home, *señor,*" she told him frankly.

"Only yours?" Delgado *tsk-tsked.* "How disappointing." He shrugged. "I came to bring you and Lupe dresses that belonged to Cordoba's late wife. He thought you might want to dress for dinner. I knocked at the door of your and Lupe's room, but no one answered. I suppose Lupe was sleeping soundly, eh?"

Sandoval saw Tess quickly look away from Delgado, but too late. He'd seen some hint in her expression that whatever his sister was doing, it probably was *not* sleeping.

"*¿Señorita?* Are you trying to hide something from me?"

Sandoval spoke up. "Cordoba came courting, Diego. Your sister and he are probably strolling the grounds somewhere."

"Ah, I see." Delgado's lips formed a smirk of satisfaction. "*¡Bueno!* I told Lupe she should latch onto him if he was still interested. She could do much worse than to marry a rich, old fool who would die soon and leave her a wealthy landowner, eh?"

He didn't wait to see if they agreed, but laid one of the garments, of a purple so dark it was nearly black, on the bench, saying, "That one is for Lupe." He held out the other, a rich, deep blue, to Tess. "I think this will look very well on you, *señorita.* I look forward to seeing you in it."

Tess took it and the other, nodding. "It'll be nice to wear something else for a change," she said, indicating her drawstring blouse and split skirt as if she had nothing more weighty on her mind than what she wore, and had not noticed the subtle tensing of Sandoval's muscles.

"We dine at eight," Delgado said, turning on his heel to go, then back again. "Oh—I almost forgot—as I left the upper floor, servants were bringing up buckets of hot water and a couple of hip baths, so you ladies can bathe the dust of the trail away. If Lupe lingers too long under the grape arbor kissing Cordoba, her water will be cold, eh? Just the thing to cool her hot blood," Delgado joked.

His eyes met Sandoval's across the room, and there was finally sympathy in them, sympathy that Sandoval, despite his handsomeness, could not compete with Cordoba's wealth for Lupe. Sandoval's expression was convincingly aggrieved.

"Welcome, ladies, you grace my humble table," Cordoba said, rising along with Delgado and Parrish as Tess followed Lupe into the dining room. With a gallant flourish, Cordoba pulled out Lupe's chair. Parrish took a step forward, but Tess quickly fired a warning look at him, for Delgado was already moving to put his hands on the elaborately carved back of Tess's chair. Parrish sank darkly into his seat on the other side of Lupe, which placed him diagonally across from Tess. Cordoba sat at the head of the table with Lupe on his right and Tess on his left.

After he had assisted Tess into her seat, Delgado bent low, murmuring into her ear, "You look truly lovely this evening, *señorita*." He probably would have kissed her cheek if Tess hadn't said quickly, "Thank you, *señor*," before turning brightly to Cordoba and saying, "Thank you for the loan of this dress, Señor Cordoba. It was very kind of you. And how lovely your table looks."

"Nonsense, my dear lady," Cordoba said, but his face beamed at her praise. "It gives me pleasure to have lovely ladies at my table again. And it is but a simple supper." He wore a dark frock coat with a gold brocade waistcoat over an immaculate white shirt and looked immensely dignified.

"You are too modest, *querido,*" Lupe purred, her slender fingers caressing the older man's wrist. "This is truly a magnificent feast."

For once, Lupe spoke the truth. The linen-covered table fairly groaned with silver platters and gold-rimmed, fine-china bowls full of roast beef, chicken, sliced pork in an aromatic sauce, spicy-smelling rice dishes, salads, bread. The gilt-edged plates were embellished with the Cordoba crest in the middle. The gold-rimmed crystal goblets sparkled; the silverware was heavy and ornate. Tess could faintly hear the buzz of conversation outside in the courtyard where Delgado's men were feasting, too, though she guessed their menu was much less sumptuous.

Tess sighed with pleasure at the idea of eating a meal that didn't include beans and tortillas, even as she remembered to bow her head and give thanks. *Thou preparest a table before me in the midst of mine enemies.*

Dishes were passed and for a few minutes there was nothing but the clinking of silverware against fine china and appreciative remarks about the deliciousness of the food.

Tess wished she could gaze openly at Parrish. Like Delgado, he had no fancy clothes, but he'd clearly bathed, shaved, and changed his shirt. He outshone any man she'd ever known. When Delgado turned to him to corroborate a story about one of their raids, she took advantage of the time to drink in the sight of him.

Despite his obvious reluctance to take his eyes off Lupe, Cordoba was the consummate host, making sure everyone's plates were heaped with food and their goblets never empty. Tess was relieved to see her glass had been filled with water rather than wine.

She could almost have enjoyed herself if it hadn't been

for Delgado's closeness and his wandering eyes—the neckline of her borrowed dress was too low for her comfort. Tess grabbed the lacy shawl she had draped over the back of her chair and wrapped it around her shoulders, acting as if she felt a draft.

"Diego tells me you are a photographer, Señorita Hennessy, and that you have been taking pictures of him," Andrés Cordoba said. "What a surprising pastime for a young lady, to be sure."

Tess sensed Delgado holding his breath, probably wondering if she would embarrass him in front of their host by telling him the full story of how she had been brought to the outlaw against her will. Little did Delgado know how safe he was from that, now that she was determined to delve into his memories of Parrish's sister.

"It's my profession, sir, rather than a pastime," Tess corrected Cordoba, though she smiled to soften it. Out of the corner of her eye, she saw Delgado relax a little. "As soon as my work with Señor Delgado is done, I hope to go to New York to work for the famous Mathew Brady."

"I am hoping to talk her out of leaving, however," Delgado told him. "I had wanted my picture taken, yes, but once I beheld this charming lady, I was captivated—by her beauty, her fire."

"Ah..." Cordoba said. "I wish you luck, my good friend."

Tess felt distinctly uneasy as Delgado placed an arm casually but possessively around her shoulder. She did not dare look at Sandoval. She could not indignantly remove Delgado's arm if she hoped to pump him later for information.

Cordoba stood again and lifted his goblet. "I would like to propose a toast," he proclaimed, "to Diego Delgado, a friend and business partner who is about to become a relative, and to his lovely sister, Lupe."

Delgado, on Tess's left, pretended—not very convincingly—to be mystified. "My good friend, whatever do you mean?"

Cordoba smiled broadly, and it made him look ten years younger. "Perhaps I should have asked you for your permission before I approached the lady, but I hope you will forgive me, Diego. Your lovely sister has consented to become my bride—but only with your permission, of course."

At his side, Lupe preened and even managed a maidenly blush. Tess wondered how she did it.

"But this is wonderful news!" Delgado cried, jumping up and coming around behind Tess to embrace Cordoba and his sister in turn. "But of course I consent and give you my heartiest blessing!"

Since Delgado, his sister and Cordoba were all wrapped up in the moment, Tess felt it safe to exchange a triumphant look across the table with Sandoval. The remainder of her captivity would go so much more easily if she didn't have to cope with Lupe's ever-watchful eyes, her scorn for Tess and her attempts to get Parrish alone.

"In that case," Cordoba said, reaching inside his waistcoat, and taking Lupe's hand with his other hand as he sat back down next to Lupe, "I would be honored, my dearest, sweet Lupe, if you would wear this betrothal ring as a symbol of our love."

The ring was a large emerald cabochon set in gold. "Oh, Andrés, it's lovely," cooed Lupe, smothering a wince as Cordoba pushed the slightly-too-small ring onto her finger. Tess wondered if the ring had been Cordoba's late wife's; if so, her fingers had been more slender.

"And when is the wedding to be, since you have already settled everything else without asking the consent of her brother and head of the family?" Delgado demanded with mock severity. "I would assume you will need a little time to prepare, but that my sister will be unwilling to leave your side in the meantime, eh?"

Cordoba's smile dimmed a little. "Ah, that is the only, slight flaw in my happiness," he admitted. "I have asked Lupe to remain with me until the wedding, even promising her a trip to Mexico City to commission a wedding gown fit for a queen, but she insists on departing with you on the morrow so that she can have her seamstress in Santa Elena sew her a dress. She says you and she will return in a month for the wedding."

Tess could hardly hide her dismay as Lupe, confident that her new fiancé was looking at Delgado, winked at Parrish across the table and then smirked at her. So they were not to be free of Lupe's presence, after all! What was Lupe hoping to accomplish? Tess didn't believe Lupe's excuse for leaving tomorrow in the least.

This time Delgado was genuinely surprised. "But, Lupe, are you sure that's what you want to do? Surely the seamstress in Santa Elena is not the equal of a dressmaker in Mexico City...."

"Oh, but I promised Señora...ah, Gutierrez she could make my wedding dress someday," Lupe said with sighing regret.

"I am willing to grant my beautiful *novia* her slightest wish," Cordoba said, kissing Lupe's cheek, "no matter how I will miss her until her return. But it is too bad that circumstances did not permit you, Señorita Hennessy, to bring your camera. I would love having a photograph of my beloved, above all things, to comfort me while we are apart."

"Perhaps I could return for the wedding," Tess offered, hoping she would be long gone from the outlaw band by then.

"Oh, but she is quite talented at drawing, too, Andrés," Lupe said. "Perhaps she could do a sketch of me after dinner so you would have that, at least. You would do that for us, wouldn't you, *mi amiga* Tess?" she coaxed, as if she and Tess had become fast friends. "And perhaps you could draw a picture of my dear Andrés for me, too. I would carry it next to my heart," she declared, dramatically pressing her outspread fingers over that organ.

Tess stifled a desire to roll her eyes. If only she could draw Lupe as she saw her true personality—greedy, grasping, faithless—to warn the old man.

Cordoba took Tess's agreement as a matter of course. "Ah, that would be wonderful. No wonder you've become fond of this talented lady, Diego."

Chapter Fifteen

They left the next morning at dawn. The bandits were in good spirits, after a night spent feasting and not having to sleep in the open, and Delgado's mood was buoyant, too, since he had pocketed a handsome sum from Cordoba for the stolen livestock and the other plunder. Lupe seemed equally glad to be back on the trail, after kissing Cordoba goodbye and giving him a merry wave as she rode away.

"I'm surprised you can leave him so easily," Tess said, after they'd ridden out of sight. "He seems a kind man."

Lupe eyed her suspiciously. "Cordoba? Bah! He's nice enough, all right, but he's a dried-up old stick next to an hombre full of *brío* like Sandoval, here," Lupe said, winking at Parrish, who was riding on Lupe's other side. "I'll settle down into the lap of luxury as Cordoba's wife soon enough, but there's no sense depriving myself of a stallion before I have to settle for an old gelding. We have some unfinished business, do we not, *querido?*" she said, fluttering her thick, black lashes at Parrish.

Parrish stared pointedly at Lupe's heavy betrothal ring,

winking in the light of the rising sun, then kneed his pinto forward until he was riding next to Delgado.

Lupe wasn't the least abashed. "Men!" she said with a husky chuckle. "They get so jealous. But I'll make it up to him," she added, with a secretive smile.

Lupe thought that Sandoval was jealous, instead of disgusted at her? Tess was glad that she knew the truth about Sandoval's feelings, and marveled that Lupe could deceive herself as well as she could Cordoba.

"In any case, Tess," Lupe went on, "how could I tamely stay with Cordoba when I have a job to do? I'm here to chaperone you amid all these wild men." She chuckled, then lowered her voice. "I'm also here to make sure you don't try anything foolish, like escaping. Diego wants you, *gringa,* and what my brother wants, I'm going to see that he gets."

Delgado, perhaps hearing his name mentioned, turned to look over his shoulder, and all the menace faded from Lupe's sharp features. "And besides," she went on, her tone merry again, "I haven't had the chance to shoot anyone yet. That's always the high point of going raiding for me."

Lupe was baiting her, Tess knew, and struggled not to tighten her hands on the reins. "What will your betrothed say when you return to him without a wedding dress?" she asked. "There's no seamstress in Santa Elena, is there?"

Lupe laughed again. "Of course not! But who says I'll return without a wedding dress? Perhaps I'll find one to steal."

More than ever before, Tess understood why Parrish and the Rangers were determined to put an end to raiders like the Delgados—both of them. The cause had become hers, too.

Delgado decided to strike a little settlement just across the river from Reynosa that day, a place so small that it could hardly be called a town as yet, but big enough to boast a post office, a small general store, a cantina and a church. They paused just after crossing the river, studying the town, while Delgado announced his plan.

"We'll take the post office," Delgado said, indicating himself and two men. "They should have a little cash, and then we'll pay a visit to the cantina. I'm sure they're overstocked, and would be glad to donate their excess to us, eh? Sandoval, you guard Lupe and Tess, and take Elizonda and Aguilar, and see what the general store has to offer, eh? Maybe they'll have some pretty cloth for your wedding dress, sister."

Tess tensed, wondering if this was the time she'd be caught in the crossfire and killed—or Sandoval would be.

Sandoval shot Tess a look, his eyes eloquent with regret and an unspoken promise to protect her, even if it cost him his life. Tess lifted her chin and tried to smile back at him, so he wouldn't worry, but she knew it was unconvincing.

Lupe turned around in her saddle. "Don't even think of trying to escape, *gringa*—"

A bell began to peal in the steeple of the small church just then, interrupting her.

"What's that? Is it a signal?" Delgado hissed, starting to wheel his horse around. "Let's get out of here!"

"No, wait, brother," Lupe pleaded, catching hold of her brother's arm. "Look—we could not have planned it better!"

The church door had opened, and as they watched, a throng of people spilled out on the lawn. As they watched, a man and woman walked out, arm in arm, the woman dressed in white. A bride.

"Lupe, no, please!" Tess pleaded, guessing what the woman had in mind. "Have a heart!"

Lupe flashed her a look of withering scorn. "A wedding party!" she crowed. "What luck. Rich pickings there, brother. There will be jewelry at the very least, and from here, it looks like that wedding dress would fit me just fine...."

"Lupe, please don't spoil her wedding day," Tess said again. "I'm begging you."

"Don't be silly, *gringa,*" Lupe said with a derisive laugh. "As you pointed out, I need a bridal gown."

"Lupe, perhaps we ought to leave the wedding party alone," Sandoval said. "Just think how much easier it will be to rob the businesses in town—probably most of the people are at this wedding."

It had been daring of him to speak up, Tess thought. But Sandoval's effort to appeal to Lupe's logic failed simply because it ran counter to what Lupe wanted to do—and possibly because he'd failed to return her blatant overtures.

"We? The last I knew of it, Sandoval, my sweet, you were merely my brother's lieutenant. Do not presume to advise me," she snarled. "Diego, what do you say? Am I to have this wedding dress I want, or will you listen to the whining of the *gringa?*"

Diego, who had been watching this byplay, shrugged. "Señorita Tess, I'm sorry, but we are outlaws, after all. What could be easier than robbing that flock of pigeons, and then the stores they have left unguarded?"

He started to gesture them forward, but his arm froze in midair as another sound intruded on their ears: the clatter of horses' hooves, the creak of leather and the jingling of bits. As one, they whirled in their saddles.

A mounted patrol of blue-coated soldiers was approaching, a score of them, Tess saw at a glance. All of them had pistols in holsters, and carbines strapped to their saddles.

"The cavalry!" Delgado cried. Beside him, Lupe swore viciously, even as her brother called, "Scatter, *muchachos!* Rendezvous at the hideout beyond Reynosa!"

Even as the bandits began to wheel their horses in different directions, the officer at the head of the patrol shouted, "Halt! I'm Captain McCoy of the U.S. Army and I am ordered to detain any suspicious parties of Mexicans. Halt or we'll shoot!"

Sandoval had used Delgado's distraction to maneuver his horse close to Tess's. "Tess, *go to them,*" Sandoval whispered urgently. "Ride toward them with your hands up. You'll be safe! You could go *home!*"

Before she could refuse, however, and whisper back that she wasn't leaving till she found out about Sandoval's sister, the first volley of bullets buzzed past like angry wasps. One of the bandits—the one called Mérida, Tess thought—screamed and fell out of his saddle.

Lupe grabbed the reins of Tess's horse. "You're not getting away so easily, you fool!" and spurred her own horse toward the river. Tess grabbed her saddle horn as Dulce followed willy-nilly, and held on for dear life, while Sandoval brought up the rear, firing behind them to cover their escape.

They rode hard for miles south along the Rio Grande before Lupe, Tess and Sandoval shook their pursuers and felt safe to swim across. It was hours before they were able to make their way to yet another of Delgado's hideouts on a *riachuelo* feeding into the Rio Grande on the Mexican side. Delgado and several of the other outlaws were already there, and others trickled in afterward.

Tess, exhausted, unsaddled her lathered mare, rubbed her down, then lay down with her head against her saddle. Lupe was at her quarrelsome worst, now that she had been deprived of her prize and her joy in bringing misery to an innocent crowd of wedding guests, and she had been trying to pick a fight with anyone who came near her. Tess planned to feign sleep to get away from her, but the next thing she knew, it was evening.

It wasn't long after the usual supper of beans and tortillas that the men started passing around the bottles. Tess made herself comfortable by the fire with her sketching pad and a bit of charcoal. She'd seen Parrish walk away from the camp shortly after he'd finished his meal, and it wasn't long before Lupe got up and followed him.

Tess wondered if Lupe had heard Sandoval's whispered suggestion that she should seek refuge with the cavalry, and was going to vent her displeasure about it. But given her treacherous nature, it seemed more her style to denounce Sandoval to her brother. No, she was probably attempting yet again to snare Sandoval with her wiles. If so, the woman was unbelievably persistent.

Dear God, help Sandoval walk the tightrope between revealing his true dislike of Lupe Delgado and being forced to pretend desire for her.

"Ah, you've been drawing again, I see," Delgado said, folding his legs and sitting down beside her. The outlaw leader carried a bottle of brandy, which must have been a gift from Cordoba, and his first exhalation informed Tess that he'd already imbibed some. Tess wanted to find some reason to excuse herself, but this was her chance to draw him out, and she must take it.

"Yes," she said, looking down as he did at her rough sketch of how she imagined the raid this morning if the cavalry had not come along—the bride and groom and their guests, all with their hands up, the bride with tear-drenched cheeks as Lupe, cruelly smiling, held a gun on her. Behind her, an amused Delgado sat on his horse, watching.

The outlaw leader picked up the pad, studying the drawing more closely. "You draw with painful honesty, *señorita,*" Delgado observed ruefully. "Perhaps we will not show this one to Lupe, eh? You feel sorry for the subjects of our raids?"

"Oh? I thought she'd enjoy it, since this was how she wanted things to go," Tess told him. "And yes, I do feel bad for them. They're only trying to make a living and have an occasional celebration." Being bluntly critical was no way to coax this man into bragging about himself, yet she had to answer honestly, didn't she?

"As am I and my men," Delgado countered, "though not an honest living, I'm sure you would say."

"No."

"I must commend you for trying to stop my sister from robbing the wedding this afternoon, even though you knew it had little chance of succeeding. It was only chance that the bluecoats came by when they did. You knew your protest would draw her wrath to you, yet you did it anyway. You have the heart of a lion, *señorita.*"

"You give me too much credit," Tess said, waving the idea away. How was she to work this conversation around to Delgado's past? "A bride shouldn't have to face robbery on her wedding day, of all days. I'd think that since Lupe was about to be a bride herself, she could have a little compassion for a woman on her wedding day."

"Lupe is a hard woman," Delgado admitted. "Life has made her so. Perhaps she should have been born a man—

even a general, eh? She would have made a ruthless soldier."

"All men are not ruthless and bloodthirsty—even soldiers."

Delgado shrugged. "Don't worry about Lupe. I won't let her harm you. Though heaven knows, it's hard to control her tongue."

"I'd rather you kept her from harming the people you steal from," she said.

Delgado said nothing. Night sounds surrounded them—the crackling of the fire, a bawdy song some of the men were singing, the screech of an owl in a tree nearby, the call of a distant coyote summoning his mate.

"You don't like being with us, do you, Tess Hennessy?"

"I would rather be at home, with my family, naturally. They're probably worried sick."

"I had hoped you would have learned to appreciate the outlaw life a little by now, if not Delgado. Do you hate me, Tess?"

Appreciate the outlaw life? Did he seriously think—

"No, I don't hate you," she said. She couldn't help being a little amused that he'd referred to himself in the third person.

"Because your faith forbids you to hate, eh?"

"I dislike what you've done in having me kidnapped, of course. But you haven't harmed me." Tess watched him warily. Just as Parrish must take care with Lupe, so must she walk a fine line with Delgado. Swallowing hard, she said, "I can see that you have a lot of ambition and energy in getting what you want. But I don't really know you, Señor Delgado."

"Diego, please."

He leaned closer to her, and Tess had to stifle the urge to scoot away from him. *Lord, please give me the right words to say.*

Chapter Sixteen

"You say you don't really know me, Tess," Delgado said. He spread his hands wide. "Here I am, an open book. Ask me what you will. I would like you to know me very well, eh?"

Again Tess felt that warning tickle of ice on her spine that warned her to proceed carefully. Very, very carefully. She drew in a breath, wanting to draw back, to increase the distance between them, but that would telegraph the discrepancy between her words and her feelings, so she forced herself to remain still. "I...I tried to ask you about something, if you will recall, that first night in camp. But I'm afraid my approach was a little...um, *confrontational.* I've often been sorry for that." Tess fluttered her lashes at him as she had seen Lupe do to Cordoba, praying it didn't look like she had just gotten dust in her eyes instead.

It worked better than a proverbial charm. Delgado smiled sympathetically. "Ah, Tess, there is no need to berate yourself about that night. I understood. You had just been captured, and you did not know what to expect. And you have *this* that influences your temperament, eh?"

He caressed the hair on the side of her head. "I like a woman of fire, Tess. So ask, and do not be afraid."

She had to school herself not to shrink away from his touch, even while praying it did not go further.

All right, what did you do with Pilar Morelos?

If only it were that simple.

"Very well," she said, making her tone brisk. "At dinner that night, I asked you to tell me about your early days, when you first turned to the outlaw life. I'd still like to hear about that time. What was it like?" Tess knew she had to make her questions general at first, and gradually lead into specifics, or he would become suspicious.

Delgado smiled in remembrance, his eyes losing focus. To her relief, he leaned back, away from her. "Ah, those were the days, *señorita.* I would ride into a town, sit in the cantina and spin my tales of how the devil Texans had killed my family, and tell how I planned to wreak vengeance on their behalf and for all Mexicans who had suffered at the Texans' hands. I was raising an army, I declared, of brave, like-minded men. Everyone would buy me tequila and clap me on the back and tell me what a fine fellow I was." He took another long draft on his bottle of brandy.

"Young men flocked into the cantinas to join up. I made them sign—or make their mark—on a pledge of loyalty in their own blood. That paper gave me the right to cut the throat of any man who betrayed me. Not that most of us could read, mind you, but knowing the consequences of betrayal impressed on them that Diego Delgado was serious.

"When I had enlisted everyone who was interested," Delgado went on, arms around his drawn-up knees, "we would go on to the next village. Our army swelled with each town we visited."

"I imagine the ladies found you fascinating," Tess dared to say.

Delgado grinned, too lost in his memories to be modest. "*Sí.* I had women cooking my meals, washing my clothes, volunteering to ride along, not to be outlaws, you understand, but to be close to me. But I refused, wanting to keep my band quick and fast. And besides, there were always more women in the next town for Delgado—and the ones I didn't want, I let my men have."

There was no end to this man's ego, Tess marveled, striving to keep her distaste from showing on her face. He'd apparently forgotten he was trying to woo the very woman to whom he was bragging of his conquests.

"I notice you said *women,*" Tess murmured. "You liked them older? Not…girls?"

He blinked at the question, and Tess hoped she hadn't gone too far in her haste to get the information Parrish needed.

"I suppose you *could* say that, yes… In those days I liked my lady friends…ah, shall we say *experienced?* They didn't expect impossible things of a man always on the move. They didn't weep—much, anyway—when it was time for Delgado to leave. Ah, but there was a girl once…"

Did he mean Pilar?

"Tell me about her," she encouraged, leaning forward.

Delgado inclined himself toward her. "This girl, she lived in—"

"Diego, what are we doing tomorrow?" Lupe said, bursting into the circle of firelight and shattering the moment. Tess wanted to gnash her teeth in vexation.

Even in the flickering firelight, Tess could see the bright patches of scarlet flushing Lupe's cheeks and the angry glint in her eyes. She reminded Tess of a cat whose tail had been caught under a rocking chair.

So Lupe's little tête-à-tête with Sandoval hadn't gone as she had hoped. Tess found that immensely cheering in the midst of her own frustration.

"Sorry—was I interrupting something?" The look Lupe threw at Tess was anything but apologetic.

Delgado frowned at her, shaking his head as if to clear it. "What do you mean, what are we doing tomorrow?"

Lupe gave an elaborate shrug. "Where do we raid?"

"I haven't decided yet," Delgado growled. "Why must we discuss it this minute?"

Lupe ignored his question. "Let's rob a bank, brother. What do you say? We haven't done that in a while."

"Why do you want to do that? It's more hazardous, and dollars must be converted to pesos."

Lupe shrugged. "It's more of a challenge than stealing from gringo ranches. And I don't imagine Cordoba would mind exchanging them for you. Or it could be my dowry—a dowry of dollars."

Delgado shot a considering look at Tess. "I don't know, Lupe. Banks are more dangerous. I wouldn't want Tess to get hurt. She is our guest, after all."

Lupe's face hardened, and she leaned down to her brother. "Oh, well, if you're going to let a *gringa* rule your choices, then you will no longer be the Scourge of the Border. Bah! Next you'll be saying you want to buy a *rancho* and settle down."

Delgado was instantly on his feet, his fist cocked. "Shut your mouth, woman! You do not tell me what to do!"

It was a mistake, Tess thought, for Lupe to mock her brother in front of anyone, let alone her, since Delgado was trying to impress her. Delgado always had to be master of any situation.

Lupe recoiled, her expression transfiguring from scornful and mocking to that of a hurt child. Tess watched in amazement as Lupe's lip quivered and tears welled up and spilled from her eyes.

Even more astonishing was the change in Delgado. His angry, tense features immediately softened, and he gathered his sister into his arms. "I'm so sorry, little one, I did not mean to yell," he soothed her. "Forgive your cross brother, eh? We will do anything you want tomorrow, anything."

Couldn't Delgado see through his sister, see how she was playing him?

Lupe knuckled the tears from her eyes and gave Delgado a tremulous smile. "*Really,* Diego? Do you mean it?"

"Of course," Delgado said, just as Parrish entered the circle of light. "Sandoval, tell the men. We're robbing a bank tomorrow."

Parrish's face was impassive. "Tomorrow? It's Sunday. The bank will be closed."

All of them stared at him in surprise, Tess included. She had completely lost track of time.

Lupe swore under her breath. Delgado gave her a one-armed hug. "Ah, don't fret, *hermana.* We'll do it the next day. I'll take you to church tomorrow instead, and Tess, too. That will be nice, eh? And our bank robbery will go that much better for having an extra day to plan it."

The town of Mission came into sight about five miles after they'd crossed the river. Lupe grinned at Sandoval, clearly exultant that they were about to unleash terror on the unsuspecting townspeople of Mission and rob many of them of their life savings—and that she would be in the thick of it.

Parrish didn't acknowledge her look. Apprehension tightened his spine as if he were stretched out on a rack. He hoped desperately that no innocent citizens would be harmed today. He had to find a way to bring this charade of his to a close, with the Delgados both captured. Or killed. It didn't matter much to him which way they paid the penalty for their crimes.

He risked a glance at Tess, sitting rigid in her saddle, her freckles standing out against her pale skin. She stared straight ahead at the town. He thought he saw her lips moving—in prayer?

He and Tess should be anywhere but here. At that moment Sandoval would have given anything, even his soul, to be calling on her at Hennessy Hall, taking her to barbecues, riding, picnics, to church on Sundays…. He'd been completely stupid to involve her in his convoluted scheme to bring Delgado to justice. He'd never foreseen that the outlaw leader would do anything more than have Tess take a few pictures, then let her go. But you could never quite predict what a snake would do, so he had no excuse.

"Let's *stage* a robbery at the bank in Santa Elena," Sandoval had suggested last night at the campfire. "Those townspeople would be happy to pose for you, knowing it wasn't real, and no one would get hurt. Tess could even use her camera then."

Sandoval had felt a flash of hope when he saw Delgado rub his chin thoughtfully. He was considering it.

"And the camera would show that the bank teller and customers were as Mexican as we are, not lily-white *Americanos,*" Lupe had snapped scornfully. "Anyone would know it was faked."

Her remark convinced her brother, of course.

Now Sandoval was in the ridiculous position of being a Texas Ranger about to help rob a Texas bank. Now he'd have to not only get Tess to safety, and find Pilar—he'd also have to find a way to take the money back from Delgado when they escaped, or he'd never be welcome on either side of the border.

At that moment he hated Delgado more than he ever had. Delgado had led them all to church yesterday, the hypocrite, and today he was leading them in a bank robbery.

"Sandoval, I want you to stage a diversion at the north end of the town," Delgado ordered. "That will draw the sheriff and deputies, if he has any, away from the bank. Maybe you can even get them to chase you out of town, then lose them and double back to the border. Garza and Rivera, stand as lookouts on either end to the street. Prieto, Aguilar, take the rear exit of the bank into the alleyway. Don't let anyone in or out. Elizonda, watch for snipers from the right side of the street, Barriga, the left. Zavala, Dominguez, Lupe, you're with me in the bank."

"What about Tess, *jefe?*" Sandoval asked. "Why don't we leave a man guarding her here, so she can watch, but she's not in danger?"

Leave me with her, he wanted to say. Let someone else divert the sheriff.

He'd try his best to talk Tess into fleeing toward Chapin, given the chance. He knew, though, there was no chance Delgado would agree.

Lupe's narrowed eyes were hard as obsidian. "You're very solicitous of her all of a sudden, Sandoval. Should we worry about that, brother? Perhaps, Sandoval, the gringo blood is singing more loudly in your veins today than the Mexican?"

"Not at all," he said, with a calmness he didn't feel,

keeping his eyes from Tess. "I'm sure Diego wouldn't want Tess caught in the crossfire, as she would be if the citizens put up a fight. Why not let her come with me, *jefe?* Then she would see some action, but not be in so much danger."

And I could at least watch out for her, he thought.

Lupe glared at him.

Delgado straightened in the saddle. "Tess will come in the bank with us, of course. How would she be able to make one of her excellent drawings of my exploits if she doesn't experience a real bank robbery? She will soon have enough material to write an entire book about me, eh? Dominguez will guard her. They'll stay near the door, out of the way, and be the first out when we make our getaway."

The rack of apprehension along Sandoval's spine tightened to the point of agony. Dominguez, the very bandito Tess disliked the most, the one Tess had told him she'd struggled with during her kidnapping and had kneed in the groin. The man still ogled her whenever Delgado wasn't looking. Dominguez would care less than nothing if Tess came to harm.

"Diego, let *me* come inside. Dominguez can stage the diversion," Parrish said.

"Sandoval, you're sounding like my old maid aunt. No more arguing," Delgado snarled. "Do as I told you."

Delgado had assigned Parrish where he couldn't see what was happening to Tess, couldn't protect her. *Lord, it's up to You to keep her safe. Please, if You never answer any prayer of mine again, shield her.*

He shot a cold warning look at Dominguez—Don't let anything happen to her, if you value your life, hombre.

Dominguez smirked.

"Let's go," Delgado said, and brought his arm forward. They walked their horses toward Mission, in no apparent hurry, doing nothing to draw any watcher's attention to the fact that disaster was fast approaching.

Chapter Seventeen

Tess locked eyes with Parrish one last time before, grim-faced and silent, he reined his horse away from the rest of them to skirt the town. What kind of diversion would he mount? Would he be successful in drawing the sheriff's attention away from the bank? And then, would he be able to escape? Would she ever see him again, or would one or both of them be killed today? *Please, Lord, protect us!*

They entered the town, silent and unobtrusive as a breeze, and fanned out as Delgado had specified. She saw no one on the street except for an old codger whittling in front of what looked like a saloon next to the bank. Delgado, Lupe, Zavala, Dominguez and Tess dismounted in front of it, tied their horses to a hitching post and climbed up onto the boardwalk. Tess's legs felt like pudding.

Dominguez grinned nastily at her. "Afraid, *gringa?*"

She ignored him.

Just before Delgado reached for the door, they all paused to pull bandannas over their faces. The bandanna Tess wore was a spare one of Dominguez's, and it stank of stale sweat. Surely she was in the middle of a nightmare, and any moment she would wake up in her bed at Hennessy Hall and find that her time among Delgado's banditos had all been a bizarre dream. Only Dominguez's iron grip on her shoulder with his left hand, and her sidelong view of his long-muzzle pistol held in his right as he pushed her through the door convinced her that it was all too horribly real.

"Hands in the air, everyone!" shouted Delgado, and everyone whirled around.

"It's *Delgado,*" the teller quavered. The bank president and three of the four customers raised their arms obediently. The fourth, a woman who had been standing in front of the teller's window, swooned, collapsing like a suddenly empty sack. Tess envied her. If only she were that delicate sort of female! Then she wouldn't have to endure the next few minutes. In fact, copying that woman's action might be the very smartest thing she could do. The outlaws would have to leave her behind!

Tess let herself waver as if she were about to lose consciousness.

Dominguez's fingers on her shoulder clamped down like talons. "Don't pretend to faint, *gringa,*" he whispered in her ear. "I'd take pleasure in shooting you."

Tess went rigid.

"Yes, it is Delgado himself, and a few of his amigos," Delgado agreed with a beatific smile, as if he had been announced as the guest of honor at a party, "come to relieve you, the good citizens of Mission, of your excess *dinero.* Be wise and hand the money over without any problems, and all of you will live to appreciate the virtue of poverty, yes? Give us any trouble, however, and you will be sorry—the very last feeling you ever have," he added, brandishing his pistol. All geniality had vanished.

"Is anyone back there?" Delgado asked the short, gray-haired bank president, motioning to a door to the right of his desk.

"No, no," the man said, nodding his head so violently that his jowls wobbled like a turkey's wattle. "That's my private office…for meetings…"

Tess heard the sound of gunfire then, coming from the north end of town. Parrish had begun his diversion. Everyone tensed, a couple of them uttered cries of alarm, but no one took his eyes off Delgado and his pistol.

Except for Tess, who couldn't help looking over her shoulder out a window behind her at the jail across the street. No one tried to run out the door. No one appeared at its window.

Lupe held out the large gunnysack she had been carrying folded up under her arm, and motioned to the teller with her pistol. "Fill it up with the money—all of it. And the rest of you start removing your jewelry and pocket watches," she ordered, jerking her head at the paralyzed customers. "Don't try to hold anything back, or it will go worse for you."

Just then the door to the right of the desk banged open and three men burst out, the one in front yelling, "Drop your guns, Delgado, you and your men!"

Chaos erupted. Customers screamed and dropped to the floor. Lupe let go of her sack and fired in the sheriff's direction, while Delgado aimed at one of the deputies behind him, collapsing him with a wound in his chest that blossomed into an obscene crimson flower. The wounded man managed to fire once more, but the bullet went wide, missing Delgado and embedding itself in a wall, sending plaster flakes flying. Dominguez shot at the other deputy, but he threw himself behind the desk, firing around it a second later. Zavala went down, moaning. Then the sheriff fired at Dominguez, but he ducked behind Tess. She threw her hands up in the air, had time to think, *Lord, help—!*

A flash of fire scorched the side of her head. Everything went black.

No one had come running out of the jail after his first shots into the air. Garza, the only bandito positioned where Sandoval could see him, shrugged and went back to staring at the bank.

Sandoval fired into the air again. All at once the window of the nearest house was thrown open. The long muzzle of a rifle poked out and immediately spat bullets in his direction, kicking up the dust around his horse's hooves, causing the pinto to dance and whinny.

He fired at the window, shattering the glass. Then, from the other end of town, a rider came galloping toward him, shooting as he came.

Finally, some response! Sandoval kicked the horse in the ribs. *"Hyaah!"*

The pinto needed no encouragement to take off.

Once he'd left his pursuer far enough behind, Sandoval galloped in a wide arc for an hour before heading for the river. By now, God willing, Tess would be safely across the Rio Grande with the others and waiting at the agreed-upon rendezvous in one of Delgado's hideaway valleys. He wondered if all of the bandits had made it out of the town, and if the man who'd ridden after him had been the sheriff.

The pinto was lathered and blowing by the time Sandoval arrived at the valley. He knew he should have slowed the horse, sparing him, when no one had chased him to his crossing point, but he was driven by anxiety for Tess. Nothing else mattered till he knew she was all right.

The drawn, haggard expressions on the faces of Garza and Aguilar, posted at the entrance of the valley, did nothing to reassure him. They looked up when he trotted past, but he saw none of the usual exhilaration that followed a successful raid. He rode on until he spotted two horse-blanket-covered forms on the ground.

Jumping off the paint, Sandoval ran to the blankets. *Please, God...don't let one of them be Tess....*

He yanked the blanket back and saw with unspeakable relief that both corpses were men—Zavala and Dominguez.

But Dominguez was supposed to have been assigned to Tess. Where was she?

He turned on his heel, his eyes seeking Delgado among the banditos until he spotted him kneeling in the shade of a cedar elm by a supine, skirted figure. *Tess?* He ran toward them.

It was Lupe, her head pillowed by folded horse blankets. She and Delgado looked up as he broke into the circle.

"Where's Tess?" Sandoval demanded without preliminaries. "What happened?"

"*Muchas gracias* for your solicitude on *my* behalf," Lupe whimpered. "I'm wounded! See?" She pulled part of her riding skirt up to show a thick bandage around her calf. A spot of blood the size of a *centavo* showed through.

"The bullet went on through," Delgado said. "She'll be all right, thankfully." But his eyes were troubled. "Sandoval—"

"It *hurts,*" moaned Lupe, interrupting. "Will you sit with me, Sandoval?"

Sandoval ignored her. "*Where is Tess?*"

Delgado got to his feet. "Sandoval, I'm afraid I have some bad news. Tragic news..."

Now Sandoval saw the pallor underlying the bandit leader's bronzed cheeks, and he froze for a moment, then lurched forward unsteadily, grabbing Delgado by the shoulders. "What are you saying? What happened?"

"Amigo, they were waiting for us inside the bank. It was an ambush."

"Who was waiting?"

"The sheriff," Delgado said dolefully, "and two other men. They jumped out of a side office in the bank and shot at us. I killed one of them, I think, but Zavala was badly wounded and died on the way here, God rest his soul...."

"What about Tess?" Sandoval couldn't care less about Zavala at the moment, didn't care that he was shouting now at the most feared outlaw in the Rio Grande Valley.

"When they started firing, Dominguez ducked behind Tess, the cursed *cobarde!* Tess—oh, amigo, I don't know how to tell you this—I saw them shoot Tess. She fell down, her face all bloody...she must be dead. When we reached this valley I shot Dominguez myself for his cowardice. He got the *señorita* killed! I should have listened to you, should have let you stay with her...."

Sandoval felt as if his blood had frozen. *Tess, dead?* Then what Delgado had said repeated itself in his brain. "You said she must be dead. You don't *know?* Why didn't you bring her with you?"

Delgado's eyes were haunted with pain. "Sandoval... my sister and Zavala were both wounded. Tess wasn't moving...there was so much blood...I was sure she was gone. Everyone was shouting and screaming...."

Sandoval felt his hands clench into fists. He wanted to pummel Delgado into the earth, then choke him. "I'm going to get her," he said. "Dead or alive, I have to *know*." Lord in heaven, how was he going to face her parents and Sam Taylor, if Tess was dead?

Delgado stared at him. "Don't be loco, hombre. If she wasn't dead then, she is by now. My heart is full of pain to think this, my friend, but we must face it. Don't stick your neck in a noose for nothing!"

"I'll need a fresh horse," Sandoval said, as if Delgado hadn't spoken. "Fresher than mine, anyway."

Delgado's shoulders sagged. "Take my black," he said. "But you're going to your death, amigo. Those gringos will be out for blood, and any Mexicans will do."

"Bah! He's only part Mexican," Lupe's voice mocked from the ground a few feet away.

"Shut up, Lupe," snapped Delgado, surprising Sandoval with the fury in his tone. "If he can use his Anglo blood to bring my Tess back, alive or dead…" His voice broke and he turned away.

Someone was sponging her forehead, and every stroke shot fresh waves of burning pain spearing deep into her skull. Tentatively, Tess opened one eye, and when she was able to focus, she beheld an elderly, bespectacled man sitting by the cot on which she lay. Looking behind him, she saw floor-to-ceiling bars. She was in a jail cell?

Then she remembered Dominguez shoving her in front of him, the flash of fire coming straight at her head, the sudden, overwhelming pain before everything faded away….

"You're awake," the man said. "You speak any English?"

"Of course I do," Tess said. "I'm American. I—"

"Take it easy, missy. I'm Doc Waters, and you got yourself creased by a bullet. Lucky you weren't killed," he murmured. "Or maybe not so lucky," he said, with a meaningful look at the bars. Outside she heard a rumble of voices, but she couldn't make out what they said.

"Wh-what do you mean?"

"Your amigos killed a deputy. Or maybe it was you who shot him—I dunno, I wasn't in the bank, but they said they found a pistol near where you fell."

"It wasn't mine! I wasn't even armed," Tess cried, but her indignation only made her pounding headache worse. She put a shaky hand up to her forehead and felt something sticky. When she looked at her fingers, they were streaked with blood.

"Yep, scalp wounds bleed a lot," the doctor said. "The blood had clotted, but when I started cleaning the wound it commenced t' bleed again."

Tess didn't care about that. "What am I doing in jail? I didn't want to be in that bank with Delgado any more than any of the customers—"

"So it *was* Delgado," interrupted another man, who had appeared beyond the bars. "Thought so, but I wasn't sure."

"Who are you?"

"Sheriff Mason," the grizzled, stocky man said as he let himself into her cell with a ring of keys. "And I'll ask you the same question. What's an American girl doing ridin' with Mexican bandits, robbin' banks?"

"I'm not a bandit," she protested. "I'm Tess Hennessy, and I was kidnapped by Delgado's men—"

"Sure," he retorted. "Mighty convenient t' claim that, now that you're sittin' in my jail, girl."

Tess pushed herself up on her elbows. "You can't possibly believe I wanted to rob that bank!"

He stooped over her. "Don't you tell me what I cain't believe!" he cried, wagging a thick finger at her. "All I know is a good man was killed by you an' your Mex friends t'day."

"*I* didn't kill him," she cried. "I'm a photographer, and Delgado had me abducted because he wanted his picture taken, and—"

"A woman photographer?" he retorted skeptically. "So where's your camera box? I didn't see anything of the sort! You think you can spin some yarn, and I'm gonna buy it? You'll have to do better than that, Miss Hennessy."

"I can draw as well as photograph, and Delgado wanted a sketch of the bank robbery done later. I'm telling the *truth,*" she protested, when his expression remained skeptical. "I live at Hennessy Hall, near Chapin, and my parents are Patrick and Amelia Hennessy. You could contact them—does Mission have a telegraph? They'll tell you what I'm saying is true." She closed her eyes, not wanting this man to see her pain at the thought of her parents being informed their daughter was in jail, charged with attempted bank robbery.

"Mebbe you're tellin' the truth and mebbe you ain't," the sheriff said. "An' no, this town don't have no telegraph office. You kin tell your story to th' judge tomorrow morning—*if* you're still around, that is."

"If I'm still around?" she echoed. "Where would I be?"

He pointed at her window, where the rumble of voices had grown to an angry buzz, like a swarm of wasps confined to a tiny bottle. "Hear that? Remember I said a deputy was killed? Well, his older brother is the biggest rancher in this area, and he wants someone t' pay fer his brother's death. He organized a posse to catch them murderin' bandits, but by th' time they was all mounted up, the bandits had scattered. He's wantin' t' lynch someone, an' he's too mad to care if it's a woman."

Tess stared at him, feeling the rough scrape of hemp tightening around her neck, choking off her air.... "But I'm innocent! You can't let that happen, Sheriff. Not without a trial—"

"I'll be here all night, doin' what I kin t' save your skin," he said grudgingly. "But you hear 'em out there," he repeated, jerking his head toward the sound. "He's mad as a teased snake and he's gettin' the rest of 'em all riled up. I ain't about t' get hurt protectin' some girl who thought it'd be a lark to ride with outlaws."

Chapter Eighteen

Yes, she heard them out there, all right. There had been individual voices muttering threats and ideas about what should be done with her, but just then they united to chant, "Lynch the redhead! Hang 'er high! String 'er up!"

The doctor, having rolled a wide strip of clean linen around her head, got to his feet. "Well…I've done all I can…perhaps I'd better be going…." He shook his head uneasily. "Mason, don't you let them take this young woman. Whatever she did, she's at least entitled to a trial," he added as he motioned for the sheriff to let him out of the cell.

"Whatever she did?" Even the doctor thought she was guilty?

"Doctor Waters, on your way out, would you ask the brother of the deputy who died to come in here? I want to talk to him," Tess called to the physician.

Waters turned around in the doorway between the jail's two cells and the sheriff's office, blinking in surprise. "Miss Hennessy, are you sure that's wise?"

It had been an impulsive act on Tess's part, and she

wasn't sure at all, but she nodded. "It's certainly better than sitting here listening to them planning what tree to throw the rope over," she said. Surely, if she talked to the grieving man, she could make him see that she was innocent.

Waters looked to Mason for permission, and at last the sheriff nodded. "I don't think it'll do any good, but you can try, Miss Hennessy. Doc, you tell Amory I'm only lettin' him in, no one else."

A minute later, Tess heard heavy footsteps approaching the cell, and looked up.

Backlit by the sunshiny office behind him, Amory at first appeared only as a dark, hulking shape against the bars of her cell, but even from this distance the reek of stale whiskey reached her nose.

"You th' red-headed witch—" it came out *wissch* "—who kilt my brother Bill t'day?"

"My name is Tess—Teresa, that is—Hennessy," she said with a calmness she was far from feeling. "And I didn't kill your brother. I've never fired a gun at anyone. I was with Delgado and his outlaws not of my own free will, but because—"

"*Shuddup!* You jus' shuddup, y-ya hear? I don' wanna lissen t' yore lies!" the man shouted at her, rattling the bars in his fury, his red-rimmed eyes glaring at her. "You can't trust nothin' no red-haired wumman says—an' I oughta know, 'cuz my no-good wife was one! You jes' enjoy the air yore breathin' right now, mishy, 'cuz purty soon it's gonna be choked right outta ya!" With that parting shot, he turned on his heel and lumbered unsteadily out of the jail, slamming the door behind him.

The hum had quieted while Amory had been inside, no doubt so the men could hope to overhear what was being said. Now it rose to a buzz again.

Sheriff Mason shot her an "I told you so" look. "If you got any other good ideas, I'll be out there at my desk." He let himself out, then locked the cell behind him.

Where was Sandoval? Had he been killed during his attempt to stage a diversion? He couldn't have been captured, or he'd be in the other cell.

"Sheriff Mason, were there…that is, I don't remember…were any of the outlaws killed?" she asked as he reached the doorway.

He turned around. "I wounded the Mex woman—in the leg, I think—and Edgerton, the other deputy, wounded the one that wasn't standing next to you. Gut-shot, he was, so I don't reckon he'll live, but Delgado drug him onto a horse and rode outta Mission holdin' onto him."

"No one else?"

Mason studied her. "One of the men told me some fella was shootin' his pistol in the air down t' other end of the street. He chased after him, but he lost him. Why? You got a sweetheart among them banditos, even if it ain't Delgado?"

She shook her head quickly. "No, I was just wondering."

So Zavala was probably dying, if not already dead, and Lupe had been wounded. For a moment, Tess wished fiercely that it had been Lupe who had been more gravely hit. The whole idea of robbing the bank had been hers, and the responsibility for the deaths of the deputy and Zavala could be laid squarely at her door—and at her brother's, too, for agreeing to it.

Delgado would have told Sandoval he'd seen her go down, shot in the head. Sandoval must think she was dead, too. Was he even now mourning her, holed up in some hidden valley with the other outlaws, not knowing she was still now in as much danger as she had been during the bank robbery? If so, she was truly on her own.

"My sister'll be bringin' us some supper in a while. Mebbe you oughta get some rest till then."

Rest? Tess fought an urge to laugh hysterically, knowing it would only make her headache worse. Would this supper be her last meal? *Lord, help me!*

Sandoval waited in the darkness, watching as the mob outside the jail trudged en masse down to the saloon. They were going to use whiskey to shore up their determination to storm the jail. One of them had knotted a rope into a hangman's noose. He'd seen the fellow twirling it around all through the evening while the men talked about the killing of the deputy. A few had been uneasy lynching her since she was a woman, but they were shouted down by their fellows who said they had to make that redhead pay since she was the only one captured. She must be a bad woman, to be riding with outlaws, anyway.

As soon as they were gone, Sandoval led the two horses—he'd declined Delgado's black in favor of a less flashy, brown horse, and Tess's sorrel to a hitching post in front of the jail. He climbed up onto the boardwalk and peered through a curtain. A kerosene lamp inside revealed the sheriff sitting with his feet propped up on the desk, his eyes closed.

Parrish knocked at the door as if he had every right to be there.

Within, he heard a thump as if chair legs had just hit the floor, and a second later the sheriff was pulling back the curtains and opening the window a crack.

"Who're you? I kin tell ya right now, ain't no one visitin' my prisoner for any reason."

Sandoval flashed the badge he'd brought out of the hidden pocket in his pants.

"Texas Ranger, huh? C'mon in, then. I'm Sheriff Mason," he said, offering his hand. "What kin I do for you?"

"I'm Sandoval Parrish," he said after the sheriff shut the door behind him, "and I understand you're holding Tess Hennessy here."

The older man nodded. "She helped rob a bank today. One a' my deputies was killed."

"So I hear," Sandoval said with a somber nod. "Well, she's been riding with the Delgado gang for a while now, so she's wanted for several crimes. I'm here to take her to Brownsville for trial."

The man's relief was palpable. "Thank God. Sounds like she'll pay for her crimes, then, but at least no one can say vigilantes took her from *my* jail. Them fellas was about ready t' lynch her. C'mon back here," he said, beckoning for Sandoval to follow him into the cell area. "If yore quick y' kin be gone afore they're done drinkin'."

Sandoval hid a smile, realizing Sheriff Mason hadn't thought to ask him how he knew Tess was in a jail cell in Mission.

The jangling of the ring of keys jerked Tess awake in her dark cell. She blinked at the flickering light of the lantern. Then she shrieked, seeing only a dark form standing behind the sheriff as he opened her cell door.

Had Amory come back to drag her outside?

"Calm down, Miss Hennessy, it ain't those boys who been loiterin' around beneath your window, don't worry. This here's a Texas Ranger, come for you. Says you're already wanted in other robberies with them greasers, so I reckon you'll get your fair trial afore th' rope, at least."

She saw now that it was Parrish who stood behind the

sheriff, and relief flooded over her. Tess saw him shake his head in warning, and she turned back to the sheriff. "But what about...what about the mob out there? Won't they try to—"

"You don't hear 'em, do you? That's cuz they're all down at the saloon gettin' likkered up. Mr. Parrish and me figgered it was a good time to take you away, 'specially as they're probably tryin' to get drunk enough t' come force their way inta th' jail."

She looked over Mason's shoulder into Sandoval's face, but nothing in those dark eyes gave him away. He appeared stern and even contemptuous as he stared back at her, exactly as a Ranger should look when he was about to take custody of a notorious female criminal. She saw his eyes rake over the angry furrow on the side of her forehead where the bullet had scraped her scalp.

"You wanna borrow my handcuffs?" Mason offered, reaching for a pair of metal restraints that hung from a hook on the wall outside the cell. He was only too ready to give any assistance to this Ranger who was going to take the source of his trouble off his hands.

Sandoval shook his head. "Thanks, but this'll work, I reckon," he said, pulling a length of braided rawhide cord from his pocket. He made an abrupt gesture at Tess. "Hands out in front, miss."

Tess watched as he bound her hands, keeping her face poker-straight with an effort. It would make Mason suspicious indeed if she grinned at the Ranger who was supposedly taking her to justice!

"We'll be going now," Sandoval said as he took hold of the cord between her hands. "There's a lot of riding between here and Brownsville. I want to get far away from here before I make camp, so if Delgado comes looking and finds she's not in Mission, he won't ride on and find us."

Mason's brow furrowed as if he hadn't even considered such a possibility. "You don't think he'd dare come *here?*"

Sandoval gave a whistle and shook his head. "I wouldn't put it past him. Miss Tess here was his *amante,* his sweetheart. If I were you I'd keep a sharp eye out tonight."

"Sweetheart, huh?" Mason gave a disgusted snort. "She tried to tell me she was only with him to take pictures. I knew she was lyin'!"

Tess glared at both of them.

Sandoval didn't rein in until they were at least five miles out of town on the Brownsville Road.

"Oh, Sandoval, I've never been one-hundredth so glad to see *anyone* in my entire life!" she began, only to have him hold up a warning hand.

Positioning his horse next to hers, he listened in silence for a minute or two, but no sound rode on the breeze that tickled the palms and wild olive trees except the hoot of a sleepy owl. Then he grabbed her into his arms and kissed her, and they were laughing and she was crying, too, as he undid the cord that bound her wrists.

"Sandoval, they were going to *lynch* me!" Her voice quavered as she said the words. "Without a trial! They didn't even care that I might be innocent—they just wanted someone to pay for the death of that poor deputy...." She wept in earnest now as he held her, all her pent-up fear flowing out of her with her tears.

"Hush now, you're safe, love. Thank God that bullet only grazed you," Sandoval murmured, caressing her head near the wound. "Delgado thought you were dead...."

"But you came anyway...."

"I had to *know,*" he told her, and she saw in his eyes that the possibility that she might be dead had shaken him to the core. "I wasn't about to leave you in that town, alive or dead. I'm taking you home."

She drew back in surprise. "*Home?* I can't go home yet! We're not done—I haven't found out about your sister yet."

"Tess, we're only about fifteen miles from Chapin. You could be back at Hennessy Hall by dawn. I can't take you back to Delgado, back to danger, when you're so close to home!"

She stared at him, tempted. How wonderful it would be to ride down the palm-lined lane to the Spanish mission-style house that had been home to her all her life, to be embraced by her mother and father, to sleep in her own soft bed and not the hard ground...but if she gave in, Sandoval would never know if Pilar was dead or alive, for he'd already given up hope for his sister. It was likely that Sandoval wouldn't even be able to return to Delgado, for the outlaw leader might learn that Tess had not died, but had been taken by a Texas Ranger whose description fit Sandoval Parrish. Then he'd never be able to accomplish *his* goal of publishing Delgado's picture far and wide so the outlaw could be captured.

"I won't go home," she repeated. She looked away from his expression of incredulity and gazed instead at the river they had been riding alongside. "Can we cross here?"

Chapter Nineteen

"Tess! You are alive! *¡Gracias a Dios!*" exclaimed Delgado, pulling Tess into his arms as soon as he helped her down from her horse. Tess flashed a startled, alarmed look at Sandoval as Delgado embraced her and kissed her on both cheeks. "But how on earth did you rescue her, amigo?" he asked, turning to Sandoval. "Did you storm into the jail, guns blazing, or did you sneak in and knock the sheriff in the head with your pistol? You are a miracle worker. I am indebted to you forever!" He released Tess and embraced Sandoval.

Sandoval shrugged. "I used my Anglo blood, as you suggested," he said. "I told them I was a Texas Ranger, and had heard one of the Delgado gang had been captured, and that I was taking her to trial in Brownsville on an earlier charge. Good thing I arrived when I did—the brother of the dead deputy was inciting the men of the town to lynch her."

"Thank God you were in time," breathed Delgado. "If they had harmed Tess, I would have slaughtered every man, woman and child in Mission—this I swear!"

Sandoval relaxed a bit, seeing his last dramatic statement had distracted the outlaw from questioning him further about his ruse.

But Lupe was not so easily diverted—probably because she would not have cared if Tess had been hanged. "You just walked into the jail and told them you were a Ranger, and they believed you, without any proof?" she challenged from her nearby nest of blankets under a tree. "Even an Anglo is not so gullible, I think."

"Of course not," Sandoval said shortly over his shoulder at her. "I had proof. Remember that time we were ambushed by that contingent of Rangers just as we were about to cross the river down by Matamoros, Diego?" Sandoval had set up the ambush with his fellow Rangers in an attempt to kill or capture Delgado, only to watch as Delgado and his men fought their way out of it. One of the Rangers had been killed in the action, as well as two of Delgado's men, and there had been several wounded on both sides.

Delgado nodded.

"Well, while Dominguez searched the dead Ranger's pockets and Zavala took his boots, I pocketed this." He held out his badge, hoping Delgado would believe his tale.

Delgado did. "You are one clever fellow!" he cried, clapping Sandoval on the back. "I am proud to ride with you, amigo! Hombres, let's give a cheer for Sandoval!"

Everyone cheered but Lupe. No doubt she would have preferred that Sandoval had brought back Tess's lifeless body, if he returned with her at all, Sandoval thought. He could tell Delgado's sister was still suspicious of him. He and Tess would have to be extra careful of Lupe from now on until they escaped—which was going to be as soon as possible, Sandoval vowed—even if he had to kidnap Tess again.

Lupe made an elaborate show of struggling to her feet. Delgado was instantly at her side, murmuring worriedly, putting her arm about his shoulder and helping her. She grimaced as she limped over to them, her upper teeth clamped over her lower her lip as if to smother an outcry of pain.

She stopped in front of Tess. She reached out a hand to touch the red furrow on the side of Tess's head. "Ah, *señorita,* you will have a scar there. What a pity," she said, oozing false sympathy.

Tess tensed. Sandoval imagined she was probably fighting the urge to slap Lupe's hand away, but she only shrugged and said, "No matter. My hair will cover it. I am lucky to be alive. But you were wounded, too, I hear? I don't remember—the bullet knocked me out."

"It is nothing," Lupe said heroically. "A mere scratch. But I'll make those Anglos pay for what they did! Zavala died, you know. And Dominguez." She affected a mournful face.

Sandoval noted that Lupe didn't mention that Dominguez had been executed for his cowardice in not protecting Tess.

"Yes, Sandoval told me on the ride back here."

"We buried them before you arrived. Tomorrow we will return to the canyon," Delgado said.

"Return to the canyon camp?" Lupe protested. "But I don't want to! I want to rob another bank, and this time succeed."

"Be realistic, Lupe!" Delgado snapped. "We've lost two men, Tess nearly died and you've been wounded yourself. We're going back to the canyon hideout for a while, and that's the end of it."

Lupe stuck out her lower lip at the rebuke, then glared at Tess.

Delgado's tone was softer when he spoke again. "For tonight, all is well. We have Tess back with us, safe and sound, thanks to Sandoval! We rest now, eh?"

They reached the camp in the canyon at dusk the next day, after riding all day. Fernando Aguilar had scouted ahead; Sandoval had guarded the rear in case of pursuit. They arrived without encountering any problems, however—unless one considered Lupe's constant complaining about the pain of her wound.

"Welcome back, *señorita,*" Esteban said, smiling a shy welcome while he assisted Tess to dismount with one hand, his other still resting in a sling.

"Thank you, Esteban. How is your shoulder?" Tess asked, while Sandoval led their horses to the corral.

"It still aches and it is numb at the same time," he admitted. "It is kind of you to ask, Señorita Tess. I see you were wounded, too." He pointed to the makeshift bandage tied about her head.

"God was watching out for me—it could have been worse." Tess smiled at him, wishing this nice man could find some honest way to make his living so he wasn't in danger of being shot ever again.

"And how is my mule?" Tess asked. She had seen the beast prick up his long ears and bray at her from the corral. "I hope Ben hasn't given you any trouble while we were gone."

Esteban grinned. "That *mulo,* he is a stubborn fellow. On some things, we have agreed to disagree. But inside, I know he has a good heart."

"Come over and get your supper, Señorita Tess," Delores called, beckoning. Since Aguilar, the scout, had arrived ahead of the rest, she had been able to ready a hot supper for their arrival.

Gratefully, Tess accepted.

"And what is this Fernando tells me about Tess being captured by the Anglos, and nearly hanged, and Zavala and Dominguez killed?" Delores said, casting a baleful glance at Delgado. "Shame on you, Diego, for exposing Señorita Tess to such danger! Your desire to show off cost the lives of two men, and nearly hers as well."

Tess's jaw dropped, amazed at the frankness of the old woman's condemnation. She tensed, expecting a wrathful reply from Delgado, but to Tess's surprise, the outlaw leader merely hung his head, chastened as a schoolboy.

"*Sí.* I realize now it was foolish of me," Delgado admitted. "Fortunately, Sandoval was able to snatch her from the jaws of death through a clever ruse." He recited the whole saga for the benefit of Delores and Esteban, who listened raptly.

"May all the saints bless you, brave man!" Delores exclaimed to Sandoval, when the tale was fully told. She rose heavily to her feet and planted a kiss on both his cheeks. Everyone laughed as Sandoval tried to duck and insist it was nothing.

Lupe had been glowering sullenly from her seat by the fire during the entire recital. "Delores, did Fernando tell you *I* was wounded, *too?*" Dramatically Lupe flung back a length of her skirt to expose the small hole in the fleshy part of her calf with its surrounding swelling and redness. "I might have lost my leg, Delores!"

The old woman nodded placidly. "But you did not, just as my Esteban might have died of his wound, but he did not," she said, nodding in the direction of her son, who was passing out second helpings of tamales.

Lupe frowned for a moment, then tried again to capture the conversational spotlight. "Esteban, did Fernando tell you I am betrothed to the rancher Andrés Cordoba? He is old, but very wealthy. I imagine, like all the other men, you will miss me, no? I am to return for the wedding in a month."

"To the contrary, I rejoice in your good fortune!" Esteban exclaimed. "Why didn't you just stay with him? Does he have a sister who needs a husband? I could go back with you."

His fellows howled with laughter, and even Delgado chuckled.

"Diego, I think it's time I returned to Santa Elena. I'll leave in the morning. For now, I'm going to bed," she added. "I've had enough of these louts." With an exaggerated limp, she headed toward her brother's quarters.

"Good night, sister, pleasant dreams," Diego called after her. "She's overtired," he added a moment later, to no one in particular. He stood up. "As I am also. Señorita Tess, *buenas noches*. I hope you sleep well, too. You have been a very valiant campaigner, never complaining. I am much impressed."

Tess watched him go, then flashed a dismayed look at Sandoval. She had hoped to get Delgado talking again, especially when Lupe had flounced off.

After Delores politely refused her assistance with the dishes, Tess strolled over to the corral to greet her mule. She spent several minutes scratching Ben's ears. The mule's blissful snorts lightened her heart, but she still felt restless, so using the light from the campfire to light her way, she wandered down to the creek.

She found a comfortable seat on a flat rock, and had just bowed her head in prayer when a voice behind her said, "Tess, I'll give you through tomorrow evening to talk to Delgado. After everyone goes to bed I'll ready the horses.

We're leaving in the dead of night whether you've gotten the information out of him or not."

Tess whirled in dismay. How had Parrish crept up on her like that, in boots, over uneven, rocky ground? "But, Sandoval," she began, "if I haven't learned where he took her—"

"If you haven't found out anything, I'm taking you *home,* Tess. I love you, and I won't take another chance of losing you, don't you understand?"

"So you'd chance losing your sister forever instead?"

He was silent for a long moment, his face in shadows. "You're the only one who thinks there's any reason to hope," he responded, his voice flat, his eyes bleak. "I probably lost her years ago, soon after he took her away. Pilar wasn't strong like you, Tess. You're so brave, even after what happened to you yesterday, but I wish you wouldn't even risk trying. What good will it do if you find out she's lying in some unmarked grave?"

Strong like you. Brave. Tess felt anything but strong or brave. She was full of apprehension that Delgado would suspect her motive, or would try to force his attentions on her. But if Sandoval thought of her as strong, and with God's help, she could do anything.

"I love you, too, Sandoval," she said, reaching a hand up and feeling the roughness of his unshaven cheek. "And because I do, I have to find out what happened to your sister. She might be alive."

When their lips met, the taste was bittersweet.

Chapter Twenty

Delgado set down a bottle of tequila the next evening after supper when Tess entered his quarters, carrying the dried and mounted photographs she had taken that day.

"This is quite a nice collection of pictures you have put together, Señorita Tess," Delgado praised.

She looked at the walls around her. Four of the photographs she had taken when she'd first arrived in the camp had already been mounted and hung in ornate frames that had been among the booty. Three of them were of Delgado, the other of Lupe. The paintings and photographs that had formerly been framed in them, precious to those from whom they had been stolen, no doubt lay in the pile of trash to be burned.

"Thank you. I think I have enough pictures for the book I will write about you," she told him.

He looked inordinately pleased. "You are making it more than a collection of pictures? A full biography of the daring Diego Delgado and his *bandoleros?* Ah, that will be very fine. Everyone will want a copy."

Then she saw alarm flash across his hawkish features.

"You propose to take all the pictures away from me to make your book?" he asked, waving at the stack of matted pictures to which she had just added.

"No, no, don't worry," Tess assured him, "I have negatives of all of the pictures I have made. I can make copies from them, and leave the originals with you."

It would never happen, of course. The only negatives she would be taking with her were the two portraits she had made of him, full-face and profile, that were even now secreted in Sandoval's saddlebags. All the rest of the negatives and her photography equipment, and Ben, she would have to leave here—at least for now. She hoped Esteban would continue to care for the old mule.

"But that implies *you* will be leaving, *señorita,*" Delgado said.

She shrugged. "I'll have to leave eventually," she told him, hoping she had not tipped her hand too much. "For one thing—"

Delgado moved closer. "But why, Tess?" he interrupted. "I want you to stay here with me, ride at my side. It will be very lonely here when Lupe goes to be Cordoba's wife."

If she goes through with it, Tess thought cynically. Lupe had not left for Santa Elena this morning as she had threatened last night when Esteban had refused to be jealous. Delgado's sister had been flirting with Esteban today as if her life depended on his responding to her wiles. Just before Tess had entered Delgado's quarters she had seen Lupe sashay up to the young Mexican, hips swaying.

Just then Delores came in, looked at his near-empty bottle of tequila, and without a word brought another down from the shelf, setting it by him, along with a glass that she set on the desk near Tess.

"Will you have some tequila, *señorita,* or is it still

only water for you?" Delgado asked, his hands poised on the bottle.

"Nothing, thanks."

He topped off his own glass. "That will be all, Delores. *Gracias.*"

The old woman nodded and shuffled silently out.

"And Lupe is counting on you to take her wedding photograph," Delgado went on.

"That's just it," Tess said, "I will need to go home between now and the wedding to replenish my supplies. After the photographs I processed today, I'm afraid I'm out of chemicals to develop any more," she explained. "I could come back as soon as I have done that."

Please believe me, she pleaded silently. Don't make me swear to a lie.

Delgado, much too close now for her comfort, laid a hand caressingly on her cheek. It took all her will not to let herself shudder.

"You are so sweet to offer that," he purred, "but I am sure your dear mama and papa would not let you out of their sight once you return, especially since they know who you have been with, the notorious outlaw Delgado. You could not help being kidnapped, but it is another thing to return of your own will, eh?"

Tess feigned a rebellious pout that would have done Lupe credit. "I'm a grown woman," she said, "I'm not about to let them tell me what I can and cannot do anymore."

"Yes, you are, aren't you?" he said, staring boldly at her in a way that made her distinctly uncomfortable. "I love your spirit, *querida.* But there is no need for you to go home, Tess. We can purchase your chemicals in Mexico City, after all."

"But that's so far away," she protested. "I wouldn't want to put anyone to the trouble of—"

"You make it sound as far as the moon, Tess. I would find it very pleasurable to journey there with you to buy your chemicals."

"I—I'll think about it," she said, knowing that if all went as planned, she would never travel anywhere with Delgado ever again. She needed to change the subject, if she was ever to get the information she must have before the end of this night. "About my book, Señor Delgado—"

"Diego," he corrected her. His warm breath, laden with tequila, fluttered a curl at her forehead. "I would think after all we have been through these past days, you could call me by my given name, as I am doing, *Tess.*"

"Diego, then," she agreed, pretending to ignore the intimate tone of his voice and his alarming closeness. "Diego, if I am to write a book about you there must be words as well as pictures, you know."

He nodded. "Yes…I will be most happy to render you any assistance you may need with this project, Tess, of course."

"Well…" Tess pretended to hesitate. "Do you have time to talk now for a while?" she said, indicating the table and chairs behind him.

His black eyes gleamed, and then he turned a pair of adjacent chairs around so they faced each other, and indicated that she should sit in the one on the right. "I am at your disposal, Tess. My time is yours."

Gingerly she sat down, wishing he hadn't put the chairs so close together that their knees could almost touch, wishing she dared to push it back, wishing that she was wearing her sturdy, long-sleeved shirt instead of this thin drawstring blouse. She wished Sandoval or even Lupe were present, too. But she had deliberately sought him out when he was alone, because Delgado might not be so frank if another person were present to dampen the atmosphere of intimacy. It was up to her. And the Lord would protect her, wouldn't He?

Please, Jesus, be with me. Keep me safe. And let me discover what I need to know.

She took a deep breath. "Well...we were talking the other night about your early days as an outlaw, when you were first gathering your band of men. You had just begun to speak of a girl you knew once."

He blinked in confusion. "A girl? I think I told you, Tess, there were many girls—many women. To my regret," he said, his face full of a sadness that, she was sure, was pure pretense. "If I had only met you sooner..." He leaned toward her—again, too close.

She sat back in her chair, as far as she could without being too obvious. "But it sounded as if this girl was different. The others were experienced, you said. Women of the world. They enjoyed your attentions, but understood it was temporary. But this girl..." she prompted.

Recognition flashed in his eyes. "Oh, yes, I know who you mean now. I must have been speaking of that girl from Montemorelos."

Montemorelos, she recalled. Yes. That was the name of the town near the Parrish rancho.

"What was her name?"

Delgado sat back, his eyes losing focus. "Her name...I can see her so clearly—small, with the most perfect heart-shaped face, the most glorious hair, black as a raven's wing, thick and smooth as satin...a waist a man could span with his hands..." He pantomimed what he was saying. "Her lips were like rosebuds. She was the only daughter of an Anglo rancher who had married a *méxicana* and settled there.... Her name began with a *P,* I think. Pabla? Pepita? No, that's not it. Pia? Pía means pious, and she was very devout, this girl, but I don't think that was it...." Something flashed in his eyes. "*Pilar!* That was it, Pilar. I don't remember her family name, though."

Thank you, Lord! "That doesn't matter," Tess said with a nonchalance she was far from feeling. "Tell me about her—about your romance."

Delgado's eyes were suddenly sharp again. "I'm not sure I should, Tess. I do, after all, want you to think fondly of Diego Delgado—*very* fondly, *querida.* And this tale does not reflect well on me. I had the excuse of being young, perhaps, but still...."

"You must think of me as your biographer right now, Diego," she reminded him. "Not as your...your friend."

"My very...good friend," he murmured thickly, slurring his words, reaching out to touch her hair. "What has this tale to do with the story of Diego Delgado, the greatest outlaw of all time? I think I should tell you of some of the great raids, the big prizes I have taken."

To come this close and then have him refuse to say more about Pilar? Tess fought a feeling of desperation, and knew she had to tread carefully. "Telling me about the women in your life reveals you as a full, well-rounded man, a man of feeling, with human failings," she said. "A man other men can sympathize with."

He sighed. "I suppose you're right. You are so wise, Tess Hennessy. Very well. I will tell you, but you must promise not to hate me, eh? I am not the same man as I was then."

Tess didn't believe for a moment he had changed. He merely desired her, and wanted her willing. She didn't hate him, though. She hated what he did, and what he had done, but hating him was a useless emotion and one not becoming to a Christian.

"Go on."

"I first saw Pilar entering the church in Montemorelos just as I happened to pass by, and I was smitten with her beauty. I couldn't believe she was alone, not with some relative or at least a duenna! I followed her inside, but she went immediately into the confessional, so I went back outside and waited for her. I cannot imagine what she was going to confess, for she was the most innocent female I have ever known. Coveting an extra sweet, perhaps? Anyway, when she came out I introduced myself to her, and asked if I could escort her somewhere. I would have offered to buy her a drink at the cantina, but this was not a thing a gently bred girl like Pilar would have agreed to do, especially not with a stranger, you understand?" He yawned. "I'm sorry, I cannot imagine why I'm sleepy, after doing so little today."

Perhaps from drinking so much tequila? Tess thought.

Delgado took another deep draft from his glass before continuing. "She was shy, *so* shy. She blushed when I first spoke to her, and said she could not, since we had not been formally introduced. She said her duenna, some elderly aunt, was ill, but it had been a full week since Pilar had made her confession and she did not like to miss it, so she had stolen out of the house to do so, intending to go right back. I told her it was a matter of honor to me that she was safe as she walked home, and if she did not allow me to walk with her, I would be so devastated that I would die of grief. At last she agreed."

Tess could not imagine any girl believing such fulsome flattery, even if she had enjoyed a very sheltered upbringing, but apparently it had been so.

"I was my most charming self," Delgado remembered.

"It was obvious she did not know I was the outlaw who had been recruiting other young men to join me, so I soon had her laughing with me and chattering away as if we were old friends. Her *rancho* was perhaps a mile away, but the distance seemed like nothing.

"I meant to leave before anyone saw me," Delgado went on, steepling his fingers, "but I was so beguiled by her beautiful eyes—and she by my compliments and my funny stories—that we lingered under the arbor, talking. It was obvious to me that she had never flirted with a man before, and she was enjoying it immensely. I was just stealing a kiss when her father found us there."

"Oh, dear," Tess murmured. "Did he know who you were?"

Delgado chuckled ruefully. "I'm afraid he did. He was a big, strapping Anglo, and he snatched me up by my shirt and said if he ever saw me near his daughter again he would kill me. He threw me to the ground, and my cheek scraped against a stone. When I got to my feet I was bleeding. Pilar was very distressed and protested, but he ordered her into the house. She obeyed him, but not before I saw the sympathy in her eyes."

"So, how did you manage to see her again?"

Delgado grinned. "It wasn't easy. After that she was never alone. If she came to town that elderly aunt was always with her, or her gangly younger brother."

Sandoval.

"He was very vigilant, that brother. And he never came to the cantina, where I might have corrupted him with drink. But I was determined."

"What did you do?"

"I bribed an old man in town to write Pilar a love letter from me, and paid a child to deliver it to her secretly. I told her I would wait under the arbor that night, and if she did not come I would understand, but I said I had fallen in love with her. I told her I craved more of her kisses, more than I craved my next breath."

"How romantic," Tess said, injecting admiration into her voice. She could well imagine the appeal of his approach to an innocent like Pilar—the thrill of a secret rendezvous with a handsome stranger who had been hurt by her father because he'd dared to kiss her….

"She sent back a note saying she would be there, that she would kiss the wound on my cheek. It was exactly what I wanted to hear."

Delgado's face was changing now. Gone was the wistful romantic. As if he'd forgotten he was telling this story to Tess, his features became sly, cunning, predatory. "That night I lured her into my room at the cantina. I made her mine with promises that we would be married as soon as we were far enough away from Montemorelos. We made a plan to steal away at dawn, before she had been missed. I left word for my band of men to join us in that town. It was a risk, of course."

"That her father would find you?" Tess asked, fascinated in spite of her horror at the cold-blooded way Delgado spoke of ruining Pilar's innocence.

Delgado shrugged. "That, too, but the risk I meant was the risk that my men were not loyal enough to obey my order without my being there. We had not been together that long, of course. But they came, just as I had instructed them." He smiled triumphantly at the memory.

"And Pilar?" Tess reminded him.

"She was completely in love with me, and even with her romantic idea of being an outlaw's wife—free as the wind, answering to no one but her loving husband."

He smothered a yawn again, and rubbed his eyes. Tess was tempted to apologize for keeping him from his bed.

"But her father never caught up with her? And you never married her?"

"No… We rode east for a while. We heard the Anglo was looking for us, so we headed west, north, south. We lived off the land. I had gathered all the men I needed, and eventually we stopped hearing of him chasing us."

Tess thought of Sandoval and Pilar's father, overcome with grief, never finding his daughter, and finally dying. Was *her* father grieving like that, too? The thought made her heart ache.

"By this time," Delgado continued, "naturally, Pilar had begun to suspect my promises were worth nothing. But it was not until we came to Monterrey, and she found me with another woman, that she realized that I was never going to marry her."

"What did she do?" Tess asked, keeping her voice level, nonjudgmental. As if she were asking about the weather, when the question meant everything.

Delgado rubbed his eyes, and it was a long time before he spoke. His speech was becoming quite slurred now. "She wept. But she did not rage at me, or demand I marry her or even apologize for my unfaithfulness. She had begun to look sad all the time, and she had lost weight because of the hard way we lived. She wanted only that I escort her to the local convent, where she said she would take the veil."

Tess felt a twinge of hope. If Pilar was in a convent, then she was safe. "So you left her at a convent?"

Delgado shook his head. "I was tired of her. I had other things to do. I came to a brothel before I found a convent, so I left her there."

It was all Tess could do to control her reaction of shock and anger, to remain still in her chair and keep her voice calm.

"And you never saw her again? Never went back to see that she was all right?"

"No. I was a busy man. We had begun to raid across the river by this time, and I was caught up in the thrill of being the most feared outlaw in Texas." He smothered another yawn. "I'm sorry, I don't know what has gotten into me...." He closed his eyes.

"Perhaps we should continue our talk tomorrow," Tess said. She had gained the information she needed, but how could she tell Sandoval his sister was in a brothel? He would be so angry he'd want to kill Delgado on the spot!

She could not think of that now. What could explain his sudden drowsiness? Delgado drank every time liquor was available, but she'd never seen him overcome by it.

"No, please, Tess. Perhaps if we take a walk..." Delgado rose, wobbling to one side, but catching himself on the table.

Something wasn't right. "Really, it's getting late. We'll talk tomorrow."

"At least give me a good-night kiss." The word came out *kish.* Delgado lurched toward her, his arm outstretched to grab her, then fell forward, and lay prone on the stolen carpet.

Tess paused only long enough to hear him snore.

Chapter Twenty-One

Tess gave a start when she crossed the threshold into the night and a dark shape detached itself from the adobe wall.

"Did the tequila do its work?" Delores said, rising with some difficulty.

Tess automatically reached out a hand to help her, wondering what the old woman meant. "Um…yes, he must have drunk a lot of it before I came to show him the pictures. He…fell asleep, right on the floor…." She was sure she looked guilty to Delores, even in the shadowy light, even though she was mystified at the sudden nature of her deliverance.

Delores chuckled. "You think he is merely *borracho?* Oh, no, *señorita,* Delgado has been drinking tequila since he quit his mother's milk. The tequila he was drinking contained a sleeping potion I added. He will sleep like the dead until morning. That will help you make your escape, no?"

Tess's jaw dropped. She stared at the old woman's amused face, then darted quickly past her to check at both sides of the hut and in back of it to make sure no one lurked there, eavesdropping. She stared across the creek, where some of the others were still sitting by the campfire, or in some cases, already rolled up in their bedrolls.

"You *know?* You drugged him to help me escape?"

The old woman nodded, her lips curved and her eyes still dancing with delight.

"Of course. You cannot stay here much longer, *señorita.* Delgado wants to make you his woman, and Lupe is out for your blood. You must get away from here."

"Yes..." How much did Delores know? Did she know Sandoval was part of the plan? Did she know he was a Texas Ranger whose ultimate goal was to capture Delgado?

"But why are you doing this?" Tess asked, hoping Delores's answer might indicate how much she knew.

"Because you are a good woman, and you do not want this—to be his *ama,* no? Lack of willingness would not matter to Delgado, but it matters to me. And I want to help you because you took such good care of my son."

Tess saw a figure cross from the corral and step onto the narrow bridge. She tensed, holding up a warning hand to Delores, but in a moment she saw that it was Sandoval.

"That is the man you love, yes?" Delores murmured as he approached, but it was more a statement than a question. "He is the right man for you."

Tess could only nod.

"Everything is ready. Is Delgado sleeping?" Sandoval asked both women. So Delores knew of Sandoval's part in the escape plan, at least.

"Sí," she said to Sandoval. "He will be no threat to you till morning. And my Esteban will do his best to distract Lupe until the sleeping potion takes effect with her, too."

So Esteban was part of the conspiracy, also. Now

they only had to sneak with two horses past several sleeping men.

Sandoval looked probingly at Tess. He had to know right away if she'd been successful, but he wouldn't ask the question in front of Delores. All of their survival might depend on Delores not knowing. The Delgados wouldn't hesitate to torture the old woman if they thought she knew anything.

Fortunately, Tess understood immediately and nodded with a tremulous smile.

She had discovered what had happened to Pilar, and she was alive! Tess knew where she was! Tears stung Sandoval's eyes. He fought the urge to let out a cry and resolutely blinked the tears away. There was no time for that now.

"Once I'm sure everyone's asleep, we'll leave," Sandoval told Tess. "Between now and then, bundle up your clothing in the saddlebag you'll find by your pallet."

Tess nodded her understanding.

"Esteban's much more recovered than he pretended to be, Tess," Sandoval went on. "He's worried that Ben will bray when he sees us leave and wake someone, so he's going to hold Ben's head while we're leading the horses out of the canyon. Then, when we're discovered gone, and everyone's haring off after us—in the direction they *think* we're going—Esteban's going to hitch Ben to your camera wagon and, with any luck, bring your precious camera and mule home by another route. He'll deliver the negatives of Delgado to your assistant, Francisco, who will take them to your godfather. That way they can be published much sooner than if we were bringing them, since we're going in a…a different direction," he said, after a glance at Delores. "He'll also assure your parents you are all right and coming home as soon as you can."

Tess clapped a hand to her mouth, clearly overcome with joy. "You've thought of everything, haven't you?" she cried. She hugged him fiercely for a moment, then turned to Delores, kissing the surprised woman on both cheeks. "*Gracias,*" she breathed, through her tears. "Tell your son I thank him, too...." Clearly too moved for words, Tess was silent for a moment. "Esteban is a good man. And I—I don't know why, but I love that old mule. And the camera..."

"*De nada, señorita,*" Delores said, beaming. "I have wanted to get my son away from the life of a bandit for a while now, and he's finally seen the sense of an old mother's pleas. I am glad he can help you while helping himself."

"But what about you?" Tess asked, worry furrowing her brow. "I don't want Delgado taking his fury out on you when he realizes we've escaped."

The old woman chuckled. "I have a place to hide that that fox would never suspect. I'll wait there for my son to come for me when it is safe. Meanwhile, I'm going to drink some of the spiked tequila myself, so that when Delgado and Lupe wake to discover you two are gone, I'll be as hard to wake as they are now. Maybe they'll think you drugged me, yes? 'Ah, that red-headed *bruja,*'" Delores said, mimicking Delgado's voice, "'We had no idea she was so devious!'" She laughed at her own joke. "Now, don't you two have things to discuss?" she said, making shooing motions toward Tess's hut.

"So he left Pilar at a *brothel* in Monterrey?" Sandoval repeated, when Tess had finished telling him what she had learned from Delgado. His stomach churned with nausea, his throat felt thick at the thought of his sister, broken and disillusioned, believing she had no alternative but that—a girl whose faith had always been important to her, who had never skipped her prayers. A girl who'd wanted to be a wife and mother, just like their mother. She'd asked to be taken to a convent, but he'd taken her to a brothel instead.

It was too bad he could only kill Delgado once, and that he couldn't do it right now, this minute, and with his bare hands.

Tess nodded, watching him with wide eyes, as if she feared he would explode. She reached out a hand and gingerly touched his shoulder. "*We'll find her, Sandoval.* We have only to ride to Monterrey and ask at every brothel until we find her. Is it far?"

"About fifty miles from here," Sandoval said. "Almost due east. Tess, I *looked* for her in *Monterrey*—it's the biggest city in Nuevo Léon," he protested. "I went to every *burdel.* I offered money as a reward. No one knew anything about her."

"Perhaps she hadn't come yet," Tess pointed out. "Delgado said she rode with him for a while before he left her there."

He winced inwardly, imagining his delicate, innocent sister living as he had been living, always in the saddle, roaming from place to place, eating poor provisions cooked over a fire or in shabby cantinas and, in her case, gradually losing hope in the man she'd been unwise enough to trust with her love. And then he had abandoned her to an unspeakable fate.

"Then, as long as we're lucky enough to evade Delgado, we should be able to find her.... What's wrong?" Tess asked.

How could he explain to an innocent girl like Tess what life must be like for Pilar in such a place? He could not imagine Pilar surviving it a week, let alone five years. He almost prayed that she was dead, that God had taken her to heaven to rescue her.

"What if she didn't stay there, in the brothel?" he asked, afraid to give voice to the full horror of his thoughts. "What if she was too full of despair after what had happened to her, and she couldn't bear the life of a—" He couldn't say the word. "What if she lost all hope, and became ill and died?'"

Tess pulled him into her arms. "What if she managed to find a way to escape such a place? You must hold on to hope, my love. I cannot believe God would allow us to find out where he left her," she said against his chest, while he allowed the tears he had held back to slide down his face, wetting her hair, "only to close the door in our faces, Sandoval. No, I believe we will find her in Monterrey. But we must have faith until we get there."

He pulled away only enough to look down at her, smiling through his tears. "You have enough faith for both of us, Tess. It's why I love you."

"I love you, too. She'll be there, Sandoval," she told him. "You'll see."

But there was more he had to know. "Tess, Delgado…he didn't hurt you…before he passed out, did he?" He already hated the man for what he'd done to Pilar, but if Delgado had even come close to molesting Tess also, it would be hard to leave camp without making the outlaw pay for hurting the woman he loved.

"No," she assured him quickly. "I saw in his eyes that he wanted to…" she said, flushing. "And I *was* afraid I'd have to fight my way out of there. But he passed out at just the right time. God bless Delores for her cleverness."

"Amen to that! Now, here's what we're going to do…"

* * *

"It's time," Sandoval said, waking Tess with a gentle touch.

Tess started awake, her gaze darting around the room before settling on him. "I can't believe I fell asleep," she murmured. "I felt tight as a fiddle string when you told me to lie down for a while." She sat up, stretching out her arms.

"It's good that you could get some rest," he said, watching fondly as Tess rubbed her eyes and smoothed back a few curling, errant strands that had escaped her braid. "We have a long way to go."

"I'm ready," she said, getting to her feet. "But how will we get past the guard at the mouth of the canyon?"

"The plan was for Esteban to go out and offer to share a bottle with Prieto to help him while away the lonely hours. The trick will be for Esteban to pretend to drink when the bottle is passed to him, without actually drinking, but in the dark that shouldn't be too hard to accomplish. We need him to be alert later to drive the wagon away while everyone is off chasing us. So if Prieto has imbibed enough, the only bandits we need to worry about are the ones sleeping out there. Are you ready?" he said, nodding toward the door.

"I think we should pray first," she told him.

"Yes. You go ahead," he said. How could he expect the Lord to listen to him when he'd doubted God cared ever since Pilar had disappeared? God would listen to Tess.

Tess surprised him by taking his hand before she bowed her head and closed her eyes. "Father, we come to You believing that You can do anything, and that You'll give us safety as we leave the canyon tonight. Please stop the ears of the bandits as we walk past them. Make us invisible to their eyes. Prevent the horses from whinnying. And keep

Delgado and Lupe and Prieto deeply asleep. Help us to find Pilar. Oh, yes, and give Esteban protection and success in bringing Ben and the camera home, and give Delores safety too as she escapes. For we ask it all in Jesus's name, amen."

"Amen," he said, adding his own silent prayer—*Lord, I don't know if You will do all this, but please, at least get Tess safely home. It's all my fault that she's here, so if anyone has to pay for my foolishness, it should only be me.*

Tess met his eyes after he raised his head. "Now we can go."

"Wake up! Wake up, you fool!" Lupe cried, kicking her brother again, viciously, in the ribs.

Diego Delgado slitted his eyes open and snapped out a hand, catching the offending foot. He jerked on it, succeeding in yanking Lupe off her feet to fall heavily on him.

She cursed at him and struck him with a fist.

"Quit that!" Delgado shouted, and shoved her off of him. "Why are you abusing me, Lupe? I was only sleeping—what have I done to you that you would treat your brother this way?"

"Let go of me, and wake up, you stupid oaf! While you've been sleeping, your little redhead has flown the coop, and Parrish with her. I *told* you he was not to be trusted, that half-breed. We have to go after them!"

Delgado roared, fully awake now. He sat up and, grabbing Lupe, jerked her into a sitting position, too. "You say they're *gone?* Where? When?"

"I don't know," she muttered. "I just woke up myself—and I wasn't on my pallet in there," she said, jerking her head to indicate the curtained-off room that separated her sleeping area from her brother's.

"Where were you?"

"Lying in a bedroll by the campfire." At her brother's knowing snigger, she pounded the floor with her fist. "I can assure you, brother, I'd never sleep there! I don't even know how I got there."

"What do you mean?" Delgado said. He had risen to his feet and was already strapping on his gun belt.

Lupe looked confused. "The last thing I remember, I was sitting on the bank of the creek," she said, pointing toward the mouth of the canyon, "talking to Esteban and sharing a bottle with him—flirting, if you must know the truth. I remember getting very drowsy…and then the next thing I knew, the sun was shining in my eyes and Esteban and the rest of the men were all waking around me!"

Delgado rubbed his chin, a murderous certainty growing within him as he searched his memory of the night before. He remembered telling Tess about that girl from his past, while he drank. He remembered getting unusually drowsy, which didn't make sense. He'd always had a good head for tequila. And he'd never slept on the floor, not with his good bed—a prize he'd taken from a rancher near Brownsville—a few feet away.

"We were *drugged*," brother and sister said in unison.

"Where's Delores?" he said. "Tell her to make us something to break our fast. We ride within the hour."

"Good luck with that," Lupe snapped sourly. "I found her asleep in the *gringa's* hut. I think she was given the same thing we were, because I pinched her till she woke, but she went right back to sleep."

"Then we'll ride without eating," he decided aloud. "We can catch up with them faster that way. They couldn't have gotten that far yet," he said, but it sounded like wishful thinking, even to him. "I'll kill that traitor when I see him!" he said, his hands tightening into fists. He'd trusted Sandoval like a brother, and made him his second-in-command because of his intelligence, even though he had only joined the banditos during the last year.

"Yes, I'll kill him," he snarled, "slowly and painfully. And I'll make Tess Hennessey wish she was dead."

Chapter Twenty-Two

"Thank you, Lord," Tess murmured, when the opening to the canyon lay in the distance behind them. So far, God had answered Tess's prayers. Despite the fact that one or two of the sleeping banditos had stirred in their slumber, none had awakened when first Tess had stolen past, then Sandoval had walked the two horses by their sleeping forms. Esteban had lain among them, presumably feigning sleep. They had seen no sign of Delgado or Lupe. Prieto had snored at his post, rifle propped against a boulder.

Dawn was breaking when they reached the little village of Santa Clara, not far from the border between the Mexican states of Tamaulipas and Nuevo Léon.

"It's not a big village, but we'll stop here, if we can find a place," Sandoval announced, peering at the dusty village from their vantage point on a little bluff. "Sleep awhile."

"I—I can ride farther if you want, after we water the horses," Tess assured him, thinking he was trying to spare her. The thought of stopping, when they were still so close to the canyon hideout they'd fled only hours ago, made her nervous.

His eyes swept back to her, caressing her with his approval. "I know you can, sweetheart, but even though I don't think they'll figure out we've gone this way, it's probably better that we travel by night and hole up during the day."

It was then that she saw the fatigue that shadowed his dark eyes. He'd been awake all night, while she'd had the benefit, at least, of a short nap.

"All right, whatever you think best," she acquiesced, "but where will we hide the horses?" The pinto gelding Sandoval rode was memorable for his flashy color, as Tess was for her red hair. But Tess could hide her hair under the broad-brimmed hat she wore.

Sandoval must have had the same thoughts, for he said, "You stay here. I don't want anyone to remember seeing you, or these horses."

Tess looked uneasily over her shoulder.

"No one's been following us," he said. "But take this." He handed her one of his two pistols. "If anyone threatens you, use it."

No one passed by Tess except a boy herding a dozen goats, who stared at her curiously but did not stop. Sandoval returned within minutes. Santa Clara boasted no inn, he'd discovered, and the rooms attached to the back of the cantina housed the owner and his family. But the priest at the small church, Father Aldama, had been able to direct him to a farmhouse on the edge of town where his sister, Josefina Padilla, a widow, lived.

She agreed to give them shelter for the day and hide their horses in her barn for the price of a few pesos—but not before she'd peered at them through her spectacles and interrogated them.

"Are you running from the law? I won't have outlaws

under my roof," she informed him, leaning on her cane and staring up at Sandoval, who was a foot and a half taller than she.

Tess watched as Sandoval swept his hat off his head and gave the widow a smile that would have melted ice. "No, Señora Padilla, we're no lawbreakers. As a matter of fact, we're fleeing from outlaws. You have perhaps heard of Delgado and his band?"

"Diego Delgado? Bah!" The widow spat in the dust. "I would kill him myself if I got the chance. He lured my nephew into joining him, and Antonio—may God forgive him—was killed the very next time they raided across the border. That man and his cutthroats give Mexicans a bad reputation. What are your names?"

"It may be safer for you not to know, *señora.*"

The diminutive widow digested that fact for a moment. "What am I supposed to call you, Juan and Juana? I'm not afraid of that fool! Tell me your names."

Seeing she wouldn't take no for an answer, they did so.

"Are you two married?" she asked, directing her question at Tess.

Tess felt herself redden under the woman's scrutiny. "No, *señora.*" She chanced a glance at Sandoval, and the look in his dark eyes caused Tess's blush to flood all the way to her scalp.

The widow saw it. "I'll give you two rooms, then. I'll have you know I'll stand for no mischief under my roof."

"Yes, *señora,* we understand," Sandoval said meekly.

The old woman showed them to two rooms at opposite ends of a long back hall.

"I'll wake you when the sun goes down, and give you something to eat before you go on your way," she promised.

Tess had doubted she would sleep, but she did not wake until the old widow came in bearing a basin of hot water, soap and a towel. She'd evidently done the same for Sandoval, and even unearthed her late husband's razor, for when Tess and Sandoval met at Josefina Padilla's table to enjoy a meal of spicy chicken stew, they both looked and felt a great deal better than when they had lain down.

After she had served them, Josefina sat down and ate with them—or rather, she took an occasional bite while they answered the numerous questions she peppered them with. They soon found themselves telling her their entire saga.

Josefina gasped at the perils they had endured and the danger they were still in, growled in outrage when she heard what Delgado had done to Sandoval's sister and shed tears when they explained why they were headed to Monterrey instead of Texas. But it was their growing love for each other that seemed most to capture her fancy. It was plain that the widow was a romantic at heart.

"So you love one another," she concluded after the meal, while they drank her delicious but strong coffee and munched on freshly baked, pastel-colored cookies. When they both nodded, she leaned forward, placing her hands on the table. "You will marry?"

Tess's gaze flew to Sandoval, and he met it steadily, asking a question with his eyes and receiving her answer, all without words. "Yes," he answered for both of them.

"When?" Josefina demanded, her birdlike eyes avid for his reply.

Sandoval looked at Tess. "I imagine that will be once we have safely reached Tess's home, *señora,* and I have asked her father for her hand, and a proper wedding can be planned. The kind of wedding she deserves, where she wears a beautiful dress like a queen as she places her hand in mine."

"Humph!" the widow said, crossing her arms over her chest. She looked vastly disappointed, almost disgusted.

They both looked at her, startled. It was the last thing they had expected her to say.

"Pardon me?" Tess said at last.

"You said you love one another. Yet you plan to travel alone together all the way to Monterrey, and with God's help, find Sandoval's sister, and return to Texas again, still unmarried. All so you, Tess, can have a proper, fairy-tale wedding. I can see that your motives are honorable, Sandoval, but this is not right."

Tess looked uneasily at Sandoval, and then back at Josefina.

"But we must find Pilar, if it's possible, before we can think of going home," Tess pointed out.

"Indeed you must," Josefina agreed. "But you are in love and you want to be married, and here you are in a place where my brother is the priest! He can marry you this very night. However much the Lord approves of your plan to find Pilar, you are not guaranteed tomorrow, you know. I have been a widow for ten years. My Tomás and I thought we had forever, but we did not," she said, wiping a tear from the corner of her eye with a lacy handkerchief from her apron pocket. "Do you really want to wait for some other day when you can wed at home, when you could be man and wife this very night?"

Sandoval cleared his throat. "Perhaps you would not mind if Tess and I stepped outside and discussed this alone for a few minutes?"

"Of course," Josefina said, gesturing toward the porch just beyond the back door.

Tess followed Sandoval outside on shaking legs. Was this really happening, or was she still lying in the back bedroom of the widow's house, dreaming? What would Sandoval say?

For a moment they just stood there in the gathering darkness, staring up at the stars, then through the window at the widow bustling to clear the table, then at each other.

"Sandoval, please don't let Señora Padilla pressure you into something you're not ready to do," Tess began. "I mean, we've hardly had a normal courtship...perhaps you'd prefer to wait until we're home, and can see each other in regular circumstances. Perhaps you wouldn't even like me then, let alone love me. I'm spoiled and selfish and I like to have my own way—"

To her astonishment, Sandoval threw back his head and laughed. "*You're* selfish? *You* like to have your own way? Tess, you're speaking to the man who had you *kidnapped* to achieve his goal to capture Delgado, who didn't concern himself about the danger it could put you in. And you fell in love with me anyway!" he said, taking her in his arms and gazing down at her.

"Yes, I did," she admitted, feeling she could never have enough of gazing into his dark eyes and seeing the love for her that radiated from them.

"I was wrong to have you taken as I did," Sandoval said, "but in one sense I'm not sorry at all, because now we're here together like this. I don't think you'd have ever given me the time of day back in Chapin, would you? You looked so suspiciously at me at your godfather's barbecue."

"You looked dangerous," she told him honestly. "And mysterious. I was afraid of you, a little, but more afraid of the immediate attraction I felt. I was afraid of what it would cost me."

"Your independence, you mean? I know you have a goal, too."

"Yes..." she said, moved that he could so completely understand her and crystallize her thoughts so effortlessly. She'd never been so well understood before—not by her mother, who loved her but had no understanding of her dreams, not even by her father, who sympathized with her goals.

"Loving you means I want you to be yourself, Tess," Sandoval told her earnestly. "If you want to go to New York and be a photographer, we'll find a way to do that."

She couldn't believe her ears. "But what would *you* do? You're a Ranger. You live to enforce the law in Texas. That's who you are. I understand that."

Sandoval shrugged. "I reckon there's law to enforce in New York, or anywhere you are," he said.

She tried to imagine this tall, rangy man who'd been bred for the big sky over the warm Rio Grande Valley living with his view hemmed in by the tall buildings of a vast city, buffeted by the cold winds and snow blowing in a northern winter. "You'd be like a fish out of water," Tess said. "And so would I," she murmured in a whisper, and knew it was true. Photography would always be important to her, but Brady's studio in New York City no longer shone in her imagination like the promised land. The promised land was anywhere Sandoval Parrish was.

"I don't think I want to go to New York City anymore. Not to stay, at least. I'll probably never be a conventional wife like my mother, but I love you. And I want to be your wife this very night."

"You don't want to wait and be married in your church at home? In a beautiful dress? I'd wait for you, you know—it's not tonight or never. Don't little girls dream of such a wedding?"

"Little girls dream of the dark, handsome stranger," she said, reaching up to caress his raven-black hair and his angular cheeks, "who turns out to be their white knight."

Her mouth fell open as he knelt and took her hand. "A white knight always kneels to ask his lady's hand in marriage," he explained. "Tess Hennessy, will you do me the honor of marrying me tonight?"

Father Anthony Aldama was bemused at his sister's request, but nonetheless, obligingly dressed in his vestments and followed her back to her farmhouse, listening as they walked to her accounting of Tess and Sandoval's story.

"This is hardly a usual situation," he said, when he arrived. "But no matter. If you are Christians and you love each other, and you want to be married before journeying off to find your sister, Señor Parrish, I can only approve. Are you ready?" he asked, beckoning them forward.

"Wait, wait!" Josefina interposed herself between the couple and her brother, moving quickly for a woman using a cane. "I have just the thing for the bride…." She left the parlor, and returned in a few minutes carrying a lacy white mantilla that smelled of the lavender it had been packed away with. She draped it over Tess's head.

"I wore it to my wedding," she said, kissing Tess on each cheek. "You do not have a proper wedding dress, but at least you have a veil."

"Thank you," Tess said, embracing Josefina. She met Sandoval's admiring gaze over the widow's back. His eyes told her she was as lovely as any bride ever born, the only woman he wanted.

"You are ready now?" Father Aldama said. "Dearly beloved…"

Afterward, when he had pronounced them man and wife, he said, "Will you stay here tonight, Señor and Señora Parrish? My sister can come back to my little house next to the church so you may have the privacy a newlywed couple needs."

Sandoval's heart gave a leap of joy as he saw Tess smiling at being addressed as his wife. "We appreciate the offer," he said, sensing Tess would not mind his decision, "but it's probably best if we go on tonight as planned. The less time we are here, the less danger for you both if Delgado figures out what direction we went." And there was something he liked about the idea of their wedding night taking place under all the stars in God's heaven.

"Delgado, humph!" piped up Josefina. "I'd like to see him try to bother me and my brother. I'd beat him with my cane!"

Tess and Sandoval knelt for the priest's blessing.

Chapter Twenty-Three

They rode on until the middle of the night and finally sought refuge in a grove of venerable live oaks some distance off the road. After tethering the horses to a rope line stretched from the trunk of one tree to the other, Sandoval set to making a bed out of their combined bedrolls.

Tess deserved something better than this for her bridal bower, he thought. There was a glade in the middle of the ring of trees where the sun was able to reach, so the ground was grass-covered, but it would still be a hard bed. "I should have taken the priest and his sister up on their offer of the farmhouse," he murmured, watching as she approached the blanket and sat down on it. "Once we get back to Texas, Tess," he promised hoarsely, "you'll never have to sleep in the open again."

"Shh," she said, leaning back on her elbows and beckoning to him to join her. "Look, you can see the stars, and even the moon." He sat and peered through the space between the branches, admiring the celestial view with her. Then he turned to admire Tess, the way she looked by the light of the moon and the stars.

Thank You for this most marvelous gift, Lord, this woman whom I do not deserve, whom You have given to me as my wife. And if I can believe that You gave me Tess, I should be able to believe You will also allow us to find Pilar.

"Sandoval..."

At first Tess did not know what had awakened her—the light of morning filtering through the leaves? The gentle breeze? Then she realized it was Sandoval, no longer lying supine and relaxed next to her, but standing tensely with his back to her, facing the direction of the road, one hand loosely holding the pistol he'd set next to him when they'd gone to sleep.

Tess shifted quickly from her back to her stomach and levered herself up on one elbow, peering at the space between the trees where a man sat on a bony brown horse, his eyes shifting from Sandoval to her and back. She was thankful that the cool night had impelled her to don her clothes again before sleeping. Underneath the blanket, she reached surreptitiously for the other pistol.

His broad, flat face and short, broad-shouldered stature revealed a heavily Indian heritage. Probably his ancestors had dwelled in Mexico long before the Spanish conquerors had come exploring. But his Spanish, when he spoke, was as pure as Sandoval's.

"*Señor, señora,* I apologize for disturbing you. I saw a flash of white as I walked past, and wondered if it was the lost goat I was looking for. But as I came closer, I realized it was a horse instead," he explained, smiling as he nodded over his shoulder at Sandoval's pinto. That he was lying, Tess knew by the battered old shotgun he held at the ready. She froze in place, knowing Sandoval needed no distractions right now.

Lord, help us!

"I mean you no harm," the man said, but he made no move to put away the shotgun. "That's a nice horse, that pinto."

"Yes, he is." Sandoval did not turn his head away from the man to look at his horse. "As it happens, I would be willing to trade him for yours."

The man blinked in surprise. "Why?"

"He doesn't get along with my wife's horse."

It was a patent falsehood, for the pinto gelding, who had raised his head alertly when the man started speaking, had returned to grazing with his head just inches from that of Tess's mare.

A grin spread across the man's broad, coppery features. "This is my lucky day," the man said. "You have a deal, *señor*." Darting glances full of avid curiosity at Tess, he dismounted, laid down his shotgun and offered Sandoval the reins of his nag.

Sandoval did not relax his vigilance, and kept the gun in his hand. "I'll keep my own saddle," he said.

Disappointment flashed across the man's face, then he shrugged as if to say, "you can't blame me for trying." He loosed the cinch on his own horse and pulled off the saddle; then, while Sandoval remained on guard, put his old saddle on the pinto.

"*Gracias.* It was a pleasure doing business with you, *señor*," he said, reining the horse out of the grove and back toward the road.

Tess waited until the fellow was out of sight to come out of her blanket. "There was no lost goat!" she cried, her voice indignant. "You shouldn't have had to trade your pinto for that sorry piece of horseflesh." Then she felt bad when she looked in the rawboned brown horse's steady, honest eyes.

Sandoval was philosophical. "You're right. I never gave him a name, but that pinto could really run. But the man went away feeling he'd gotten a prize, instead of staying and making trouble. I didn't like the way he kept looking at you."

"Neither did I," Tess admitted.

"I'd been thinking of trading the pinto for another horse somewhere along the way, anyway," Sandoval said. "His markings were too memorable. I still have money from my share of the booty. Now if Delgado comes asking about a man riding a black-and-white pinto, they won't tell him about seeing us."

"You can't get much less memorable than this horse," Tess said, but laughed as the nag nuzzled her hand.

"I can buy another horse at the next town or *rancho* we come across," Sandoval said. "We'll keep this old fellow for a packhorse."

Tess wondered what Delgado and his sister were doing now. Were they still searching furiously for them somewhere between the canyon hideout and her home in Chapin? Had Esteban, with her precious camera and mule, and above all the important negatives of Delgado, managed to evade the outlaw leader? Had Delores, his mother, escaped safely?

Five days later, after encountering no further trouble, they arrived in Monterrey, a city tucked at the foot of the Sierra Madres. The closest mountain was notched at the top like an uneven *M*.

"That's *Cerro de la Silla,* Saddle Hill," Sandoval announced from the back of the bay gelding he'd bought along the way. He peered out over the city and sighed. "There were a lot of brothels when I was here before. But maybe we should check into lodging first, and find some food? It must be nearly noon."

"That sounds good." He was nervous, Tess realized, worried that they'd look at each bordello and still not find Pilar.

Near the main cathedral they found a decent inn that also provided stabling for their horses, and down the street, a humble restaurant that served excellent tamales. Then, refreshed, they began their search.

Sandoval had remembered that the seedy part of town, where most of the brothels were located, lay to the east of the grand plaza. It took them fifteen minutes to walk there, but once they had reached it, it seemed like another world to Tess.

The narrow, winding street was lined with cantinas and two-story buildings whose upper verandas jutted out over the street. On several of these, handfuls of women in gaudy-colored wraps lounged on couches and chairs, chattering with each other and calling out raucous greetings when they spotted Sandoval, despite Tess's presence at his side.

Sandoval stopped. "I'd better take you back to the inn," he said, glancing upward and then quickly back at her. "You shouldn't be here."

"I'm staying," Tess said, and essayed a grin. "You might need protection from *them.*" And then she remembered that one of those women could possibly be Pilar, and sobered. *Please, Lord, guide us to the right place, and as soon as possible.*

They went into the first brothel, *Casa de Marías.* A frowsy older woman dozed in a threadbare armchair.

"Buenas tardes, señora," Sandoval said, then repeated himself more loudly until the woman blinked, startled and

nearly fell out of her chair. Bleary, beady black eyes focused on Sandoval with apparent difficulty.

"Good afternoon, sir," she said with a drowsy smile. When she spotted Tess at his side, though, her eyes narrowed and she crossed her arms over her chest. "I have enough girls. I don't need any more. You might ask Florita down the row, though—she keeps foreign women for her customers. Me, I think they're too much trouble."

"No, you don't understand," Sandoval said curtly. "This is my wife. We're looking for a woman named Pilar Parrish, or maybe Pilar Morelos."

The woman shrugged, clearly bored now that there wasn't any money to be made from Sandoval. "All my girls are named *María.* It's easier that way. I have María Angela, María Filipa, María Rosa…"

"No María Pilar?" asked Tess.

The woman shook her head, setting her jowls waggling. "She's not one of my girls. I don't know her."

"Thank you," Sandoval said, and they left.

It was the same story in the next five *burdeles.* No one knew of a woman named Pilar, or of any woman who might have been brought by Delgado five years ago, though some had heard of the outlaw.

Tess's heart was heavy as she saw Sandoval's shoulders sagging in disappointment as they left each establishment. There was only one more place to try.

At the seventh house, the elderly proprietress, who seemed afflicted with some kind of tremors, shook her head. "No, I don't have any girls named Pilar."

"Thank you, *señora,*" Sandoval said, already turning to go.

"But wait, *señor,*" she said. "She was brought by an outlaw, five years ago? I wasn't here then, you understand, but the woman who ran this place before me told me about all the girls, and that sounds like Magdalena."

Magdalena. Mary Magdalene had been a prostitute Jesus healed of evil spirits. Tess felt a spark of hope flicker in her heart.

Beside her, Sandoval had paled and gone still.

"C-can we see her?" Tess asked, because her husband seemed unable to speak.

The woman shook her head, the voluntary motion accentuated by her palsy. "She's not here."

Sandoval stifled a groan and Tess's heart sank. "She's not here anymore? Where did she go?"

The woman held up a hand. "I'm sorry, I meant she's not here right now. I sent her to the cantina to buy some more tequila for the customers. If I didn't send her out on errands occasionally, that one would never go outside. She's very quiet, doesn't mix much with the other girls. Keeps to herself. Some customers don't care, I suppose, but she's not a favorite. Ramón—he's the owner—he tells her always she needs to be more friendly."

Something in Sandoval's tight face must have warned the old woman, for she stopped. "Who is she to you, *señor?* Why are you looking for her?"

"If this Magdalena is really Pilar, she's my sister. And I'll be taking her out of here."

The old woman looked alarmed. "Oh, *señor,* Ramón would never allow that."

Sandoval's jaw set in a hard line. "I have money. I'll buy her freedom—"

He broke off as the door opened behind them, and a young woman entered, her arms laden with a boxful of a dozen or so bottles.

Tess stared at her, and beside her, Sandoval was doing

the same. It was hard to see her features, for she kept her head down, avoiding their gaze.

"Señor Alba says he'll put this on Ramón's bill, Joaquina, but Ramón needs to pay him soon. I'll just take them to the back."

Sandoval cleared his throat. *"Pilar? Pilar Parrish?"*

Chapter Twenty-Four

"S-*Sandoval?*" she queried, in a hoarse version of the voice Sandoval had thought he'd never hear again. *"Is it really you?"* She set down the case of bottles with a clatter of glass.

"Yes. *Yes!*" he cried, starting forward. His sudden movement seemed to alarm her, and she took a step back; then, as if realizing he told the truth, she took trembling steps forward, her arms outstretched, until they met midway.

He stood holding her, both of them shaking, while he smiled through his tears at Tess, who stood beaming at both of them.

At last he loosened his hold on her but, still touching her upper arms, smiled down at her tearstained face. She was still lovely, he thought, though older, and a world-weariness had settled in her eyes where shining joy with life had once lived.

"Why don't you come into the reception room?" Joaquina suggested from behind them, beckoning to a door that led off the entrance hall. "It's never busy at this time of day, and you will have some privacy to visit."

They followed her as she ushered them into a medium-size room where chairs were lined up against the walls. Here was where the women of this house greeted their customers in the evening, Sandoval realized with a pang as they pulled three chairs into a circle.

"I thought never to see you again in this life, brother," Pilar said shakily, as soon as they had sat down.

"Pilar…may I call you that? I will call you Magdalena if you prefer…"

Pilar shook her head. "You may call me whatever you like."

"Pilar, I have been searching for you ever since…since you were taken away. I had given up and begun to think you must be dead. I would not be here if Tess—" he beckoned for Tess to join them "—my wife, had not helped me discover where you were and insisted we come and find you."

Pilar shifted her gaze and, leaning forward, embraced Tess, kissing her cheek. "Thank you. It is so much more than I deserve. I am in your debt."

"You owe me nothing," Tess assured her. "We thank God He has led us to you."

"But what are you saying, 'much more than I deserve'?" Sandoval said, his voice impassioned. "None of what happened was your fault. I knew Delgado had taken advantage of your innocence and lured you from home."

"Before I say anything more, I must know where that monster is. We've heard of his doings, even in Monterrey. He…he did not come with you, did he? How did you find out where I was?" Her eyes darted to the door, as if she expected Delgado to materialize there.

"No, no, of course we wouldn't bring him with us," Sandoval said quickly. "Please don't worry. I'll never let him come near you again." He briefly summarized how they had come to be here.

Pilar listened, her eyes widening at some parts, her jaw dropping at others. "So you are a Ranger, but you have posed as an outlaw in an effort to bring him to justice? And you *kidnapped* Tess in an effort to achieve your goal, all because she can take photographs?" She shook her head disapprovingly, then turned to Tess. "And you not only *forgave* my brother for what he did, but *married him? Why?*" She blinked as if the story was almost beyond comprehension.

"I love your brother," Tess said simply. "However unconventional his methods are, I discovered he is the man the Lord planned for me to marry."

Pilar looked from Sandoval to Tess and back again, still shaking her head. "So, you, too, brother, have received more than you deserve."

Sandoval nodded.

"God gives all of us more than we deserve," Tess said.

"Pilar, we came to take you out of here," Sandoval said. "You don't have to stay here any longer."

Pilar stared back at him, her eyes bleak, and shook her head. "It is enough that I have seen you again, and know that you are happy. This is my life now, brother. There is nothing left for me out there," she added, nodding in the direction of the front door. "What would I do, where would I go, after what I've done? No, Sandoval, I will stay here."

"Pilar, what are you saying? You can't mean you like this life!" he cried, taking her hands in his. "You can go home—either to Montemorelos, which I will deed to you, or join us in Texas. Our mother will be overjoyed to see you. She has grieved for years, not knowing if you were dead or alive."

Pilar's eyes were huge in her still-beautiful face, and now they gleamed with tears, like rain on onyx. "*Madre?* She…she's still alive?"

Sandoval gave her hands a squeeze, sure that mentioning their mother would convince Pilar. "Yes! She lives on my ranch in Texas, but if you decide to go to Montemorelos, she might want to come back there. I am willing to share her, of course," he added with a laugh—a laugh that soon died when he saw Pilar's face subside into hopelessness again.

"You must not tell her you found me," she told him flatly. "It's better that she thinks I am dead than living in a brothel."

"But why? Are you blaming yourself for being here, where Delgado brought you? None of what happened was your fault. You were *innocent,* sister," he repeated.

Pilar shook her head, her eyes brimming with a sorrow too deep for words. "I was innocent when I first met him, yes. But then he seduced me with his blandishments and flattery, until I was willing to plot and scheme and lie to be with him. I thought he loved me because he said so, and I left with him because I was addicted to his kisses and caresses. I *gave myself to him,* Sandoval, knowing we had made no vows before God, because I couldn't bear to breathe without him. *I* did those things, brother. It was *my choice,* don't you see?" She struck her chest with a clenched fist. "And now I am here, where I deserve to be. My sin is too deep for me to go anywhere else. How could I go home to our village, where everyone knows what I've done? I would be shunned like a rabid dog!"

Sandoval knew she could be right about Montemorelos. People's memories were long, and they might treat Pilar like a pariah, as if she could contaminate them. "Come with us to Texas, then. You could start all over again."

"Pilar, no one's sin is too deep for forgiveness—" Tess began.

"Mine is!" Pilar cried, and with a shout of anguish, she jumped to her feet and ran from the room. A moment later, they heard the sound of feet running up the staircase.

Sandoval would have gone after her, but Tess stopped him. And then Joaquina entered the room.

"That is enough for now," the old woman said. "Your coming has been a major shock to Magdalena—or Pilar, as you call her. She will have much to think about. In addition, it's time for her to get ready for work tonight."

The idea of his sister conducting business as usual in this place filled him with horror. "But I don't want her doing that! I want to take her out of this place, with us."

The old woman was polite, but firm. "I'm sorry. You're welcome to come back tomorrow, if you wish. She has little to do then."

Tess spoke up. "*Señora,* may I speak to my husband for a moment?" She glanced meaningfully at the doorway, then back at the woman.

Joaquina looked from Tess's earnest eyes back to Sandoval's, while Sandoval fought the urge to run upstairs after his sister.

"*Seguramente, señora.* But please understand my position. Señor Ramón holds me responsible for what happens in this house. He would not like it if he believes you are upsetting one of his girls so that she cannot work, and might not allow you to come back."

Sandoval would have told the old woman just what Ramón would have to accept, but for the tightening of Tess's hand about his arm.

Joaquina turned on her heel and left the room.

"Sandoval—"

"Tess, don't try to tell me that I must accept my sister staying here, doing…what these women do. I'll carry her out kicking and screaming, if I have to."

"Yes, you could do that," she said, "but, don't you see, you'd just have this Ramón and every other bordello owner coming after you, probably armed to the teeth? And Pilar isn't ready yet. She's convinced she deserves to be here. We will have to spend more time with her."

He stared at her, hardly able to tolerate what his wife was saying. "You're saying we must let her 'work' at night, while we come to visit during the day? I can't do that."

"I understand how you feel. You have money, you said. So what's to stop you from paying for her time? Come back tonight, and pay for the whole evening. We can take her for some dinner, if she's willing and they'll allow her to go, and then we can talk to her."

He stared at Tess, hardly daring to hope that would work. "Do you think the old woman would let me do that? After I told her I'm determined to take Pilar away from here?"

Tess shrugged. "You won't know until you try, will you? I think she has a kind heart, but she wants to keep her position safe—she probably has nowhere else to go, either. It wouldn't hurt to give her a little…shall we say, *incentive?*" She pantomimed rubbing a coin between her fingers.

Together, they went back to the entrance hall, where the old woman had resumed her seat on the sofa, where she was munching on a pastel cookie from a dish of them.

"Does Ramón allow his girls to be hired for the entire night, and leave the house?" he asked Joaquina.

"*Sí, señor.* It happens occasionally. But I warn you, the price is not cheap." She named a figure.

She had told the truth. The price was not cheap. But Sandoval's share of the money from riding with Delgado was the Mexican equivalent of some three hundred dollars.

"What time do the customers start coming?"

"We usually see no one until seven, *señor,* though we're open from noon till the wee hours."

"I would like to book Pilar's time for the entire evening then, starting at six o'clock." Sandoval said. "And here's a little something so you do not feel it necessary to tell Ramón I'm her brother." He dropped a handful of pesos into the woman's palm.

"Ramón will be very pleased," Joaquina said with a conspiratorial wink. "Magdalena—Pilar—is so shy and withdrawn she is always the last one chosen. And I am not going to tell Pilar who is coming for her."

Sandoval felt the pain of the woman's last sentence like a punch in the gut. "You think she might not be willing to go with me?"

Joaquina shrugged eloquently. "Who knows? She gave up hope long ago. I can't remember when she's left this place, except to go across to the cantina to buy bottles. It's as if she doesn't exist outside this place, as if she's hiding from the world. We will see you back at six."

It had been a long journey to Chapin, one fraught with peril. Esteban had traveled, always looking over his shoulder for pursuing outlaws, northward beside the Rio Grande. Once, Esteban had only avoided being seen by Delgado, Lupe, and his former compadres by hiding in a thicket of mesquite and cedar and holding the mule's nose as they swept past. He'd kept off the roads after that until he came to a ford that boasted a ferry so he could keep the contents of the wagon dry.

Now, after picking up Tess's assistant, Francisco, in the small town of Chapin, they'd arrived at the plantation home of Samuel Taylor. Esteban waited in the parlor, clutching the precious negatives wrapped in oilskin, while Francisco went with a maid to fetch the retired Ranger.

Samuel Taylor came into the room, his eyes narrowing at Esteban. "He speak English?" he asked Francisco.

"*Sí,* Señor Taylor, he talk it better than me," the youth told him eagerly. "He knows where Tess is!"

Taylor turned to Esteban. "That true?"

Esteban nodded warily.

"What's this yarn Francisco's telling me about you having a picture of Delgado that my godchild took? Where's Tess and that rascal Parrish?"

He listened while Esteban explained in his heavily accented, halting English; then, when Esteban had finished telling him how Parrish had sent him here to have the negatives developed and sent out while he went with Tess to find his missing sister, he sighed deeply.

"I don't know what Parrish was thinking not bringing that girl straight home to her mama and papa. They're worried sick, even though they've gotten a couple of messages sayin' she was all right. But if I know Tess, she probably talked him into letting her go along," he mused aloud. "Headstrong, that girl. In need of a firm hand."

"Señor Sandoval has that," Esteban assured him, daring to grin. "And he loves Señorita Tess."

Samuel Taylor looked at him sharply, as if he hadn't expected to be answered. "You don't say."

"Yes, I do. And she loves him!"

The older man blinked. "We'll just see about that. If he lets my godchild come to harm, there won't be enough of him to bury, I can promise you that. And don't bother to assure me of something you can't know," he warned Esteban. He shifted his stare to the package Esteban carried.

"Well, what are we waiting for? Francisco, can we go develop this negative and see if your amigo here really brought me a picture of Delgado?"

"Of course, *señor!*"

"Then run to the barn and tell my stable boy to saddle my horse. Lula Marie!" he bellowed. "I'm goin' into town."

Chapter Twenty-Five

Delgado's curses were bloodcurdling when they returned to the canyon after their fruitless pursuit and found no campfire burning, Esteban and Delores gone, and the photography wagon missing as well.

One of the bandits silently took Delgado's and Lupe's horses, avoiding their furious gazes, while the rest of them quietly unsaddled their mounts. No one wanted to give the outlaw leader cause to redirect his wrath to him.

"The pictures the *gringa* took are still there," Lupe assured him, after running inside her brother's adobe to check.

"Bah! As if that matters!" her brother snarled at her. "They've taken some of the negatives, if not all of them—of that, you may be sure. My face will soon be plastered all over the valley, and beyond. Maybe yours, too! But how could Esteban and Delores have gotten away with that heavy wagon so quickly? Delores is an old woman. We should have come across them."

"Perhaps they did not travel together," Lupe pointed out.

Delgado gazed at his sister, considering her words.

"You're probably right. But where—" He stared into the fire one of the men had hastily kindled, remembering the last conversation he'd had with Tess that evening before so mysteriously passing out.

"*Monterrey,*" he said aloud. "Sandoval and Tess went to Monterrey. That's why we did not find them!"

"But why—"

Delgado told her about Pilar Morelos. "And that traitor Esteban, his shoulder miraculously healed, must have driven the wagon out of here and managed to avoid us. By now he's probably arrived somewhere in Texas where he can have the negatives developed. I will have to think of the most painful way possible for him to die when I catch up to him. But he will die no more painfully than Sandoval Parrish, that treacherous half-breed."

"I always told you you shouldn't have trusted him, brother. His heart is Anglo, after all."

"*You* seemed content enough to overlook that for a while, sister!" Delgado snapped.

"So, I was fooled," she retorted. "So were you, by that cursed redheaded *bruja.* You wanted to wed her, remember? Are you still enchanted with the thought of her lily-white face?"

He would have slapped Lupe then, but she danced out of reach, and her hand came up holding the dagger she always carried in her waistband. "Have a care, *hermano,* and remember that *I* am not the enemy. Sandoval Parrish and Tess Hennessy are the ones who've played you false. Save your fury for them. I will help you achieve your revenge, if you let me be the one to carve a design in that lovely face until it's not so lovely anymore. Then you can have her and do what you will."

Their shared laughter was chilling.

* * *

The Metropolitan Cathedral bells were just tolling four when Tess and Sandoval left the street of the brothels and cantinas. Realizing they had some time to kill before they could return for Pilar, they toured the cathedral, admiring its baroque loveliness, so different than any of the churches at home. Tess wished aloud that she had her camera, to attempt to capture its grandeur in a photograph—or at least with her sketchpad and pencils.

After that, they happened upon a goldsmith's shop and belatedly purchased a simple gold wedding ring for Tess.

"I'll buy you a better one someday," he told her, placing it on her finger.

But she shook her head, laying a finger on his lips. "I only want this one. I'll always remember Monterrey when I look at it."

Pilar was sitting alone in the reception room when Sandoval entered, and rose when she saw him.

"*Buenas noches,* sister. You look lovely."

And she did. He had worried what sort of clothing his sister would have available, but although her white silk blouse nestled low over her shoulders, she looked perfectly respectable.

"*Buenas noches,* Sandoval." She smiled crookedly. "Joaquina wouldn't tell me who was coming, but when she said he had paid for the entire evening in advance and was coming to take me out of here at such an early hour, I guessed it was you. I'm not usually in high demand, and no one ever offers to take me out. You always were persistent, brother. Where are we going?" she asked, as they walked into the entrance hallway.

Pilar stopped stock-still as Tess emerged from the

shadowy interior doorway. Tess had worried aloud that the owner of the establishment, Señor Ramón, would get suspicious if he saw a couple arriving for Pilar, but Sandoval had not been willing to let her wait on the street in such an area. God must have been watching over them, for Joaquina told them Ramón had not arrived yet.

"Good evening, Pilar," Tess said. "We wanted to take you out for dinner, so that you and your brother could get reacquainted and I could get to know you. Is that all right?"

Pilar looked like a wary wild mare that might bolt at any moment. Nevertheless, she shrugged her shoulders and said, "Sure. Why not?" But something in her guarded eyes warned Sandoval they would need to keep the conversation light, at least at first.

In one of the streets that led away from a plaza they found a restaurant that served excellent food at a reasonable price, and soon the three of them were laughing and talking like old friends. Pilar regaled Tess with a number of tales about Sandoval as a pesky younger brother full of mischief, and Sandoval responded in kind, telling Tess about how Pilar would achieve her revenge by making it seem that Sandoval had been the one who had stolen a hunk of freshly baked cake off the kitchen windowsill, or placed a toad in their old nursemaid's bed.

Sandoval felt full of joy as he and Pilar reminisced about old times at their home near Montemorelos. Then Pilar asked about their father.

"He is dead, sister," he said gently, reaching out to take hold of Pilar's hand, while Tess looked on in sympathy.

Tears ran down Pilar's cheeks. "I knew he must be when you did not mention him along with our mother."

"When?" Pilar asked.

"Almost five years ago." He did not say, Shortly after

you left, he died of a broken heart. He saw that Pilar guessed as much, however.

They let her weep, but soon she was smiling through her tears to hear how their mother thrived on Sandoval's ranch, where she did the cooking.

"Ah, if only I could taste *Madre's pan dulce* again," Pilar said with a heavy sigh—then looked startled, as if she hadn't meant to say it aloud.

"Pilar, you *could,*" Sandoval told her. "You could leave with us tomorrow. Just say the word."

Already, though, Pilar was sitting back in her chair, shaking her head. "No, I couldn't."

Sandoval leaned forward. "Why not?" he said earnestly, keeping his voice low so the other customers wouldn't hear them. "I have some money. I'll give whatever it takes for Ramón to let you go. And if he won't take money, I'll take you from him—at gunpoint, if necessary."

Now Pilar leaned forward, too, and whispered back. "Even if Ramón would allow me to go, I've told you, Sandoval—it's too late for me. I can't forget what I've become, or change it. Let's not discuss it any further."

Sandoval looked away, fighting the urge to argue with his sister, to somehow force her to see that he couldn't leave her where she was. He noticed that they were among the last customers remaining. The evening had flown, and he guessed the restaurant owner was ready to close his establishment. Sandoval paid their bill and they left.

"This has been wonderful, Sandoval, Tess," Pilar said, when they were once more out in the street. "I will remember it always. Thank you. But perhaps you should take me back now. You are newlyweds, after all." She laughed when Tess blushed in the lamplight.

"If we take you back now, you…will not have to…" Sandoval's voice trailed off.

"Work?" she said, her expression guarded once again. "No, you paid for the entire evening. Besides, Joaquina gave me the key to the side entrance. I can go up to my room without going through the entrance hall. Ramón won't even know when I return."

"May we…see you again tomorrow?" Tess asked.

"You will still be in Monterrey?" Pilar asked, looking surprised. "Sandoval, you ought to ride out to Saddle Mountain with Tess. I hear there's a lovely view of the city."

"I'd like to, but I'm worried that Delgado may have figured out where we've gone and be heading this way. I don't think he'd come into Monterrey looking for us—there are too many people around—but we'll have to be on our guard when we leave."

Mentioning the outlaw made Pilar's expression somber again. "Brother, you should leave at dawn—tonight, even. You shouldn't take a chance on him catching you. You have a wife to worry about now."

Sandoval's heart ached for her. "I'm not leaving without you, Pilar. Or at least until I convince you to leave the brothel and go somewhere else."

"Go where? Another brothel?" Pilar's laugh was harsh. "It's too late for me, Sandoval—I told you that. I can never forget what I am—what *he* made me."

"Pilar—"

"Sandoval, it's late," Tess said, interrupting him. "We're all tired. Let's agree to see Pilar again tomorrow—if you're willing, Pilar? We could come earlier in the day, and stroll through the plazas, perhaps have lunch somewhere?"

Sandoval saw that Tess was holding her breath, clearly fearing Pilar would refuse to see them anymore.

"I suppose," Pilar said at last with a shrug. "Anything is better than lolling around with those women, watching them trying different hair arrangements and listening to them chatter about the baubles their customers bring them."

Sandoval couldn't sleep that night, imagining how it would feel to leave Monterrey with Pilar remaining in a brothel, until at last his tossing reawakened Tess. Taking his hand, she insisted he share his worries with her.

"We must pray that Pilar becomes convinced that God loves her and will help her start anew," she said sleepily, after he had confessed his worries. "I think, now that Pilar sees that she has a choice, she is paralyzed at the thought of having to make a decision. She probably thinks it's possible that the new life could prove to be harder than the life she lives now. At least, where she is now no one expects too much of her."

"But, how?" he asked. "You heard her tonight, Tess. Her mind is set."

"God will give us the right words when we need them."

When they returned to the brothel at midmorning the next day, Joaquina informed them that Pilar was sick and unable to leave her bed. Tess's heart sank. She didn't believe that Pilar was ill—she was trying to avoid them, and so avoid making a decision.

Pilar had given the old woman a note to deliver to them, though, she said, handing Sandoval a folded piece of paper. The old woman's eyes were alight with curiosity. Tess suspected the woman was illiterate, or she would have read it already.

Sandoval unfolded it, looked at it, then handed it to Tess.

"Go home, brother," it read. "It has been wonderful to

see you again and meet your lovely Tess, and I am happy for you. But you cannot change what happened to me. Go with God, and remember, tell our mother I am dead. Pilar."

Tess looked into Sandoval's sorrowful eyes, and knew they couldn't give up so easily.

"Tell her I want to see her—just me," Tess told Joaquina. "Tell her we won't go away until she agrees to speak at least with me."

Joaquina nodded, and five minutes later she was back, breathing a little hard from her exertion. "She will see you, *señora,* but only you. Her room is the third one on the right upstairs."

"Let me try, Sandoval," she said. "I'll try to convince her to see you."

Sandoval pulled her into his arms. *"Thank you,"* he breathed, against her ear. "I love you for trying."

"I have to go to the market, since Pilar won't leave her room," Joaquina told Sandoval, after they had watched Tess ascend the stairs. "You may wait in the reception room."

Sandoval nodded and watched the old woman leave. He tried to pray, but his prayers seemed to go no farther than the ceiling with its exposed beams.

Tess knocked, but received no answer. Checking to make sure she had counted the number of rooms from the stairs correctly, she knocked again, and at last tried the door. It was unlocked. *Help me, Lord.*

The room was lit only by an ill-smelling tallow candle sitting in a bowl of melted wax. As Tess's eyes grew accustomed to the light, she saw a figure lying on her back in the bed, the dingy covers pulled up to her shoulders.

"I'm here, Pilar," Tess called out. "Thank you for agreeing to see me."

For a long moment, she wondered if Sandoval's sister was going to acknowledge her presence, but at last, slowly, Pilar turned on her side, gesturing for Tess to sit in the rickety chair beside the bed.

"Well, it didn't sound as if you'd take no for an answer." Pilar's eyes, so like her brother's in their color, shape and expressiveness, were shadowed with violet smudges. The lids were swollen and red-rimmed, as if she had spent much of her time weeping. A pallor underlay the olive tone of her skin.

"Is it true what you said yesterday, when you first came here?" Pilar asked.

Tess blinked. "Is…is *what* true?"

Pilar looked down at her hands and gave a short, humorless laugh. "I'm sorry. I've been wrestling with God for hours, knowing He can hear my thoughts, even if I do not speak aloud—I forget that other people cannot. I meant, is it true what you said, that no one's sin is too deep for forgiveness?" Her eyes, desperate to believe, searched Tess's, alert for any hint that Tess would try to placate her with an easy, comfortable lie.

Tess knew Pilar didn't want to be told yet again that the fault had been entirely Delgado's. However innocent a girl Pilar had been, she blamed herself for loving the outlaw, for putting her trust in him, for becoming a liar for the sake of his kisses and more.

Understanding that, Tess did not hesitate. "Yes, it's true. Completely and totally true. If God forgave the thief on the cross, who'd spent his life in crime, He will forgive you, Pilar, for whatever you have done. God loves you. He never stopped. You have but to ask for forgiveness, but He will not impose it on you by force. You must ask."

Pilar's face crumpled. "Is it so simple? There was a baby—Delgado's baby. They said he died because I had been living such a hard life, always on the run—but I know it was because of my sin."

Tess shook her head. "Oh, Pilar, I'm so sorry.... That baby is with God now. But all of us need forgiveness from God. He wants to come into our hearts and make us new."

Pilar was haggard in the flickering candlelight. "How is it I have spent five years here, when I could have just asked God for forgiveness?" And then her face crumpled and she was sobbing in Tess's arms, crying aloud for God's mercy, while Tess assured her it was there for her already.

She wept for an endless time, and Tess held her until the storm was past.

At last, Pilar raised her head. "It's *true!* I *am forgiven.* It feels so good!"

Tess hugged her. She didn't want to hurry Pilar when she had just come so far, but dare she ask if they could share the news with Sandoval?

Sandoval paced the reception room. Above him, he heard the women start to stir and chatter, and eventually, they began to stroll downstairs past the reception room on their way to the kitchen. A couple stared boldly at him as they passed, but he ignored them.

He wondered what was happening in Pilar's room above his head, but knowing he could do nothing but wait, he began to think of the state of his own soul. Had he been trying to earn the Lord's forgiveness for failing his sister by bringing about Delgado's capture? Had he ever just accepted that God loved him no matter what he'd done, and wanted to walk with him as Father and Friend, Sandoval's failings forgiven? He hadn't.

Tess had taken that step, he realized. Probably years ago, judging by the faith that seemed to infuse her every move.

It was past time that he did so, too. Alone in the reception room, he knelt and prayed. And he knew his prayer was heard. No matter what happened with Pilar, he was at peace.

Deep in thought, Sandoval started when a knock sounded at the door. Tess entered the room, followed by Pilar, who ran into his arms.

"I am forgiven, brother. The Lord has *forgiven* me! Your wife helped me see that all I had to do was ask to find my way to the Lord."

Sandoval smiled at Tess over his sister's head. "Yes, she has a way of doing that," he said. "I've experienced it, too." He knew Tess would understand that it had just happened while she was gone.

The smile Tess returned to him was radiant with joy.

"And there's more good news," Sandoval told the two women so dear to him. "While you were upstairs, Señor Ramón stopped by to see who has been calling on you for two days in a row, Pilar."

Pilar took an involuntary step backward, her face filled with dread, her body quivering in alarm. "What did he say? Am I…still allowed to see you?"

Sandoval put a hand out and touched her trembling shoulder. "Be easy, sister, I told you I had good news," he said. "You are free to leave this place. Today. Right now."

Chapter Twenty-Six

"Wh-what are you saying, brother? I cannot just leave with you. Señor Ramón would never allow it."

"Ah, but I did, Pilar," said a heavy-set, oily-faced man who came into the room at that moment. "Señor Parrish drives a hard bargain, but at last we came to terms. I finally decided that with the money he gave me for you, I can obtain another girl who is…shall we say…more suited to her duties? Farewell, Pilar, and good luck. Oh, and leave the dresses you were given for working."

Pilar only stared at him, as if she couldn't trust her ears, until he left the room.

"As if I would wear those things anywhere else!" she said with a laugh.

Joaquina came in then. "Oh, my dear, I just heard the news. I am happy for you, my dear," she added, embracing Pilar. "If you will wait a moment, I have a small *maleta* you can have to pack your things."

Later, as the three of them sat in a sunlit plaza opposite the cathedral eating a picnic lunch of tamales purchased from an open-air stand, Sandoval asked Pilar if she had any idea where they could buy a horse for her so she could come along with them. "Ramón thinks I gave him my last *centavo* for you, and of course I was willing, but I managed to keep enough back for a mount for you, and another for me." They had already told her about being forced to trade Sandoval's pinto for the bony old horse.

"I…I hope you will understand," Pilar said carefully, looking from Sandoval to Tess and back again, "but I think I would like to stay in Monterrey for a while."

"What are you saying, Pilar? What would you do here?" Tess asked, her forehead furrowed in puzzlement.

"I…I think I will stay for a while with the sisters at the convent by the cathedral," Pilar said, watching thoughtfully as two brown-robed nuns walked by.

"Are you thinking of taking the veil?" Sandoval asked, trying to keep the apprehension from his voice. Had he regained his sister, only to lose her again behind the walls of a convent? Did she think this was the only place God had for her, because of her past?

Pilar faced him, her eyes thoughtful. "I don't know, brother. Perhaps. I…I just want to do some thinking, before I begin the next part of my life. Maybe I will visit Montemorelos, just to see it one more time. I'm not afraid of that now. And then if I do not stay with the sisters, I will find my way to you."

"But how will you come to us?" Tess asked. "We could leave some money with you—or send it to you, after we reach home."

"There is no need," Pilar said with a grin, and reached for the valise that held the few belongings she had taken away from the brothel. Opening it, she took out a gold pendant from which dangled a gold ring with a cabochon ruby as big as a pigeon's egg.

"I was given this by an old man who came to the brothel several times. He was a lonely old widower, quite wealthy, and he really only wanted to talk, to enjoy some female company. He always asked for me. When he knew he was going to die soon, he gave this to me in thanks, and told me to keep it in case I ever needed it. I'm supposed to give Ramón all such presents, of course, but I kept this one well hidden. So you see, Sandoval and Tess, I am not totally without a source of money. I will sell it to pay for my traveling expenses, or if I decide to stay in the convent," she said, nodding toward the small building that nestled at the side of the huge cathedral, "it will be my dowry."

"Will you stay with us tonight, though?" Sandoval asked her. "We won't leave until the morning, so we could get you a room at the inn. I'm not ready to part with you yet."

"I would like that, brother, and Tess, my new sister."

It was morning, and the time had come for parting. They had to begin the dangerous journey back home. While a small boy held the reins of their horses—including a handsome bay gelding Sandoval had purchased yesterday afternoon—in front of the convent gate, Sandoval and Tess embraced Pilar.

"*Vaya con Dios,* Sandoval and Tess," she said, hugging each of them in turn. "May the good Lord guard you from all harm and richly bless you. I will pray for you," Pilar told them, a tear making its way down her cheek.

Tears welled in Tess's brilliant-blue eyes, too, Sandoval noted, and felt a thickness in his own throat. "We'll send word as soon as we reach safety," he promised, when he could speak.

"And we'll pray for you, too," Tess added, embracing

her new sister. "I know you'll make the right decision, Pilar, whatever it is."

"With God's help," Pilar agreed.

"I wish there was some way to let the Rangers know when we're coming and where we'll cross, so they could be waiting to cover us," Sandoval mused aloud as they left the convent and headed for the road heading northeast out of the city. He'd decided it would be best not to try and cross the Rio Grande where it was closest to Chapin, thinking Delgado might well be expecting him to do that. Instead, he'd told her, they'd cross upriver at Roma.

Tess knew he was trying to distract himself from the pain of saying goodbye to Pilar, not knowing what his sister's ultimate decision would be.

"Yes, there's no way a letter could reach them ahead of us," she said.

And then they both saw it. They'd entered Monterrey from the east after fleeing the outlaw hideout, and they hadn't passed this way when they were sightseeing.

In a tone that indicated he couldn't believe his eyes, Sandoval translated aloud the Spanish sign over the door of the building—"Monterrey Telegraph Office. Tess, we can send a telegram home—it's perfect!"

"Patrick, I got a telegram. They're coming home!" Samuel Taylor said, brandishing the message he'd received just a half hour before. He was flanked by Esteban, whose grin was so broad it threatened to split his face.

"But why did they send it to you, not to us?"

"Because Parrish needs me to set up a Ranger reception committee. Go get your wife and I'll read the message to both of you—that'll explain it."

But summoning Amelia was unnecessary, for she'd heard Taylor's horse thunder up to the house and skid to a sliding stop at the front door. "What's that, Sam?" she demanded, flying down the stairs with a speed that belied her years. "You've heard from Tess? She's coming home? When? How?"

"This message is from her and her *husband,* Sandoval," He couldn't help but enjoy a little the way Amelia's eyes goggled and her jaw dropped open. "Yep, she and Parrish are *married.*"

"My little girl is *married?*" Patrick echoed. *"Tess?"*

"To *that man?*" Amelia cried. "The very one who had her kidnapped?"

"Now, Amelia, he's a good man, just like I told you both at the barbecue," Taylor said, conveniently forgetting the way he'd also growled at Esteban that Parrish would pay if any harm came to Tess. "Calm down. You wouldn't want her racketing about Mexico alone with him, without them bein' married, would you? And don't forget, thanks to Parrish, we have that scoundrel's ugly mug plastered all over southern Texas—and thanks, too, to Esteban, here, for bringing the negatives safely home," he said, clapping Esteban on the back. The Mexican beamed modestly.

"Yes, yes, are you going to read us the telegram, or just stand there blathering all day, man?" Patrick asked, making a grab for the telegram.

"Patience, Patrick, don't rip it," Samuel Taylor said, surrendering the paper to him. "You can read it same as I, I expect—if you don't suffer an apoplexy first."

"Married in Mexico, stop," Patrick read. "Coming home via Roma approx. three-four days, stop. Have Ranger company meet us at ford, stop. Watch for Delgado, stop. Signed, Sandoval and Tess Parrish."

"That's *all?*" Amelia demanded. "That's all he wrote?"

"Telegrams aren't cheap, Amelia," Sam reminded her. "They charge by the word, so I imagine Sandoval couldn't afford t' be wordy. There'll be time enough to pry all the details outta your daughter the bride once she's home."

"Yes, and I'm going to give that Parrish a piece of my mind for denying my youngest child the wedding of her dreams, here in our very own church with Reverend Fothergill," Amelia threatened; then she froze. "Patrick! We've got to be there, at Roma. I have to pack."

"Now, Amelia, it'll be at least three or four days before they could possibly make it to Roma, maybe more. This here message was sent from Monterrey. You'd do a lot better t' stay here and plan a big party for when they do arrive."

Amelia brightened at the prospect. "It can be their wedding reception," she said. "No matter what kind of hole-in-the-corner wedding they had, my daughter will have a proper wedding reception."

"But where are you going, Sam?" he demanded, as Samuel Taylor took hold of his wide-brimmed hat again and turned to leave.

"To send a message to the closest Ranger company, and have 'em meet me at Roma," Sam said. "C'mon, Esteban—"

"I'll be coming with you," Patrick told him in a tone that brooked no argument, then added softly, so Amelia wouldn't hear, "I'm thinking you're expecting a battle there maybe, eh?"

"It's a possibility," Sam admitted.

"Then an extra rifle won't hurt. I don't care whose wife she is, Tess is my daughter."

"Come along, then."

He followed Taylor out of the house onto the porch, bellowing for Mateo to saddle his horse.

Patrick needn't have worried about Amelia overhearing, for his wife was already hollering for Rosa, the cook, to help her plan the food for the party.

Chapter Twenty-Seven

"It's only about twenty-five miles to the border now," Sandoval announced. They had left Nuevo Léon and entered Tamaulipas again.

It was encouraging news. Only about half a day's ride, and they would be in Texas once more. Then they would be almost home. Chapin lay some fifty miles east of Roma.

"We've been blessed so far," she said.

It was true. No one had treated them with suspicion. They were just a man and his wife, traveling on horseback.

"I'll be thankful when I can go outside without this rebozo to cover my hair," she said, pointing at it. "It doesn't keep the sun out of my eyes nearly as well as a hat."

It was the closest she'd come to a complaint. He knew she had to be feeling the tension as much as he was, knowing that these last few miles could be the most hazardous of their entire journey.

The head covering would only work from a distance, Sandoval knew. Up close anyone could see from the fiery-red curl that peeped out and the blueness of her eyes that she was a *gringa*. Just tonight, when they'd left the spare room behind the little cantina and claimed their horses, the *cantinero* had stared at Tess as if memorizing her features.

"An extra ten pesos to say you never saw her or me," he'd said to the man. It was a princely sum, but there was no guaranteeing that, after they'd ridden away, the man wouldn't turn around and inform anyone who wanted to know that a couple fitting their description had passed this way. Sandoval wouldn't rest easy until they were once again in Texas and he knew that Delgado had been captured or killed.

"I imagine Papa and Mama won't want us to leave Hennessy Hall for a few days, once we get across the river," Tess was saying. "They'll want to kill the fatted calf, as they say."

"If your father doesn't shoot me on sight."

"I'm sure they'll both come to love you in very short order," she insisted firmly. "How could they not?"

"Oh, let me count the reasons," he retorted. "You could start with the fact I had you kidnapped." And then, he thought, there's my mixed blood.

She gave him a look, and he realized how pessimistic he'd been sounding. "I'm sorry. I'm not normally such a gloomy fellow." God is in control, he reminded himself.

"I can't wait to meet your mother and see your ranch," Tess said, after a moment. He'd told her about his property north of Chapin, a sprawling thousand-acre place on which he ran cattle and goats. Sandoval hadn't spent much time there before, mostly leaving it in the hands of his old foreman while he spent his time rangering, but now it would be their home. He'd have to find a way to be there more than he had in the past, when he hadn't had a wife to come home to.

"The ranch house isn't much," he warned her. "But you can put your own touches in it."

"But your mother's been in charge inside," Tess said, a little uneasily. "She might not welcome another female in her kitchen, making changes."

Sandoval shook his head. "*Madre's* been saying for years that she wanted more time to relax, and that as soon as I brought home a wife, she wanted to spend her time playing with the grandchildren we would give her. So we'll have to make the place bigger."

"*Sandoval!*" She giggled, pretending to be scandalized.

Sandoval grinned back, unrepentant. He couldn't help wondering if she was already carrying his child—a son, to carry on his name, or a daughter, who'd look just like Tess.

"And there must be a guest room for Pilar when she comes to visit," she said. "Oh, Sandoval, I can't help hoping she doesn't remain in the convent."

"I'm happy as long as she's happy, whatever she chooses," he murmured. "Though I admit I feel the same way you do and don't want her to become a nun. Perhaps she'll decide she wants to stay in Montemorelos, after all. If so, I'll deed her the *rancho*...." He froze, listening. Had he heard hoofbeats?

"Then we can visit her there, too. I'd like to see where you grew—"

"*Shh!* I think I hear horses. Quick, off the road! Take cover behind that ruined house."

The three roofless walls of the adobe house would never have hidden them in daylight, due to a window in the middle wall. As it was, they had barely time enough to ride behind it, dismount and hold their horses' heads before half a dozen horsemen rounded the curve and trotted on past. It was too dark to see if it was Delgado and his men, but Sandoval was sure it must be. Who else would be abroad at midnight?

They waited an hour behind the house before going on at a cautious walk, straining to identify every night sound. There was no more chatter. Were Delgado and his henchmen waiting for them around the next bend in the road? Each time the road curved, Sandoval scouted ahead.

They encountered no one else.

The sun rose on their right, transforming the Rio Grande ahead of them into a shining silver ribbon. A tiny village, no more than a scattering of buildings, lay between them and the river. A grove of trees obscured the tiny town of Roma on the opposite bank, but he knew it was there.

He reined in and gestured for Tess to do the same. "I'm trying to decide whether we should make a run for it. What I wouldn't give for another hour of darkness," he said, staring ahead of him.

Tess's face was sober, her eyes wistful as she stared at Texas lying on the other side of the river. So close…

"Should we see if that village ahead has an inn, and wait till dark?" she asked.

He shook his head. "This close to the river, I'd be afraid Delgado's men would be searching every building. We don't know if someone might've seen us and reported to Delgado."

"Why don't we ride upriver a ways, or downriver?"

He considered the suggestion. "The river's a lot wider, and deeper, in both directions. That's why this is such a good place to ford."

He pulled the spyglass he'd taken from Delgado's loot and studied the opposite bank of the river, and this time he was rewarded with a gleam of sunlight reflecting on metal. He peered more closely.

"There are mounted men over there under the trees," he said.

"Oh, Sandoval, it must be the Rangers!"

"I can't be sure, from this distance. Stay here. I'm going to take the spyglass and creep over to that nest of reeds yonder to get a better look."

"Sandoval, what if Delgado's men are hiding in there?"

"If they were there, I think they'd have opened fire on us already."

He was back in just minutes, but it was obvious from Tess's worried face that it had seemed like an eternity to her. "It's Rangers, all right," he reported, allowing himself to smile. "And they're here in force—looks like an entire company. I didn't see any sign of Delgado. Ready to swim for it, Mrs. Parrish?"

She nodded, trust glowing in her eyes. "As soon as we pray." She reached for his hand.

"I hope this bay can swim as well as my pinto did," Sandoval said.

In spite of the prayer, fear still gripped Tess's insides like an icy fist. "First, kiss me, please, Sandoval," Tess said, and he did.

Would it be their last kiss?

"All right, here we go," Sandoval said, unholstering his pistol. In unison, they kneed their horses forward, leaving the road so as to skirt the little village on their left. There wasn't much to the place, so their course changed only slightly.

Tess feared each step their horses took toward the water could be their last. The blood thundered in her head. She heard nothing but birdsong, the drone of dragonflies and the occasional slap of water against the riverbanks, but with each heartbeat she expected the pounding of hoof-beats behind her and a volley of gunfire.

Sandoval's bay led the way, proving he wasn't water-shy. Her mare followed willingly enough, and soon the horses' hooves left the bottom and they were swimming.

Wet to her waist, Tess let the mare have her head. She clung to the sorrel's mane with one hand and the saddle horn with the other. She could see and hear the group of Rangers easily now. They stood beneath the trees, cheering them on, their lighter skin looking almost foreign to her after she'd spent so much time in Mexico alongside men and women with skin several shades darker than hers. Then she caught sight of her father, jumping up and down, and Uncle Samuel, waving like a madman with one hand, though he still held a carbine in the other. And there was Esteban!

They were actually going to reach the opposite bank without so much as a shot fired or a glimpse of the outlaws! Had Delgado given up? She saw Sandoval's bay clamber ashore. Her mare's hooves hit bottom then and a moment later the beast was walking out of the river, water streaming off her flanks, shoulders and mane.

The Rangers surrounded them then, assisting her to dismount her horse, and she was embraced by first her father, then Uncle Samuel in turn. Through a haze of joyful tears, she saw Sandoval being embraced and clapped on the back and heard them all calling him a hero.

"You made it! You're safe. Oh, thank God," her father was saying, tears flowing unashamedly down his cheeks. "Ahem! I think it's time I met your husband?"

In spite of the noisy celebration, Sandoval heard him, and turned around now, offering his hand to Patrick Hennessy, who took it.

"Sir, I'm Sandoval Parrish, and I'm sorry for the worry I've caused you about Tess. And although it's too late for you to give permission, I hope you'll give us your blessing. I promise I'll love your daughter as long as I draw breath."

"Aye, worry me you did, and that's the truth. But you'll have a lifetime with Tess to make up for it, God willing," Patrick said. "Long life to you both, and a love that lasts for all of it and beyond. Welcome to the family, son."

Uncle Samuel was right behind him. "You couldn't have a better lady, Sandoval. And I should know—I've known this child since she was knee high to a prickly pear. I hoped you two would find a way to get together, though I had no idea it would go like this."

"Where's Mother?" Tess asked, fearing that her mother's blessing wouldn't be so easily given.

"Waiting at home for you, readying the guest cottage for you and your new husband. She's planning the biggest welcome-home and wedding reception Hidalgo County ever saw, for two days from now. Did you two sleep last night? Never mind, I can see you didn't," Patrick answered for her. "There's shadows under your eyes big as silver dollars. We'll be stopping in Roma, then, and let you catch up on your shut-eye. You'll need to change into dry clothes, anyway—which we brought, of course."

Out of the corner of her eyes, she saw Sandoval give him a grateful smile.

"No, really, I can go on. I'd rather get home sooner—" Tess began to protest, but her body betrayed her just then, a gray mist swimming in front of her eyes as fatigue swept over her in the wake of abating fear. It took half an hour and a mug of strong coffee before Tess could remount her horse.

"So no one's seen any trace of Delgado?" Sandoval asked, once they were all mounted and heading eastward, away from the river.

"Not since you sent Esteban with that picture, no," said Captain Skelly, riding beside him. "It's been posted in every spot in the road wide enough to be called a town. I've already sent a message to the governor asking for an official pardon for Esteban, by the way. Maybe Delgado's too scared to come into Texas, now that even a half-blind fella would recognize him."

"We figured Delgado might guess where y'all were plannin' t' cross, so we put together a little welcoming committee armed to the teeth for you two."

"We're just as glad you didn't need to use any of those guns, though," Sandoval said.

"Yes, I think I've heard enough gunfire to last me for a lifetime," Tess said. She glanced at Sandoval. His dark eyes remained troubled. Delgado had failed to strike during their journey or while they were crossing. She supposed it would take a while for both of them to fully realize they were safe, that they had won, for they had lived with danger for too long.

Chapter Twenty-Eight

"Now, *señores, señoras,* everyone hold still, and smile," called the voice behind the camera, underneath the heavy canvas flap.

Tess Hennessy Parrish found it easy to obey. Her husband stood beside her, tall and handsome, his arm about her waist. Her parents stood on either side of her, beaming, with her godparents and Sandoval's mother—whom Tess had liked immediately—flanking them. And it was Francisco, her assistant from the shop, with his head under the canvas flap on this hot August day, not herself. A bride had to be in the photograph, after all, not taking the pictures—even if the reception was several days after the actual wedding.

"Your older daughter's wedding dress is just beautiful on Tess," Lula Marie Taylor gushed. "As if it'd been sewn for her originally. It's a good thing your Flora's so good and quick with a needle, Amelia."

"Yes, she is, isn't she?" Amelia agreed, grinning. Her chest puffed up with pride. She was in her glory as the mother of the bride, a bride who was at last properly dressed, in Amelia's eyes, even if her complexion was an unladylike tan from her adventures in Mexico. Well, that could be amended, now that Tess was no longer racketing about with outlaws and taking their photographs. Amelia knew of a good lemon-based paste that Tess would have to apply diligently every morning and night to undo the sun's damage. It was bad enough that everyone in the Valley was gossiping about where Tess had been, but there were *freckles* dancing across her daughter's nose and cheeks.

"Your son sure is a good-lookin' fella," Lula Marie told Vittoria Parrish, who had just joined them. "So dashing, with that dark hair and those *eyes.* Why, the way he looks at Tess! And she's lookin' right back—your baby girl's in love, Amelia, and no wonder! If I was only thirty years younger and single..." she added, fanning herself.

"Remember your dignity, Lula Marie," Amelia said, although a part of her really did find herself weakening under the onslaught of her new son-in-law's considerable charm.

"What are all those tents for, beyond the back pasture yonder?" Lula Marie asked curiously, pointing.

Amelia pursed her lips. "Sandoval invited those Ranger friends, the ones who waited at the river for them in case there was trouble, to camp there for a few days."

"So they could attend the reception? That's nice, Amelia, but where are they? I don't see any unfamiliar gents at the party...." She shaded her eyes as she looked over the guests on the lawn and under the veranda.

Amelia shrugged. "I suppose they're staying in their camp out there," she said, nodding toward the back pasture. "And, yes, they're still keeping watch for Delgado. As if that outlaw would *dare* to bother us now that the picture Tess took of him is hanging everywhere! But Sandoval's convinced that Delgado won't give up and stay on his side of the river, so in the meantime those boys are eating us out of house and home," she groused.

"I'll have Sam send over a side of beef or two and a couple of smoked hams," Lula Marie promised. Then her eyes went back to Tess, standing in the shade of the veranda with Sandoval and her father. "I bet they'll have beautiful babies," she burbled, her attention easily diverted at the romantic sight.

"I've had refreshments taken out to the men, son," Tess heard her papa tell Sandoval.

"Thank you, Mr. Hennessy."

"That's Papa to you," Patrick insisted. "Or Patrick, if you'd rather. We're family, remember?"

"Papa, then," Sandoval agreed. "Thank you. I know the men appreciate it."

"I just wish they'd come and join the party," Patrick Hennessy said, half turning to gaze over his shoulder at their tents, just visible beyond the back field. "They could bring their firearms with them, if they felt the need."

"You know Mother'd have a conniption if they did that, Papa," Tess reminded him gently, "dressed as roughly as they are. It wouldn't matter to me, though."

"We'll take them slices of cake, too, once you two slice it. Isn't it about time for that, daughter?"

"I suppose so, Papa. Francisco!" she called, spotting her assistant chatting with Flora, their hands gesticulating. "Ready to take another picture?"

"*Sí,* Tess—that is, Señora Parrish," Francisco said with a grin, after giving the maid one last wink. He moved the camera in front of the veranda where the bride and groom would be cutting the cake.

Her father went to the side door on the veranda and called for Rosa to bring out her four-tiered masterpiece.

Tess and Sandoval took their places behind the table in front of the cake. Tess felt Sandoval's warm, big hand atop hers as she sank the flower- and ribbon-trimmed knife deep into the edge of the cake, and they both looked up into the camera lens. She faintly heard a soft, long whirring as the shutter opened, then closed.

And over that, in the distance, the thudding of distant hooves—coming closer.

"Riders comin' up the lane!" cried a voice from above them.

"It's Delgado! Everyone take cover!" shouted another voice.

Simultaneously, amid the roar of gunfire and the screams of running women, Sandoval dropped the cake knife and shoved Tess toward the side door. "Get inside, Tess!"

For a moment she froze, her horrified eyes taking in the sight of Delgado galloping up the lane at the head of his men, shooting as he came. Out of the corner of her eye, she saw Sandoval retrieving a rifle he'd apparently hidden in the eaves of the veranda roof, shouldering it in one swift blur, and firing back.

She spotted Lupe riding at Delgado's side, looking evil and grim as a Fury. She recognized an individual face or two of the bandits—Garza, maybe, and Mendoza—but most of them were just a blur as they galloped toward the house.

"Tess, *Madre,* go!" Sandoval shouted at her again. Other women, shrieking, some carrying children, others helping older women—one of them Sandoval's mother—were running past them toward the side and front doors.

A bullet hit the punch bowl next to them, sending scarlet liquid and crystal shards flying.

Above her, deafening gunfire erupted from every window and, above that, from the roof. The Rangers hadn't remained at their tents in the back field, she realized in that instant. After the guests had begun arriving and she and her family had gone out on the lawn to greet them, they had entered the house from the back at Sandoval's direction, stationing themselves in the bedrooms and waiting for the trouble Sandoval had been so sure was coming.

He'd been right.

A bullet whistled past her, just above her head.

She moved to obey Sandoval and flee inside. Then she saw her mother go down on the lawn in a flurry of rose-colored skirts.

"*Mama!*" All thoughts of taking cover, of safety, fled from her brain. Where was her father? Where was Uncle Sam? Lula Marie? She jumped from the veranda, heedless of her veil as it caught on a branch of crepe myrtle in the flower bed and was pulled off. Someone running past knocked over her precious camera, and this, too, had no meaning for her as she ran toward the fallen figure.

Out of the corner of her eye, she saw her father dive behind a table that had held people's used plates, pushing it down, china, silverware and all, to take cover. His back was to his wife, so he had not seen her fall, and he was firing a pistol Tess had not known he was carrying. Uncle Sam was also shooting from underneath a guest's carriage.

It was up to her to rescue her mother. *God, please protect me!*

Bullets whizzed above her, to the side of her. All Tess could see was her mother, struggling to rise. She couldn't see any blood....

"My ankle…fell…" her mother grunted as Tess reached her side. Then, as she struggled to get an arm under her mother and help her to her feet, her mother began screaming and gesturing with flailing arms.

"*Tess!* Run! Get away!"

A horseman was bearing down on them, his grinning face and the ebony blackness of his horse like creatures from a nightmare. *Delgado!*

He'd holstered his pistols and held no reins, riding with his knees like a marauding Comanche. In one swift, graceful motion, he leaned over, arms extended to pull her off her feet and into the saddle.

Time stopped. She couldn't hear the bloodcurdling cry of one of the bandits as he was shot off his horse and fell, dead before he touched the ground, or the panicked whinny of a horse grazed by a bullet, or the splintering of glass as windows and abandoned punch glasses were hit. All she could do was wait, knowing that if she fled, Delgado would ride her mother down, wishing she had some weapon other than her fists. Sandoval probably couldn't fire without the risk of hitting her.

And then Delgado was wrenching her off her feet, heedless of her twisting struggles to free herself as the horse turned in a wide circle, away from the house and the gunfire.

"*Let me go!*"

He laughed, the sound demonic next to her ear. "Not a chance, *gringa!*"

The cake knife! She suddenly realized she had been unconsciously clutching it as she had run. She still held it, wide-bladed, long and frosting-smeared.

She stabbed at him, hoping she could at least make him drop her and that it wouldn't hurt too much when she landed. But the knife was meant for cake cutting only, and wasn't sharp edged, and she was too close to him to do much damage anyway. Her stabs landed harmlessly against his leather chaps and the saddle. He grabbed at the knife. In a moment he would yank it out of her grasp and drop it—*Lord, help me!*

She stabbed again, frantically, and this time she managed to evade his grabbing hand and hit the galloping stallion in his shoulder.

The stallion reared, screaming in outrage. Delgado, caught unaware, let go of her. Stunned, the wind knocked out of her, Tess could only watch, helpless, as Delgado was forced to leave her in the grass and fight to keep his seat on the plunging beast.

Then a roar split the air, then another, and Tess saw Delgado slump, boneless as a rag doll. In the split second before he fell off the horse a few yards from her, she saw twin crimson holes flooding the front of his leather vest.

She closed her eyes and struggled to bring air back into her lungs before a blackness overwhelmed her.

Chapter Twenty-Nine

"Shh, he's dead, Tess," Sandoval was saying, before she even realized she was sobbing, or that her husband had reached her side. He held her against his chest. "He can't ever hurt you again."

Still dazed, she opened her eyes, and saw that someone was covering the body with a tablecloth, but not before she caught a glimpse of white frosting incongruously smeared on the legs of Delgado's trousers. There was no sign of the black stallion he'd ridden, or of Lupe.

"The others?" she tried to look around Sandoval's side, but he held her too tightly.

"Gone, the ones who weren't killed. Lupe was among the ones who fled. The other Rangers have gone after them, though of course the bandits had a long start on them."

"Mama?"

"She's all right, thanks to you—though I aged about a hundred years, sweetheart, seeing you running out there to her—"

"I had to help her…."

"I know," he said, kissing the top of her head. "I think

she's all right. Your father carried her into the house with your godfather's help."

"Was anyone else hurt?"

"Not as far as I know. Let me get you to the house, Tess, and we'll make sure."

Tess felt him lifting her up into his arms, and began to protest, "Sandoval, I can walk—"

He ignored her, and she was glad, for even the motion of him shifting her weight against him set her head spinning. She let her head fall against his chest as he strode over the lawn.

The door was opened as he reached it. Everyone flocked to them, exclaiming over Tess as Sandoval lowered her gently onto a brocade-upholstered couch. She saw her mother first, sitting next to the couch with her foot propped up on an ottoman and wrapped in a wet towel. Her father stood next to her, happy tears standing in his eyes at the sight of Tess. And there was Sandoval's mother, crying tears of joy and murmuring "Thanks be to God" over and over again in Spanish as she hugged her son.

"Oh, Tess, thank God you're safe!" cried her mother. "Are you hurt? When I saw that monster snatch you up I swooned. My dear girl, if my clumsiness had caused you to be kidnapped again—"

"I'm fine, Mama," Tess assured her quickly. She saw her godfather sitting with Lula Marie nearby, his arm bandaged. "Uncle Samuel?"

"One of them banditos winged me, but I'll mend, I reckon. Esteban here shot him, and although the fella was still on his horse when they galloped down the lane, he thinks he was hit worse than me. And it seems I was the only one of us hit, so we can thank God for that. I figure they came for only one purpose—you."

Tess gulped, knowing it was true. She stared at Esteban,

trying to imagine how hard it must have been for the Mexican to shoot at men he had once called compadres. "Thank you, Esteban."

He smiled steadily back at her. "I have chosen a new path, Señora Tess. I don't want to be an outlaw anymore."

"I'm glad."

"He says he'd like to work on my ranch," Sandoval told her. "As I told you, my foreman's getting old, so I reckon Esteban could work into the job. And when Delores arrives, she can help you in the kitchen."

"I am going to go look for her tomorrow," Esteban said. "She has a sister in Reynosa. She told me that she would wait there for me."

"But the other banditos—Lupe—" Tess began, alarmed that Delgado's sister might seek vengeance against the old woman.

"We never told any of them that my mother's sister lives there. I think my mother knew she might have to get away from Delgado someday. The other men…I think if they are not caught by the Rangers before they reach the border, most of them will stop raiding and go back to their villages. I hope so, anyway," he concluded with a sigh.

The friends and neighbors who had been guests at the party came forward now, expressing their relief that she was all right, and taking their leave. Doc Evans, who was already there as a guest at the reception, took Uncle Samuel into another room to tend his wound. He was followed by Lula Marie. Before long, only Tess, Sandoval and her parents remained in the room.

Amelia cleared her throat. "I have something to say to you, Sandoval Parrish."

On the couch, Tess tensed. By this time, Sandoval was sitting on a chair by the couch. She placed a hand on her husband's wrist, ready to spring to his defense. Now that the danger was over and the guests were gone, was her mother about to blame Sandoval for what had happened?

"Now, Amelia," began her father, apparently worried about the same thing.

Her mother held up a hand. "I need to say this. Sandoval Parrish, when I first saw you, and heard what they said about you, I thought you were up to no good. And if I'd had a gun, after Tess went missing and we found that note in her room, I might've used it on you."

Beside her, Sandoval said, "I understand, Mrs. Hennessy. I can't say I'd blame you. It was wrong of me to use your daughter to try to capture Delgado—"

Her mother held up a hand again, forestalling him. "Yes, it was. But she seems to have survived it all right, thanks to you. My Tess is an adventurous girl—I'm not sure *where* she gets that from, but there it is."

Beside his wife, Patrick grinned.

"I don't think she would have ever been content to just marry some planter's son around here and settle down to raise babies and give teas and help the Ladies Aid Society. She's always been different, my Tess." She smiled at Tess then, and it was a proud smile. "I want to thank you for bringing her safely home."

Sandoval rose to his feet. "Mrs. Hennessy, I—"

"That's *Mama* to you, Sandoval Parrish, or Mother Hennessy, if you must be formal. Welcome to the family. I know you're the only man the Lord could find who could keep up with my Tess."

Sandoval smiled at Tess, then went to Amelia, kneeling so they could embrace without her getting up on her sprained ankle.

"But what about this plan of yours to go to New York City and work with Brady, Tess?" her mother asked, after Sandoval had returned to the couch. The question surprised Tess yet again, especially the lack of disapproval in her mother's tone.

"Oh, I wouldn't mind going up to see his studio someday," Tess said, after gazing into Sandoval's eyes. "But now that doesn't seem so important. I'm a wife now, you know—and if the Lord blesses us with babies..." Her voice trailed off and color flooded her face. "In any case, I'm afraid the camera may have sustained some damage," Tess said, remembering how it had been knocked over in the midst of the attack. "I'm not sure it'll work anymore."

"Excuse me..." said a voice hesitantly from the door. It was Francisco. As Tess watched, he turned and began pulling something into the room—her camera.

There was a scrape on the side of the box, and a small rent at the lower edge of the heavy canvas flap in the back.

Tess braced herself, unable to hope for one more bit of good news. "Francisco, is it...?" She could not bring herself to say the word *broken.*

He held up a finger. "One moment, please." He walked out of the parlor again and when he returned, he was carrying a photograph that was apparently still wet. He held it out. It was a photograph of Ben, her mule, grazing out in the pasture.

"I took this a few minutes ago, Tess, just to test it. Your camera, she still works."

A month later, Tess and Sandoval found themselves walking into the office of the governor at the state capitol building in Austin.

"Thank you so much for coming," Governor Oran Roberts, a solemn, gray-haired and gray-bearded, long-faced man said, welcoming them into his office.

"It's an honor, sir," Sandoval said, speaking for both of them.

"I'm the one who is honored by your presence," Roberts insisted. "And on behalf of the entire state of Texas, I'm pleased to present you with these medals, with the thanks of the grateful citizens of this fine state." He pinned on each of them a bronze, five-pointed star of Texas dangling from a horizontal bronze bar by means of two slender bronze chains. "Thanks to you, the depredations committed by Diego Delgado and his band have ceased, and reports of raids by other marauding bands from south of the border have been nearly nonexistent."

Tess experienced a moment of sadness as she thought of Diego Delgado, a man whose vainglorious pride had brought about his destruction. He could have done so much more with his life. He could have served as an example for his avaricious, cruel sister. But now he was dead.

They'd never caught Lupe Delgado, or any of the other bandits who had lived to flee Hennessy Hall the day of the attack, but reports out of Mexico had it that she had married Andrés Cordoba, the wealthy *ranchero*. Perhaps Lupe would learn from her narrow escape and turn her life around—or at least make only this one last man wish he'd never met her. Tess resolved to pray for her, and for all the men who had been part of Delgado's band.

"I was merely doing my job as a Ranger, sir," Sandoval told governor. "It's my wife, Tess, who went above and beyond anything she might have been expected to do as a private-citizen photographer who happened to be of the fairer sex." He smiled down at Tess, who returned his smile, her heart glowing with pride and love for the man next to her.

Roberts's eyes twinkled underneath bushy brows. "I'm told there is much more to the story, that you actually had her kidnapped?"

Once again they found themselves telling their remarkable story.

"I've seen some of your photographs, Mrs. Parrish. A contingent of Rangers went down to the Delgado's canyon hideout—with permission from the Mexican government, I might add—and brought out the pictures Delgado had left behind there. You have a remarkable talent, ma'am."

"Thank you, sir."

"Are you planning to write a book? This yarn you've told me would make a great dime novel, complete with your drawings."

Tess smiled. "Maybe someday..." She doubted it, though.

"Might I commission you to take my photograph sometime, ma'am?"

Tess blinked in surprise. "I...I'm afraid I didn't bring my camera with me to Austin, sir." She imagined traveling all the way to Austin in the wagon and was glad she hadn't known Governor Roberts would make this request. "But we'd be honored if you'd like to visit our ranch down in the Rio Grande Valley. I could take your picture then."

"Perhaps I'll do that, Mrs. Parrish, and thank you. Mr. Parrish, do you plan to continue your career as a Ranger?"

Sandoval smiled regretfully. "I'm afraid I've tendered my resignation, sir. I was honored to serve that way for many years, but rangering is a job that can take a man away from his home for months on end. It's not a job for a man who's newly married. But I've told my captain that I'm willing to help out if Texas needs me."

"I understand," the governor said. "Congratulations on your marriage. And once again, thank you for your service to the state of Texas."

Epilogue

October—the Rio Grande Valley north of Chapin

Tess watched from under the shelter of the grapevine-twined lattice over the patio as Sandoval helped first his mother and then Pilar up into the carriage Esteban was driving. She was amused to see Esteban turn around and dart a look at Pilar, a look that Sandoval's sister returned with a flirtatious smile.

Pilar had arrived last week from Monterrey, joyous and confident, completely unlike the regretful, shy girl they had encountered in the bordello. Her time of contemplation had done her a world of good. She now knew that God loved her, and had always loved her, and she was ready to live the rest of her life in search of His will for her.

Pilar had decided to live with their mother, at least for the time being, and so Sandoval had started building an addition on the ranch house. They were going into town now to buy furniture and fabric for curtains for the new rooms.

As the carriage started down the road, Sandoval strode back to the house and sat down, smiling appreciatively as Tess handed him a glass of freshly made lemonade. For a moment both of them just savored the breeze that fluttered the tendrils of red hair over Tess's forehead. Now that the cooler days of autumn had replaced the steamy humidity of a Valley summer midday, they often sat out here, enjoying the view that spread before them—grazing horses and cattle, cotton fields and sturdy barns against the backdrop of thick tropical foliage.

"If I'm not mistaken, I think our Esteban is sweet on my sister," Sandoval said, gazing after the carriage disappearing down the road.

"And she on him," Tess responded. "You don't mind, do you?"

"Not a bit. Esteban's a good man, steady and dependable," Sandoval said, smiling lovingly at his wife.

"It's fun watching them fall in love, isn't it?" she said.

He nodded. "Our life is just about perfect, isn't it?"

It was time, Tess decided. She had waited until she could tell him alone. "It's about to get more perfect," she murmured.

"What? How?" he asked, puzzled; then, as she continued to smile, he blinked. "Tess…do you mean…are you—are we—"

"Going to have a baby? Yes. I've thought so for a week or two, but I wanted to tell just you first."

"When?"

"I think he—or she—will come in mid-May, if I'm figuring right." The baby had been conceived while they were still in Mexico, she figured, on the run, but it would be born amid peace and safety.

Sandoval pulled Tess into his embrace and kissed her. "I don't know why God gave me such gifts—I mean *you,* my darling Tess, and our coming child—but I thank Him every day."

* * * * *

Dear Reader,

Thank you so much for choosing THE OUTLAW'S LADY. I hope you enjoyed reading the story of Tess Hennessy, a woman of her time who nevertheless chooses an unusual occupation, photography, and Sandoval Parrish, a man of mixed Anglo and Mexican heritage who may or may not be on the right side of the law. It was an enjoyable process for me to portray Tess—a Christian but one whose faith has never been truly tested—as she gets to know the kind of man Sandoval really is, and grows in her faith so that she can convey God's love to him. Sandoval Parrish, bent on revenge, hasn't ever been sure of that love, but under Tess's influence, he comes to love and trust the Lord, too. I enjoy writing heroines who stretch beyond the expectations of their time, when women were supposed to prepare only for marriage to suitable husbands, heroes who are strong enough to be perfect matches for those women, and about the faith journey of both.

I enjoy hearing from readers. You can contact me through my Web site, www.lauriekingery.com, where you can read about new releases, about the writing life and my thoughts in my blog.

Laurie Kingery

QUESTIONS FOR DISCUSSION

1. How does Tess's position as the youngest in her family, the only one left at home, influence the type of person she is at the beginning of the book?

2. Tess's mother believes the only way Tess will ever be happy is if she marries. Did you ever go against your parents' wishes for your life? If so, how did it turn out?

3. Have you ever struggled to achieve a goal or join a profession that is not one usually done by your gender? What was that like for you?

4. What differences are there between a young woman's life in the 1880s and young women of today? Are all the changes good? Please explain.

5. Do you think Tess is realistic in keeping to her goal of working for world-famous photographer Mathew Brady in New York? Do you think she would have been happy? Have you ever had a goal like Tess's, only to find out when you reached it that it wasn't worth as much as you thought it was?

6. How do you think Sandoval's mixed-heritage background affects his view of the world? Do you think it would be remarked upon as much today as it was back then? Why or why not?

7. Does the relationship between the Anglo Texans and their Mexican neighbors in this story mirror in any way the relationship between America and Mexico today?

8. On her way home from the barbecue, Tess is kidnapped by raiding bandits. Would you have reacted as Tess did? Why or why not?

9. Diego Delgado is quite a charming man. Unfortunately, he is also a ruthless outlaw. Are the two mutually exclusive? Have you ever met anyone who was fascinating and charming but also dangerous?

10. Do you think Tess and Sandoval would have fallen in love if he had not had her kidnapped?

11. How would you describe Tess and Sandoval's position in regard to faith at the beginning of the book? How does this change by the end of the book? How does Tess help Sandoval to trust God?

12. Should Sandoval feel responsible for what happened to Pilar? How does that influence his character development?

13. Have you ever felt that anything you did made you unworthy of God's love, as Pilar did? What made you change your mind? Does God love people like Delgado and Lupe?

14. Sandoval does the wrong thing by kidnapping Tess to achieve his goal of bringing Delgado to justice, but how does God work it out to achieve happiness for her and Sandoval? Has anything happened in your life this way?

A thrilling romance between a British nurse and an American cowboy on the African plains.

Turn the page for a sneak preview of THE MAVERICK'S BRIDE by Catherine Palmer. Available September 2009 from Love Inspired® Historical.

Adam hoisted himself onto the balcony, swinging one leg at a time over the rail. He hoped he hadn't been spotted by a compound guard.

But the sight of Emma Pickering peering out from behind the curtain put his concerns to rest. He had done the right thing.

"Good morning, Miss Pickering." He leaned against the white window frame.

"Mr. King." She was almost breathless. "I cannot speak with you."

"But I need to talk. Mind if I come inside?"

"Indeed, sir, you may not take another step! Are you mad?"

He couldn't hold back a grin. "No more than most. I figure anyone who would leave home and travel all the way to Africa has to be a little off-kilter."

"You refer to me, I suppose? I'll have you know I'm here for a very good reason."

"Railway inspection, is it? Or nursing?"

Emma looked even better than he had thought she might—and he had thought about her a lot.

"Speaking of nursing," he ventured.

"Mr. King, I have already told you I'm unavailable. Now please let yourself down by that…that rope thing, and—"

"My lasso?"

"You must go down again, sir. This is unseemly."

Emma was edgy this morning. Almost frightened. Different from the bold young woman he had met yesterday.

He couldn't let that concern him. Last night after he left the consulate, he had made up his mind to keep things strictly business with Emma Pickering.

"I'll leave after I've had my say," he told her. "This is important."

"Speak quickly, sir. My father must not find you here."

"With all due respect, Emma, do you think I'm concerned about what your father thinks?"

"You may not care, but I do. What do you want from me?"

"I need a nurse."

"A nurse? Are you ill?"

"Not for me. I have a friend—at my ranch."

Her eyes deepened in concern as she let the curtain drop a little. "What sort of illness does your friend have? Can you describe it?"

Adam looked away. How could he explain the situation without scaring her off?

"It's not an illness. It's more like…"

Searching for the right words, he turned back to Emma. But at the first full sight of her face, he reached through the open window and pulled the curtain out of her hands.

"Emma, what happened to you?" He caught her arm and drew her toward him. "Who did this?"

She raised her hand in a vain effort to cover her cheek and eye. "It's nothing," she protested, trying to back away. "Please, Mr. King, you must not…"

Even as she tried to speak, he stepped through the balcony door and gathered her into his arms. Brushing back the hair from her cheek, he noted the swelling and the darkening stain around it.

"Emma," he growled. "Who did this to you?"

She fell motionless, silent in his embrace. No wonder she had shied like a scared colt. She hadn't wanted him to know.

Torn with dismay that anyone would ever harm this beautiful woman, he felt an irresistible urge to kiss her.

"Emma, you have to tell me…." Realization flooded through him. A pompous, nattily dressed English railroad tycoon had struck his own daughter.

"Leave me, I beg you. You have no place here."

"Emma, wait. Listen to me." Adam caught her wrists and pulled her back toward him. He'd never been a man to think things through too carefully. He did what felt right.

"I want you to come with me," he told her. "I need your help. Let's go right now. Emma, I'll take care of you."

"I don't need anyone to take care of me," she shot back. "God is watching over me."

"Emma!" Both turned toward the open door where Emma's sister stood, eyes wide.

"Emma, go with him!" Cissy crossed the room toward them. "Run away with him, Emma. It's your chance to escape—to become a nurse, as you've always wanted. You'll be safe at last, and you can have your dream."

Emma turned back to Adam.

"Come on," he urged her. "Let's get moving."

* * * * *

Will Emma run away with Adam and finally realize
her dreams of becoming a nurse?
Find out in THE MAVERICK'S BRIDE,
available in September 2009
only from Love Inspired® Historical.

Love Inspired
HISTORICAL

TITLES AVAILABLE NEXT MONTH

Available September 8, 2009

THE MAVERICK'S BRIDE by Catherine Palmer
Emma Pickering is drawn to Adam King, the rugged cowboy she meets upon arriving in East Africa. The man is as compelling as he is mysterious. And if he'll agree to a marriage of convenience, it would solve both their problems. Yet their match is anything but "convenient" when Emma's fears gain hold and malicious whispers threaten to tear the couple apart.

DAKOTA CHILD by Linda Ford
Lost in a North Dakota snowstorm, single mother Vivian Halliday prays for the safety of her infant son, tucked inside her cloak. Rescue comes in the terrifying form of Billy Black, feared by all the townsfolk. He proves, though, to be a gentle giant whose loving heart just might change both their lives forever.

LIHCNMBPA0809